DRINK WITH THE DEVIL

David Woods

Pen Press Publishers Ltd

© David Woods 2005

All rights reserved

No part of this publication may be reproduced,
stored in a retrieval system, or transmitted
in any form or by any means, without
the prior permission in writing of the publisher,
nor be otherwise circulated in any form of binding or
cover other than that in which it is published and without a
similar condition including this condition being imposed
on the subsequent purchaser.

First published in Great Britain by
Pen Press Publishers Ltd
39-41, North Road
Islington
London N7 9DP

ISBN 1-905203-30-6

Printed and bound in the UK

A catalogue record of this book is available from
the British Library

Cover design by Jacqueline Abromeit

DRINK WITH
THE DEVIL

Chapter One

It was 5.30 am on a wet April morning. Jim Grainger reached out from the small single bed, groping around until he found and silenced the alarm clock. He rose quickly to avoid going to sleep again and sat on the bed staring at his feet. Outside the wind was gusting and beating against the window. When he remembered what day it was, his heart sank. Sale Day. All the cows and calves were to be sold this morning. He sat a while longer, recalling the conversation he'd had with his boss, Andrew Jones, six months earlier.

Jim had just come in for breakfast. Andrew and his wife Ruth had obviously been up for some time because there were cold dregs in the bottom of the dirty cups on the kitchen table. Jim looked at his boss rather nervously.

"Well Jim. We've come to a decision. The farm'll be sold in the spring. We're getting on now, and it makes sense to sell up while I'm still young enough to get a job."

Jim was staggered. All he could think of to say was, "Why?"

"I've been offered a job as a storeman at the machinery dealers in town. We'll buy a small house nearby."

"And what the hell am I supposed to do?"

"You're a clever chap. And lucky enough to be able to turn your hand to almost anything."

"All I want is to work here. With the animals."

"You could get a job with another farm, and stay here with us in the meantime."

Jim had thought about this for a minute and known immediately he could not face living in a town.

Ruth Jones had given him his breakfast. "Don't worry, Jim. You're only nineteen and can get another job anywhere."

"Oh yeah. But it's not going to be the same."

Jim had known he would miss the couple who had taken him in and given him a home after years in an orphanage. His own parents had been killed in a car accident when he was a baby, and he had no other family. This situation did not worry him, but occasionally he wondered how his parents would have looked by now. Their old wedding photograph, the only one he had, indicated they were both tall and dark haired and Jim had grown himself into a tall well-built man with blue eyes and thick black hair.

After shaking himself out of a trance, he got dressed. The cows greeted him as he walked into the warm and humid cowshed, the heat generated by twenty-five hot bodies. Some of them mooed gently as he closed the door behind him and started his normal routine, cleaning behind them and then preparing the milking machine buckets.

He fed the first cow a large scoop of cow cake and then put the teat cups on. He talked to a young cow gently, as he stroked her back leg. "You'll be fine on another farm, ole girl." She turned her large head towards him, breathing heavily on his back, and he felt her hot moist breath on the skin exposed between his shirt and trousers. The teat cups were holding on all right, so he let go of them. Before he could stand up the cow gave him a lingering lick, which felt like a hot wet rasp being dragged across his back. He stood up slowly, trying not to act startled, and rubbed her behind the ears.

Milking seemed to go on forever, and he talked to each cow as he gave each one an extra scoop of cake. They seemed to respond to his soft voice, watching him with their large eyes and their ears cocked forward. They moved as he approached to milk them, and when he had finished and was alone in the dairy next to the cowshed, he felt his world was coming to an end. These cows had been his friends for four years and he would have to face losing them very shortly.

His solitude was shattered by Andrew entering the dairy, all bright and cheerful. "Good morning Jim. I'll give you a hand to wash up."

"Okay. I'll clear out the cowshed." He walked out quickly to hide his misery.

Conversation over breakfast was almost non existent, with Jim just picking at his food. Ruth was worried about him and spoke softly. "The cows'll be well looked after on a larger farm."

He just nodded. "I suppose so."

After breakfast Jim went back out to the cowshed. The cows looked at him again, expecting now to be let out to new grass, but instead found they were to be brushed down ready for sale. They mooed loudly and fidgeted. Some of them tossed straw bedding up in the air with their heads, much of it landing on Jim whilst he tried to make them look presentable.

Two lorries arrived mid morning and Jim had the unhappy task of coaxing the animals up the ramps. After an hour, all the animals including calves, had been loaded and the lorries drove out of the farmyard towards the local cattle market.

Jim stood and gazed around the old wooden cowshed, which had the names of the cows written on small blackboards above the mangers. He tried not to imagine the fate of some of the older animals, but was sure they were destined for the abattoir before the day was out.

Home Farm was set in lush countryside on the lower slopes of a hill in Sussex. It had always been a dairy farm, and the old stone farmhouse had a cheese and cream making room attached. The farm buildings were in a poor state of repair, and would need much money spent on them during the next few years. Jim guessed the farm would never be a dairy again.

During lunch Andrew Jones announced, "We've sold the farm to our neighbour, Sir William Osborne. He wants to expand his arable acreage and make Manor Farm more efficient."

"I don't think it'll make a scrap of difference. He's already got a thousand acres." Jim said dryly.

Drink With The Devil

Andrew looked him straight in the eye. "I suppose you're right."

"The first thing he'll do is sell the house and pull out all the hedges."

Ruth nodded gravely. "Yes. Then he'll knock down the old farm buildings and turn our little farm into one big field. Growing wheat every year."

Sir William Osborne lived in a large white mansion on the side of a hill. His estate included two hundred acres of woodland, which reached from the top of the hill down into the valley. Being a city financier, he only stayed in the country at weekends, and left the farm to be run by a manager.

The day after the animals went to market was deadstock sale day, when all the farm machinery and other movable items were auctioned on the farm. Neighbouring farmers arrived with items to add to the collection, placed in lots around the five-acre field by the farmhouse. It was a pleasant sunny day and by eleven o'clock the farmyard was full of Land Rovers, cars and trucks. The buyers were mainly farmers and dealers, hoping for a bargain. The first lot, a quantity of scrap iron, was sold at eleven thirty, and the slick auctioneer had sold all the rest of the items by one, well in time for his usual pub lunch accompanied by five pints of beer. He was a large fat individual with a florid complexion and a big nose, and his podgy hand gripped an old walking stock. As he walked around the field, his body swaying from side to side, he would prod each piece of machinery to indicate which lot he was selling, and then use the stick to hit the item when he declared the lot sold. He had quite a following of admirers, who would just come to the sale to see him in action. His sales talk was so fast it was legendary, but it was a different matter in the afternoon after his five pints!

Andrew Jones was delighted with the outcome of the day's events. "Well, Jim, the sale went better than I hoped."

"Oh good. At least you'll have something to show for all your years of hard work."

Jim spent the rest of the week clearing dung out of the

cowshed and calf buildings, and getting rid of the rubbish. Some of the time was spent cleaning and preparing his old 350 cc motorcycle, a B.S.A. model B31, which he bought from a neighbouring farm worker for five pounds. It started out as a wreck, which he had stripped down and re-built, hand painting the frame black and the tank green. He had fitted a large rear carrier frame, and was proud of the machine and its performance though he did not venture far, just to the local village and occasionally to town when he had to do shopping.

Jim was a solitary type, without any friends, and had never had a girlfriend. He preferred his own company and loved the countryside with its animals.

The Jones's were due to move to their house in the town in a week's time, and were getting rather concerned about Jim, as he had not made any obvious attempts to acquire another job. That evening after dinner Andrew stared at his ex-employee across the kitchen table. "What are your plans then, Jim?"

"Oh, don't worry. I'll be leaving at the weekend."

"But where are you going, for heaven's sake?"

"I've decided on a camping holiday for a while. Then I'll get a job on a farm."

Ruth frowned. "We'd like to keep in touch, and you must come and stay with us after your holiday."

"Yes," said Andrew enthusiastically. "You can apply for a job. I'll give you an excellent reference. And I'll have a word with some of the local farmers, too."

"Oh yeah. That might be a help."

Jim knew that this stage of his life was over, and he would try to manage on his own. The following Sunday he loaded up his old B.S.A. with all his possessions, and the camping gear he had collected over the last six months. He set off after a lunch of roast beef, and Ruth appeared quite upset as he started up his bike.

"You will come back to see us?"

Jim just smiled as he kicked the bike into action, and rode out of the farmyard, waving cheerfully.

Drink With The Devil

Ruth turned to her husband tearfully. "We've really let him down badly. I don't think we'll ever see him again."

"Don't get so upset. He'll be back in a fortnight looking for a place to sleep. And a good meal."

She shook her head and walked indoors.

Jim rode carefully along the narrow country lane with its steep banks either side, up the hill and then turned right along the top. He stopped and stared down on the farm buildings for a minute, then a mile farther on slowed down again as he passed through a dense forest of oak and elm trees. A quarter of a mile from the forest edge, he turned and squeezed through a gap in the hedge. The trees were more widely spaced apart here. He carried on slowly through a bed of beautiful bluebells, trying to avoid breaking the stems of the flowers. He was tempted to stop and admire the carpet of blue, but pressed on, getting out of sight of the road as soon as he could. The trees got closer together as he progressed down the hill, requiring him to weave carefully left and right in low gear, with the rear wheel skidding on the wet stony ground.

After ten minutes he stopped and got off the bike, leaned it against a tree and walked between two rhododendron bushes. In front of him was an unused shooting lodge, which had been built some time ago, of local stone with a slab stone roof. It was a single-roomed building, about twenty feet square, with a large fireplace and shuttered windows. The only furniture inside was a large table, benches around the three outside walls and a gun rack on the fourth wall.

Jim had visited the lodge many times before and had repaired the door and shutters. When it was built, rhododendrons were planted all around it, but these had grown so large the building had become almost hidden. He found it by accident one Sunday afternoon when he had taken a longer walk than usual and was hurrying home. In his haste he had tripped over a rhododendron root, looked up and there it was.

The forest and lodge were owned by Sir William Osborne,

who bought the estate just after the war, but he had no interest in shooting, and had allowed the forest to become as nature intended. No one was allowed to shoot and there was only one bridleway, which led directly to Manor Farmhouse. The only people to use the track regularly were Sir William's family and farm workers.

Jim unloaded the bike and carried his supplies into the lodge to join the other things already stacked neatly in one corner. He laid out his camp bed and sleeping bag under the gun rack, putting the smaller items on the table. The bike was left against the lodge wall and covered with a green tarpaulin.

All this activity had made him thirsty, so Jim found his enamel water carrier and walked along the side of the hill. A few minutes later he found a spring where water emerged from an outcropping of rocks, and then flowed in a stream down the hill, in small waterfalls over the rocks. He filled the two-gallon container, and drank directly from its spout. It was the purest, sweetest water he had ever tasted. The remainder of the day was spent stacking tins of food away and cutting wood for the fire, which he lit when it became dark.

He did not sleep well the first night. A breeze rustled the leaves against the building, and other strange noises kept him awake.

The next day he set off with a spade, working hard all day to dig out a small pool and dam the stream. When at last he had finished and the water flowed in one side of the pool and out the other, he ran back to the lodge to get a towel. Returning out of breath and hot, he took off his clothes and stepped carefully into the water, the coldness taking his breath away. He soon got used to it and washed himself vigorously. This was to become part of his daily routine; which came to include collecting dead branches and sawing them up, collecting herbs, edible leaves, nettles and anything his "country book" said he could eat. An iron pot was filled with these items during the day and boiled over the fire in the evenings.

After about three weeks he began to wander away from the

lodge and, one moonlit night, he reached the edge of the forest. Looking across the fields he saw the large mansion on the side of the hill. All the windows were lit up. Jim stared for a while, wondering what the people inside were like, but soon retraced his steps back to his spring with its little pool. He had become fascinated by the animals all around him. After having sat down on a rock for ten minutes, a hedgehog appeared on the other side of the pool, just a few yards away. He watched as the creature drank from the pool and hurried off. Another few minutes passed and a much larger animal approached, slowly sniffing the air.

The fox stopped dead when it noticed him and started backing away. Jim said softly, "Don't be afraid. Come and have a drink." The vixen stopped again and cocked her head to one side, looking at Jim and sniffing. "Come on, don't be afraid," he repeated. She advanced slowly and drank, hardly taking her eyes off Jim, who was sitting still and trying not to fidget. The lean agile creature turned and walked away, but ten minutes later returned with her cubs. Jim was thrilled and watched as they all drank. When they had finished he talked to them softly, and the cubs played by the edge with their parent looking on.

Jim was getting stiff from sitting so long and stood up slowly. The family took no notice, and was joined by another larger fox, who looked up at Jim before having a drink. Dawn had just broken when he finally went to bed tired, but delighted, and slept until mid-day. When he got up the rain was pitting against the windowpanes, the wind causing the cabin to creak and groan. He decided to light the fire and try some new ingredients in the vegetable stew pot.

His routine changed after the encounter with the foxes, and his nights were spent with the forest animals. He had made friends with the two families of foxes and lots of furry animals including mice, stoats and weasels. One night as he sat in his usual place by the pool, he heard a scraping, snuffling sound. A badger appeared, but scurried away when it saw him. Feeling disappointed, he called softly after it. The foxes arrived soon after and he played with the cubs, who would lightly nip his fingers when he tickled their tummies. The vixen sat by Jim and liked having her ears scratched. The badger returned two nights later, staying longer this time and drinking at the pool whilst Jim talked to it softly. The next night the badger returned with two cubs, and Jim was delighted that gradually he had been able to make friends with them.

With the arrival of autumn, the squirrels had become less timid and competed for nuts, even trying to pinch the odd one from Jim's large jacket pockets. It was great fun to have them sitting on his shoulder and being able to hand feed them. During daytime trips into the forest to collect wood, some of his animal friends followed him. The fox cubs would suddenly appear, wanting to play, and soon after their mothers would turn up to guide them in the direction of home.

Looking at himself one day in his old cracked mirror, Jim was shocked at the face that stared back at him. A long black beard nearly covered his face and his hair had grown longer. Although it was often washed, he had not bothered to comb it regularly.

The first snow of winter fell in mid December, covering the lodge roof with a full two inches. The trees looked beautiful and the floor of the forest had become a white carpet, soon criss-crossed with animal tracks. A daily routine was adhered to, but bathing in the rocky pool was a much shorter and more vigorous affair than before. Christmas came and passed without him realising - in fact he had long ago lost track of dates. Every day was the same in his isolated world, which he regarded as Heaven on earth, despite the cold. The only problem during the winter months was food, until he discovered Sir William's beef cattle were fed on reject potatoes! Nocturnal excursions became longer and took him over the nearby fields, where he filled his bag with potatoes, kale and cow cabbage — even trying mangels. These discoveries meant it was not necessary to leave the forest to buy food, and the only reminders of the outside world were his own material possessions. He had pushed his bike inside the lodge and cleaned it, wondering when he would ride it again. He kept warm during the day by sawing up wood, but began to wonder whether anyone had noticed all the dead branches were disappearing.

One day Jim heard a chain saw cutting up a large beech tree, which had fallen across a bridle path during a particularly windy night. He quickly went to investigate and saw that there were two men, one with the saw and the other pulling the sawn wood away, but suddenly the noise stopped. Jim stepped on a dead twig, which cracked loudly. The two men stared in his direction and he moved swiftly behind a tree, hoping he had not been observed but heard one man say. "Did you hear something?" Not waiting to hear the reply, Jim moved quickly and almost silently away, not knowing if he had been seen, and praying he had not.

Chapter Two

Manor Farm was dominated by the large white Georgian mansion which stood on the side of the hill overlooking the farm buildings to the left. The forest was beyond on the right. Directly below were well maintained lawns and gardens with grass meadows in the distance.

Sir William Osborne, a middle aged portly gentleman, liked to sit on his large York stone patio watching his herd of pedigree Friesians grazing beyond the gardens. He looked forward to retiring in a few years time and living permanently on the farm, but in the meantime his business took him to London during the week. His wife, Lavinia, and daughter, Angela, preferred the farm and lived there permanently. His son, Garry, had just joined his father's firm and lived in London on his own.

Angela was nineteen, of medium height with dark curly hair and a trim figure. Being a keen horse rider, she hunted regularly, and had two chestnut mares. Her mother liked her daughter to meet the right kind of men, such as members of the hunting fraternity, but Angela's experience with young men had been varied. When she left private school at seventeen, she came home and was soon lonely, missing the hectic life to which she had become accustomed. Within a short time she fell in love with one of the young farm workers, but when her mother caught them in a passionate embrace in the cowshed, the lad was promptly dismissed and told to leave immediately. She never really got over this boy, although several "suitable" young men dated her. She was not impressed by their pompous sense of self-importance, and these brief encounters normally ended when their clumsy attempts at lovemaking did not come close to the passion she had previously experienced.

Drink With The Devil

Angela turned her energies to running the farm office and riding. One particularly beautiful spring afternoon, when there was not a cloud in the sky, she decided to take a long ride. As she galloped past the front door, her hair blew in the breeze. She shouted to her mother, "I'll be gone for about three hours."

"Okay, darling, but be careful."

The mare was frisky and wanted to canter, but Angela kept her in check until they reached the flat pasture, and then off they went towards the edge of the wood. She rode around the outside until the bridle path came into view. She stopped and wondered whether to go back the way she had come or, back through the forest via the bridle path, but decided on the latter.

The mare was a gentle animal called Gemma, with long powerful legs that never seemed to tire. Angela patted her as they turned into the forest and walked between the trees, which hung low over the path. She ducked to miss some of the branches, but the path soon opened out and they moved faster. The grass under foot was long and lush, which kept their pace to a trot, Gemma's forelegs ploughing twin furrows in the forest floor. Suddenly a hare ran out of the long grass directly in front of them. The mare stopped dead, neighing and bucking, its rear end lifting Angela until she was catapulted headlong forward. She hit the ground with a thump, her unprotected head cracking against a sawn-off branch of a fallen beech tree. As she lay motionless, the horse whinnied loudly with fright and trotted a short distance down the path, before turning around to walk back to her mistress lying prostrate on the damp ground. Gemma whinnied again and sniffed at Angela's face.

Jim was wandering aimlessly through the forest, appreciating the warm weather and the scent of the primroses blooming in clumps in the clearings. He heard a horse whinny not far away, and deduced that the sound came from the bridle path, so he made his way quickly towards it. Hearing the second whinny, it was obvious the horse was distressed; later he found the path and ran along towards the sound. As he approached, the horse whinnied again and laid its ears back, looking angry and frightened. Jim stopped a few yards away. He spoke softly. "It's all right, ole girl, I won't hurt you." Gemma pricked up her ears and walked towards Jim. He stroked her neck, talking quietly to her as she whinnied softly and nuzzled against him. He looked down at the girl lying on her back. Her eyes were closed and she looked very pale, so he quickly felt her pulse and checked for broken bones. When he felt her head, he noticed a bump starting to form. Her clothes were damp from lying in the grass and he wondered what he should do.

After a while Angela groaned and stuttered. "Where am I?"

"You had a bad fall, but don't worry, I'll take care of you."

She closed her eyes as her head throbbed with pain. As Jim carefully picked her up he found she was surprisingly light, and he cradled her like a baby. Gemma sniffed her mistress again and Jim said "Come on, ole girl. You can follow."

Jim walked through the forest, choosing a route he thought the horse could follow. After five minutes his arms felt like dropping off, but he kept going to the lodge. Gemma stood by the rhododendron bush as he laid Angela gently on the camp bed. He stood up and studied her face, again wondering what he should do, when he noticed her eye lids open. He knelt down beside the bed and stroked her forehead and hair, desperately hoping she would wake soon.

Slowly Angela regained full consciousness and looked up at Jim, who was spellbound when he saw her beautiful brown eyes. Before she could speak he said. "It's all right. You fell off your horse and I'm looking after you, so relax."

She looked nervously at his face with its thick black beard, deep blue eyes and long hair. "Who are you?"

"My name's Jim. Now don't try to move in a hurry."

"Okay. I'll keep still for a few minutes."

"Good, 'cause you may have concussion."

"Where am I?"

"This is an old shooting lodge and I live here."

"What about my horse?"

"She's okay, and waiting for you outside."

Drink With The Devil

She lay still, studying this wild-looking man, who somehow made her relax.

Jim smiled at her. "Try and sit up slowly." He put his arm around her shoulder, the smell of her perfume distracting him, and he held her longer than was necessary. She sat looking around the lodge and he sat on the floor in front of her. "How d'you feel, then?"

"A bit dizzy and my head aches. Otherwise all right."

He looked into her brown eyes. "Thank goodness for that. Please tell me your name."

"Of course. Angela Osborne."

Jim's face developed a more serious look. "Your father owns this lodge, and I'm trespassing."

She smiled for the first time. "Don't worry, I won't tell on you. After all, you could have left me lying in the damp grass." She felt her damp legs.

"Thanks, 'cause I like it here."

"How long have you been living in the forest?"

"About a year, I suppose."

"Good gracious! What d'you live on?"

"All the things nature provides."

Jim seemed to tower over her when he returned with a cup of water. She looked at his well-built body whilst sipping the cool liquid, and wondered why such a perfectly built man would want to hide himself away. She imagined him without the beard and with his hair cut, and thought he could be very handsome. She even liked the sound of his voice.

"Aren't you lonely? All on your own for so long."

"Not at all. I've lots of animal friends."

"What animal friends? I see no dogs or cats."

"The forest animals. You probably think I'm daft, but they do keep me company."

She nodded, trying not to look surprised.

"Your horse is a beautiful animal. What d'you call her?"

"Gemma. My father bought her for me to go hunting."

Jim frowned and said slowly. "I don't approve of hunting.

Chasing those poor foxes till they drop, and then tearing them apart."

Angela could tell he was serious and felt deeply about animals, so instead of arguing, which she would have done with anyone else, she just said, "I can appreciate that point of view."

Jim smiled. "I'd like to show you my friends. Then perhaps you wouldn't want to hunt them again."

"Friends? Oh, I see. You mean foxes? Yes, I'd like that." Unsteadily she suddenly stood up. "It's nearly dark. I think I ought to be getting back."

"But are you fit enough?"

"Just a little dizzy, perhaps. But I'll make it."

"Come on then. Follow me."

Gemma was waiting patiently by the rhododendron bush and nuzzled up to Jim. Angela was amazed.

"She's never done that to anyone except me." She held Jim's hand and whispered. "I do feel unsteady. Please don't let me fall."

He experienced a tremor going through his body when she touched his hand, and felt rooted to the spot.

Angela smiled. "Come on. There'll be a search party looking for me."

"Okay. We'll make for the bridle path."

They walked as fast as possible with Gemma following behind, and after about ten minutes reached the path near to where it left the forest.

"On you get and Gemma'll take you home."

"Thanks for everything."

Just then a powerful torch lit the bridle path and a loud voice said "She's here, and looking good."

Angela turned to say goodbye but Jim had vanished. She nearly cried out to him but stopped herself just in time, as the figure of a farm worker ran along the path towards her.

"Are you all right, Miss? Everyone's out searching for you."

"Yes. I'm fine. Just a minor fall."

The farm worker walked beside her, lighting the path ahead with his torch.

Drink With The Devil

Jim watched from behind a tree as she disappeared from view, hoping she would return. He walked slowly back to the lodge, his mind filled with the afternoon's events. He could see her face smiling at him and remembered the strange sensation that went through his body when she held his hand.

Angela arrived home to be confronted by her mother. "Where have you been? I've been worried sick."

"I fell off. And bumped my head."

"Oh my goodness. I'd better call the doctor."

"There's no need. I'm feeling fine now."

"But where did you fall?"

"On the bridle path through the wood."

"But that was searched an hour ago."

"Oh well, I was sitting on a log in the wood." She dismounted and felt the bump on her head. "I've just got a small bump, that's all."

Her mother felt it. "I really think I should call the doctor."

"What for? I'm okay."

"Well, if you say so, darling. But you must be careful in future."

"Yes, Mummy. I will."

The search party was called off and Gemma returned to her stable.

After removing her damp riding gear, Angela decided on a bath. As she lay back in the warm soapy water, she thought of Jim and how different he was. She knew she had become attracted to him and wanted to see him again. She closed her eyes, picturing his wild-looking face in her mind, and wondered when she would hear that deep husky voice again.

The following weekend Sir William was informed of the fall, but made light of the matter. "That's a risk you take if you go riding, I'm afraid."

Lavinia was surprised at his reaction. "But she could have been hurt badly."

"That's true, my dear. But it's no good worrying about what might have been."

After Sir William returned to London the following Monday morning, Angela announced her intention to go for another ride. Her mother felt her head. "Well, the bump seems to have disappeared. Don't go far. And nowhere near that bridle path. You should wear a proper riding hat, you know."

"Yes, Mummy. I'm sure you're right."

Gemma seemed pleased to go out again and was straining against the stable door when Angela arrived and whispered. "I know where you want to go, don't I?" Soon they were off with Angela choosing a path along the side of the hill behind a tall hedge, and out of sight of the house. The path led directly to the forest and then turned and went down the hill beside it to the bridle path. As Angela turned slowly into the path, Gemma's ears were pricked as she stared into the forest. A few minutes later she started whinnying and halted. Angela looked towards the trees, but could see nothing. Suddenly, a few yards in front of them a grinning Jim appeared, and Gemma walked forward and nuzzled him.

"Hello, Jim. I thought I might see you."

She climbed off the saddle and Jim held her arm, whispering "Are you fully recovered now?"

"Yes. I'm fine, but I think my horse is about to desert me and join you in the forest."

"She's lovely."

"Will you show me your lodge again?"

Jim smiled. "I hoped you'd ask."

Gemma followed with her reins thrown over the saddle, and then nudged them in the back if they slowed down. Angela tried to remember the route they were taking, but after five minutes realised she would be lost without Jim. When they arrived she walked around the room looking carefully at Jim's possessions as he watched her in wonderment. "I can't offer you tea 'cause I only drink water."

"Water'll be fine." She sat on the camp bed sipping the cool liquid. "What a terribly spartan life you lead. Don't you want any normal home comforts?"

Drink With The Devil

"No, not really. I have all I need and besides I spend most of my time outside. Let me show you around."

"I'd like that."

They walked along the edge of the hill, Jim holding her hand and fearing she might slip. When they arrived, Angela just stared and whispered "How lovely." Just as she was looking down at the water, the clouds above parted to let a shaft of light penetrate the trees and fall on the water. The surrounding area sharpened the contrasting colours and made the water sparkle. They both stood still and marvelled at the beautiful scene. Instinctively she leant against him and did not move as his arm slipped around her shoulders. A few seconds passed as the world stood still and Angela whispered "It's nice being totally on our own."

"Well, nearly."

She looked sharply up at him. "Who can see us, then?"

"The animals and Gemma, of course."

She buried her head into his shirt-covered chest. "They won't mind."

He held her gently, feeling her heart beating against him. He could smell her perfume and kissed her forehead, feeling overwhelmed with desire and affection. She flung her arms around him and clung to him, pressing her body against him. They stayed locked together, oblivious of the world around them, until a sharp nudge caused them to part in surprise. Gemma put her head between them.

Angela chuckled. "She's jealous. Now Jim, look what you've done to my horse. You've turned her into an old softy." They both laughed and walked back to the lodge hand in hand. Once inside Angela said, "I'll have to go in a minute or my mother'll send out another search party."

"You'll come and see me again, won't you?"

"Of course. As soon as I can." She walked up to him and whispered "I want to see you a lot more."

Jim looked down into her eyes, and saw to his delight his own intense feelings reflected. She looked lovingly first into his eyes and then slowly down to his lips. He gently folded his arms around her in a loving embrace and their lips met; the sweet taste combined with the perfume of her hair, which he stroked as his other hand felt the warm skin through her silk blouse. As he drew her closer she felt the softness of his beard against her cheek, and locked in an embrace they were completely engrossed in their feelings for each other. Jim felt his whole body shake, and Angela, sensing his state of mind, gently eased away, her face flushed with pleasure.

"Oh, Jim. I'm sorry, I really don't want to leave you but I must."

"Please don't go yet."

"I must. I've stayed too long, now."

"But you're so beautiful."

"You've been locked away too long."

He flung his arms around her again and she returned his embrace, but eased away.

"I really must go now."

"Yes. I suppose you must," he said sadly.

They walked back to the bridle path hand in hand, and stopped for another embrace before Jim forced himself to say goodbye, and disappeared into the wood.

Angela returned to find her mother pacing up and down the stable yard.

"Where have you been?"

"Just out for a ride."

"You've been gone for hours."

Angela slid down and stood in front of her mother, who looked her in the eye accusingly. "Look, Darling, you're all flushed. You should have come home earlier."

Angela felt her face and found it was burning. "It's nothing. You worry too much." She led Gemma into the stable, removing the saddle as her mother walked off towards the house.

Later that evening she sat and picked at her food whilst thinking about Jim.

Her mother noticed her faraway look and remarked sharply. "Are you sure you're not suffering from concussion?"

"No, of course not. I'm just hungry."

That night she could not sleep and paced up and down her room, occasionally looking out of the window towards the forest and wondering what Jim was doing.

The wet day that followed found Angela spending a lot of time alone, thinking and beginning to worry about the future if she carried on seeing Jim.

Jim spent the days that followed wandering around the forest, and every afternoon looking across the fields towards the white mansion. At first he ate very little, but then realised he was just being silly. By the weekend a cold cloak of depression had descended, in the certainty that Angela would not return. He tried to resume his old routine, but found it far less enjoyable.

Monday was a beautiful hot day — the best day so far that year — and it was still early May. Angela completed her work in the farm office and went home to lunch, determined to have a ride in the afternoon. She set off just after two, and headed straight down the hill away from the farm buildings. Gemma kept looking towards the forest and whinnied when they were out of sight. Angela stopped and patted her neck. "I think we'll go across that way, don't you?" She said affectionately. Half an hour later they trotted up the side of the forest towards the bridle path, Gemma's ears pricking up as she surged forward into a canter. Some minutes later, when they turned on to the path between the trees, Angela dismounted and looked at Gemma. "You brought us here. Now you can find the lodge."

Having managed to keep up with Gemma as she walked off through the trees, Angela found herself out of breath and in need of a rest. She had just got her breath back when Jim arrived with a bag full of leaves and other green food, and was visibly delighted to see her. They hugged for a few moments, only pausing to make a fuss of Gemma. Once inside the lodge, Jim looked into her eyes and whispered "Angela, I've missed you so much. I've been absolutely devastated without you."

"I've missed you too, my love."

At that moment they were so overcome with pent up

emotion they flung their arms around each other again, kissing deeply.

They wanted each other so desperately, they could think of nothing else but to give each other pleasure. She kissed his eyes and nose and then whispered, "I love you so much."

He found her lips again, and then they paused for breath. "I need all of you, my love."

"I'm all yours."

He wanted to kiss her whole body and make her completely his. His kisses wandered to her neck and shoulders, and she knew she wanted him more than anything in the world and that she wanted to make him happy. As his kisses became more passionate, her flimsy blouse fell apart and he saw she was more beautiful than he thought possible. In his mind she had become the most precious person in his whole life.

Their clothes fell one by one to the floor as they explored each other's bodies with their hands, eyes and mouths until eventually Angela whispered "I want you now." They lay on the hard floor, not noticing the discomfort, and he entered her hot and eager body, both groaning with delight and desire. They kissed deeply again as their intense feelings reached towards a climax of passion which built up to the final ecstatic orgasm. They stayed motionless, not wanting to be separated, and reflected in their minds the superb pleasure each had enjoyed, hoping the other's experience had been even greater.

Angela was the first to break the silence. "That was terrific. You were wonderful, Jim."

"So were you, my love. You're so beautiful, and I love you so much."

They were still clinging to one another when depressing thoughts entered Angela's mind, and she eased away to look into his eyes. She spoke softly. "I love you very much, but I fear the time we can spend together will be very limited."

"I know what you mean. I'm an ex-farmworker living rough, and you're a gentleman farmer's daughter."

"My parents would never approve of our relationship."

Drink With The Devil

"No, I suppose they wouldn't. And if they found out I was staying here, they'd kick me out and ban you from seeing me again."

"But there's got to be something we can do. There's just got to be some future for us."

"I can't see how. You and I live in such different worlds. I'd just never be accepted in yours, and I certainly wouldn't expect you to come down to this sort of existence."

"What are we going to do, then?"

"I really don't know."

They dressed in silence. Angela left in tears and Jim was certain he would never see her again.

Chapter Three

During mid May the weather improved and for three days not a cloud appeared on the horizon. One Friday morning Angela's mother announced, "I'll be spending all day shopping in the West End, and then come back with your father."

"Okay. I'll see you this evening."

Angela waved goodbye and then ran indoors. She was desperate to see Jim again and began preparing food to take for a picnic lunch. She was delighted that such an opportunity had presented itself — she could spend a longer time with him without having to justify her absence. She could hardly contain her excitement and quickly filled her rucksack, setting off on foot. Gemma whinnied as she passed the stable. "Sorry, I can't have you distracting us today."

She entered the forest half way down the hill and made her way to the lodge, where she found Jim still asleep in bed. He woke up suddenly when she pulled his beard.

"Hey, what are you doing here so early? I didn't think I'd ever see you again."

She put her rucksack on the table and knelt down by the bed, looking at him only covered by a thin sheet. She pulled it down to reveal his hairy chest. "What a gorgeous body you have."

"It's all hairy and rough."

"But you're still beautiful." She stroked his beard and whispered, "I don't want to talk about the future today, Jim. Let's forget about it for a while."

"I agree. I'm just so pleased to see you." He reached up and pulled her down so she lay across his chest, overwhelmed with delight that she had, after all, returned. "I just can't believe you're here again. I love you so much, Angela."

"I would just die if I couldn't see you again."

Their lips merged in a long intense kiss, both relieved to be together and wishing the situation would last forever. Their tongues touched and their bodies fused together with intense desire. They felt the need to be even closer together, so he gently undressed her and they lay naked together with the innocence of Adam and Eve on his camp bed, their legs and arms entwined. They held each other so close they seemed to breathe as one, the bond between them so intense they just wanted to cling to one another. Jim thought his body would burst with desire, and her desire to please him was overwhelming. She reached down and guided his throbbing manhood into her hot eager body. They both quickly reached a climax so intense they cried out, before relaxing in the satisfying glow of fulfilment, and lay in each other's arms in silence. Jim just murmured, "Oh, Angela, I love you so much."

"I feel the same way about you. I've just had such a beautiful experience."

"Yes. Quite unbelievably beautiful."

Slowly they got up and looked at each other, neither feeling at all embarrassed at their nakedness. Jim told her how beautiful she was and then whispered, "Aren't you getting dressed?"

"What for? No one can see us." She giggled as they put their shoes on.

They walked hand in hand through the trees and bushes. The day was still and hot, sunlight penetrating the trees and landing on the ground in shafts of brilliance. The young couple lingered in the sun, appreciating the warmth of the rays on their bodies. They splashed each other in the pool, laughing and playing, oblivious to the outside world, with eyes and thoughts only for each other. After a while the chill of the water drove them out and they stood in a ray of sunlight drying one another. They walked, stopping to kiss and caress in every beam of sunlight, until they reached the lodge where Angela said, "Let's make love again. I want you."

"Good. I could make love to you for ever." He laid out all

his blankets on the floor to make it as soft as possible This time they made love more slowly than before, savouring each precious moment. He was intoxicated by her beauty, and wanted to kiss her all over as she lay back with her eyes closed, feeling his hands and lips exploring her body. Her nipples rose to his touch and she was filled with a burning desire to respond and give him pleasure in return. He kissed the inside of her legs and up to her mound of dark curly hair. She groaned with pleasure as he found her moist parts, where he lingered until she was overcome with the need to kiss him again. She lifted his head and he lay down. She kissed him, and then slowly and gently explored his body until he could contain himself no longer. He pulled her on top of him and entered her wet furnace, and their mutual feelings of ecstasy culminated in an orgasm even more explosive than before. They lay in silence, filled with thoughts of love until inevitably these thoughts turned to the subject of their future together. This negative thinking was quickly replaced when Jim said, "Let's have some lunch."

"Yes. I'm ravenous."

The sandwiches and coffee were the first conventional food Jim had tasted for months, and he decided they were good. "It's good to eat normal food again."

"I bet it is."

"There's nothing wrong with my vegetable soup, but I miss bread and cheese."

"I don't know how you've lasted so long."

They ate in silence for a while, studying each other's bodies. Jim broke the silence after staring at and fondling her beautiful breasts. "I've thought myself lucky to live in this beautiful place. Even in winter it's lovely, but with you it would be paradise."

"I don't think I could stand the hardship. Or the food."

"No. And I wouldn't ask you to. It wouldn't be fair."

"I can understand you liking it here, because it's very beautiful."

Jim looked into her eyes. "I've seen many beautiful things in the last year, but they're nothing compared to you."

Drink With The Devil

They found themselves cuddling again, but Angela broke away and looked serious. "I don't want to talk about our future today. It's been so perfect and I don't want to spoil it."

"Okay. It really has been a fantastic day."

Angela walked home, feeling elated after the events of the day. She had made love in a way she never thought possible, and it had been beautiful. She slipped into the kitchen and washed up her cups and flask whilst the cook prepared the evening meal. Her mother greeted her as she walked into the drawing room, and showed her all the clothes she had purchased that day. Including a new creation she decided would suit her daughter.

"Oh, thanks, Mum. I'll wear that for dinner tonight."

"Good idea, darling. Your father does like you to dress up."

Sir William was in jovial mood over dinner and chatted about his plans for the weekend. He complimented the ladies on their attire as he seated himself at the head of the table, still wearing his business suit.

Just as the family were finishing their meal, a clap of thunder made them all jump as rain lashed against the window. Angela thought about Jim and hoped he was all right in the lodge. The day's activities had made her extremely hungry and she ate with relish, eventually feeling satisfied and happy. The temperature in the house dropped considerably as the storm gathered strength, and they took their coffee into the drawing room in front of a log fire, these days only lit at weekends. Whilst her parents chatted, Angela sat sipping her coffee, still thinking about what had happened earlier. There were just the three of them, as their cook had gone home.

Angela began raking the fire with a long thin poker, and watching the sparks fly up the chimney, when suddenly the tranquillity was shattered by three men bursting through the door. The first man was carrying a shotgun, the two others pickaxe handles. All of them had masks over their faces, and wore identical army-type clothing. Sir William spluttered as he looked down the barrel of the shotgun. "What the devil d'you think you're doing?"

The first man spoke in a high pitched voice, slightly slurred: "We're about to relieve you of some money, you rich bastard."

All three men moved closer. Lavinia sat still and whimpered softly, and Sir William moved in front of her. "I don't keep any money here."

"You'll do as I say or die."

Angela sat still, stunned by the turn of events. She stared at the men. Two of them were of medium height and the third, pointing a gun at her father's face, was taller with a pot belly. Sir William looked nervously around at the two petrified women. "I'll do whatever you ask if you agree not to harm my wife and daughter."

"Right. Open yer safe, then."

"Yes. It's in the study."

"Go on, then. Hurry up."

The man with the gun followed Sir William into the next room. The two others approached Lavinia and Angela with pickaxe handles ready to strike. The one closest to the older woman said in a gruff tone:"Right missus. Get on yer feet and take me to yer jewellery box."

Lavinia held a handkerchief to her mouth and stared at the floor.

"Come on you stupid bloody woman. Get up."

She rose slowly and walked towards the door without looking at the masked face. The third man stood still, staring at Angela, who just watched as her mother disappeared and then studied the fire trying to be brave. Nothing happened for a while and then she heard the sound of her father opening his safe, followed by a shuffling sound of papers being strewn about. There was a short silence followed by a high pitched scream from upstairs. Angela recognised her mother's voice and shouted at the man staring at her: "What's going on?"

He moved closer and growled. "He's just havin' a bit o' fun with yer mum."

Angela cringed. She heard her father protesting to the man with the shotgun.

Drink With The Devil

"What are you doing to my wife?"

His voice was stopped abruptly with a thud, and he fell with a crash to the floor. Angela became so frightened she could not speak. She heard another louder thud and a groan. The man with the weapon came from the study with her father's briefcase. He walked through the room quickly and announced to his companion. "He won't be any trouble. Just keep yer eye on 'er while I look round."

The other man just grunted. Angela heard the gunman walking upstairs, and then after another short silence, she heard her mother scream again for the last time. By this time she was beside herself with anger, and shouted, half screamed at the man leering at her, "You evil scum." Her head sank lower as she saw him move closer while one hand fiddled with the front of his trousers. She got up quickly and tried to escape, but was too late as he struck her a stunning blow across the face with his clenched fist. She reeled backwards towards the fire, just preventing herself from falling on it.

The man dropped his cudgel, easily wrestling her to the floor. She could feel the heat of the fire on her face as he sat on top of her. She could not move; one arm was pinned under her, the other held down by a knee. She felt the top of her dress being torn down the centre, and then a rough hand gripping her breast. He moved lower, forcing her legs apart. She was too scared to move as her dress was pulled up to her waist, but her right hand was free and she moved it towards the fire. The man tore her panties off, and as he lunged forward on her, she could smell his foul beer-laden breath. It sickened her and she struggled, which forced his head up a little. Whilst he regained a grip on her she lay still, realising he was too strong for her. As he reached down and undid his trousers with one hand, holding her down with the other, her right hand found the poker and she brought it down on his head as hard as she could. The instrument lay against his masked head for a second. He screamed with pain and jumped up, wrenching off his mask.

Angela sat up, smelling burning flesh, and she looked at the poker which was still red hot from being left in the fire. Now it had hair and human flesh sticking to it. She stood up and looked at the ginger-haired individual of about twenty, as he clutched his head and bellowed. She threw down the weapon and fled from the room into the front hall, but glanced up the stairs to see another ginger-haired man about to descend. She ran out of the front door. The man behind shouted something and half fell down the stairs in hot pursuit. Angela ran as fast as she could in high-heeled shoes around the house, towards the stables, knowing her parents were almost certainly dead but could hear someone following and knew he would soon catch her.

Chapter Four

Jim spent the early evening listening to the storm raging above the forest, causing the trees to creak and groan and the rhododendron bushes to rustle and scrape against the lodge walls.

It was only a short time since he had seen Angela, but he was desperate to see her again. In his mind he pictured her lovely body, and imagined making love again in the lodge. A short while passed and he ladled himself a bowl of vegetable soup, drinking it whilst trying to think seriously about the future. It was obvious his days in the forest were nearly over. He would have to get a job, probably on a farm again, but would Angela be content to be a farm worker's wife? She might, if she loved him enough. He churned matters over in his mind for some time, and became more and more desperate to see her.

The storm continued to rage, with lightning illuminating the forest almost without a break. Thunder shook the ground as he wandered through the trees, being drawn like a magnet towards the edge of the forest and the mansion. The rain lashed at his face, water trickled down his back off his long matted hair. A steady stream was running off the tip of his beard down his jacket and his trousers were soaked in no time. But he was so preoccupied with thinking about Angela that he felt no discomfort. He passed the pool, which was filling with muddy water washed down from the hill above. Without a glance in its direction he jumped over the swollen stream and on to the field beyond the forest. He felt his shoes fill with water and thought how stupid he was not to have worn his boots.

After half an hour he could just see the mansion ahead through the sheets of rain, and most of the windows were lit as usual. He stopped, wondering if he should go any closer, but decided no one would be out in this weather, and moved forward until the stables came into view. An outside light illuminated the concrete yard and he crept closer in the shadows, hoping that perhaps Angela would check her horses before retiring, as she said she always did.

Angela ran up the path away from the house, her feet slipping on the greasy surface. She could hear the man behind getting closer and her heart was thumping as she pulled up her dress to try to move quicker. The light from the stable yard came into view and she had just reached the concrete area when the man behind dived on her legs. She was pitched forward on her stomach, the breath driven from her body as her head crashed against the rock hard surface. The last thing she saw was a flash, and then blackness.

Jim heard a noise, looked around the corner of the end stable and saw a man kicking Angela as she lay motionless on the ground. He roared as he ran towards her assailant, who looked up and literally froze at the sight of such a large wild-looking man approaching him at speed. But the man dodged to one side and was ready when Jim turned and advanced again. He had never fought with anyone in his life, and was not ready for the blow delivered to the side of his head, making him see stars. A second punch to his stomach doubled him up and he went down. When he opened his eyes, Angela's face was only a foot away, and she looked asleep. The sight of her made him desperate and he leapt to his feet, punching the now unprepared thug in his stomach as he buckled from the force of Jim's anger. Jim grabbed his jacket and trousers, lifting his body high above his head before letting him crash to the ground. Jim dived on him, battering the man's head and body with ferocious punches. He felt ribs crack as he released his anger but suddenly stopped, disgusted with himself. This feeling changed to deep compassion as he bent over his beloved Angela.

The rain had flattened her clothes against her body and her

face was white. He rolled her over gently and carried her to the nearest stable, half-filled with hay bales. He laid her out, pulling her torn dress together to hide an exposed breast. Her body felt cold, so he raced along the front of the stables to the tack room and found a large horse blanket. He folded it double, laid it carefully over her and then sat beside her, his whole body gripped with grief. He kissed her cold and wet forehead. "Please wake up, Angela."

He had a horrible feeling her injuries were worse than they had seemed before. The sound of footsteps alerted him. He looked over the stable door to see a tall man carrying a gun and peering at the body lying face down on the ground. He was saying " 'arry. Get up, you silly sod." The tall man rolled his accomplice over and stepped back in horror. "Oh, Christ." Looking wildly around, he ran back towards the house.

Jim went back and sat beside Angela, and five minutes later heard a car move away with screeching tyres. He sat on the hay bales, filled with remorse and despair. Angela showed no sign of recovery. He stroked her hair and face, talking to her softly, but when he felt her pulse it was weak and her breathing shallow. He knew he should call an ambulance, but found it difficult to tear himself away.

A short time later he looked out of the stable at the man still motionless on the concrete. He listened, thinking he could hear the sound of fire, and smoke was carried towards him with a gust of wind. The rain had stopped and he returned to Angela, kissing her forehead again and dropping to his knees in front of her. Then for the first time in his life, he prayed. Tears ran down his cheeks as he earnestly asked for Angela's good health to return. After a few minutes he got up when he heard the sound of running feet. He looked out the door as two men approached and shouted to them. "Call an ambulance. There's a badly injured girl in here."

The first man turned around and ran back shouting, "Okay. I'll do it."

The second man ran over to the body lying on the concrete.

"My God. He's in a mess." He bent down and touched the man's face, pulling his hand away immediately. "I think he's dead." He ran across to Jim. "Where's the girl?"

"Laying here."

The man looked down at Angela. "My God. It's Miss Angela."

A gust of wind blew smoke into the stable and the two horses in adjoining stables whinnied and stamped their feet. The man looked up at Jim. "Have you seen Sir William and Lady Osborne?"

"I haven't."

"I hope they aren't in the house, 'cause it's well alight. We can't get near it 'cause of the heat."

The sound of the fire engine bells stopped the conversation, and the farm worker ran off to meet it.

Jim stayed with Angela for another half an hour. The intense heat from the fire was causing the stable yard and buildings to steam, and he was just about to move her when medical help arrived. The two ambulance men ran to the man lying on the concrete, and the first to arrive said to his colleague, "He's dead. We'd better find the girl."

Jim shouted from the stable. "Over here. Please come quickly."

He helped them lift Angela on to the stretcher, and watched as they drove away with their bell ringing loudly.

Jim was getting concerned for the horses, so he put a head collar on Gemma, and led her towards the farm buildings away from the heat. A farm worker met him. "I'll show you where to put her." The man gave him a strange look. "Who are you, then?"

"Oh, I just thought I could help out." Jim ran back to the stables to find the other horse, a brood mare. She had become very agitated, with smoke filling the stable and the heat almost unbearable. He threw a rug over her, covering her eyes. He talked as he led her out, putting her in a loose box normally used for sick cows and next to Gemma, who whinnied and

Drink With The Devil

nuzzled up to him. "Don't worry, ole girl, your mistress'll recover soon." He walked back towards the burning house and noticed policemen arriving in plain cars. They ran towards the house and stables, but were soon halted by the heat and smoke.

Jim stared at the fire, thinking about Angela and how happy they had been a few hours before. Now she could be badly injured, and he had no chance of seeing her again for a long time. His depression deepened, and he felt sick when he thought about the man whom he had killed, laying on the concrete. He remembered the thud as the man hit the ground, and how he had battered him unmercifully. He turned from the fire as the contents of his stomach reached his mouth. Five minutes later, as he leant against a gatepost, the feeling of nausea subsided, but he felt weak and disgusted with himself as he staggered into the nearby cowshed. He found a cold tap, and the cold water splashing over his face brought him back to reality. He drank directly from the tap and walked outside again to be confronted by a burly-looking policeman.

Chapter Five

The ambulance took Angela to the casualty department of the local hospital, where the doctor suspected she was suffering from brain damage. He called a consultant who declared her to be seriously ill, and still in a coma she was taken to intensive care. Her other injuries included bad bruising to the ribs and arms.

Garry Osborne had just gone to bed when the telephone rang. It was the farm manager, Peter French. "I'm sorry to disturb you, Mr. Osborne, but the big house is on fire."

"Oh God. Have you called the fire brigade?"

"Of course. They're here, but we can't find your mother or father." Garry was stunned and stammered. "W-what about Angela?"

"She's injured and has been taken to hospital."

"I'll leave straight away." He dressed quickly and ran downstairs and out to his red M.G.

The policeman gave Jim a strange look as he spoke. "One of the farm workers says you were first on the scene."

"Yes. That's probably true."

"What's your name?"

"Jim Grainger."

"Where d'you live?"

Jim pointed to the forest. "Over there. In a shooting lodge."

"Where? In the wood?"

"Yes."

"You'd better come and see the inspector."

They walked across the crowded farmyard to the farm office. Jim was introduced to Inspector Brian Green, who was sitting on the farm manager's desk. He looked at Jim, carefully taking in every detail of his appearance. The police constable told the senior officer what he had been told, and the inspector turned to Jim. "So you live rough, do you?"

"No. I said I live in a shooting lodge."

"Oh, yes. And how long have you lived there?"

"About a year."

"And do the owners know about this?"

"No."

"So you're trespassing?"

"Yes. I suppose so."

"Tell me about your movements this evening."

"I went for a walk."

The inspector nearly choked. "In the middle of a storm? And only wearing shoes. You'll have to do better than that."

"I was hoping to see Angela."

"You mean Sir William's daughter? And I suppose you're friendly with her?"

"Yes. You could say that."

The inspector got up and walked around the room, frowning as he sat on the edge of the desk directly in front of Jim. "You're suggesting that Sir William's daughter would want to be friendly with a wild looking gypo, living rough in a wood? Have you looked in a mirror lately?"

Jim was stunned and just shrugged.

"You'd better start telling me the truth."

Jim looked at the middle aged balding figure and said sternly. "I am telling you the truth."

"I do hope so. Now tell me what happened on that walk."

"I thought I might see Angela checking her horses before turning in so I waited, hiding around the side of the stable in the dark." He hesitated.

"Go on. Then what happened?"

"I heard a noise, and when I crept forward I saw Angela on the ground being kicked in the side by a man." He became tense, gripping the chair, as he remembered every detail of the awful scene.

"Go on. What happened next?"

"I ran across the yard to try to save her, but the man turned on me and we had a fight. I saw what he'd done to Angela and I couldn't stop myself." He hesitated again, feeling sick.

The inspector stared at him and then walked back to the chair.

Jim continued. "I must have hit him too hard. When the fight was over I carried Angela into the stable."

The inspector was silent for a minute and then said loudly. "So you admit killing this man?"

"Yes I do."

The inspector shouted to the sergeant standing outside and he came in immediately. "Yes, Sir."

"Arrest this man. Take him back to the station, take his statement and lock him up. We'll charge him in the morning.

"Right away, Sir."

"And cuff him."

Jim was led away to a police car, feeling stunned and confused. He was jammed tightly between two policemen, who remained silent until they reached the station. "Come on, gypo," said one of them.

"Okay. But I'm not a gypo."

"Don't give us any trouble."

They took him down some concrete steps and bundled him into a small cell with a bunk against one wall. The steel door clanged shut behind him and he shuddered as he sat down heavily. He looked around the stark room, which had a dim light high above revealing a small window with bars too high to reach. He cupped his head in his hands and tried to imagine he was dreaming, but to no avail. The full impact of the situation was beginning to bear down on him. He paced up and down the room trying to calm himself down and then lay on the hard bunk with his eyes closed, picturing himself back among the trees and animals. Towards morning he eventually dozed off to sleep, dreaming about his forest paradise. His dream was interrupted by the clanging of metal doors along the corridor and, when he looked up at the small window, he could see daylight. Realising where he was, the loss of freedom and fresh air made him desperate and he bellowed, rattling the door.

A gruff voice shouted "Shut up gypo."

Jim yelled and screamed, then collapsed on the bunk. He felt his life was falling apart and there was no hope of returning to his former freedom.

* * *

Garry Osborne arrived at the farm to find it swarming with police and firemen. Peter French greeted him and took him to see the inspector in charge, who explained the situation. "I'm sorry about your parents, Sir. It appears they were inside during the evening, but they cannot be accounted for now."

"How d'you know they were in?"

"The cook said she prepared a meal for them."

Garry sat down and stared at the floor.

"I think you should prepare yourself for bad news," Brian Green said softly.

"I am."

"We've recovered the body of a ginger-haired man, who was beaten to death."

"Who was he?"

"We don't know. Could he have been a guest?"

"I don't know."

The fire brigade worked all night getting the fire under control. When Garry arrived at the hospital to see Angela, he was told she was in a deep coma and likely to stay that way for some time.

By the time he returned to the farm daylight was approaching, and firemen were preparing to search the burnt-out building with special equipment. Inspector Green had left and a new shift of policemen was on site. Meanwhile Garry was asked to identify the ginger-haired man at the local mortuary and the sight of the battered face made him feel sick, and he turned away. "I don't know him. Who did that?"

"A wild looking gypo who says he was trying to save your sister."

"Oh yes. A likely tale!"

The firemen recovered the remains of Sir William and Lady Osborne, and after forensic tests, they were both found to have shattered skulls, their bodies too badly burned to reveal any other evidence.

Peter French's wife administered Garry a stiff drink and sent him to bed. He was utterly exhausted and slept until the next morning.

Inspector Green returned to work the next afternoon to sift through the evidence. "Go and fetch that gypo,'" he said to his assistant, Detective Sergeant Mike Evans. "Better take some help. He might be dangerous."

Jim was brought in and seated at a table. The inspector looked at his face, which looked even more troubled than the previous night. What little skin that was visible was white, his eyes were bloodshot and his hair had dried matted together with grey ash stuck to it. His beard had also got flecks of ash clinging to it. The inspector smiled to himself, convinced that any jury would convict a man of murder if he looked like this one.

Jim spoke first. "How's Angela?"

"In a deep coma."

"My God. That's terrible. Poor Angela."

"Yes. Especially for you, if you caused her injuries."

Jim pulled himself upright and stared straight at his interrogator. "I love that girl. I couldn't harm her."

"So you say, now. Calm down. I want the truth about your movements."

Jim repeated his story again, the sergeant duly writing it down, and when he had finished the inspector grunted. "So you're sticking to your story?"

"Yes, of course I am. It's the truth."

"Now I'll tell you what I think. You were part of a gang of robbers who burgled the big house, and then set fire to it. You fell out with one of them, killed him and the others cleared off

Drink With The Devil

leaving you to face the consequences. Then you made up this story about protecting the girl."

Jim was stunned at these accusations and stammered. "B-but I'm not part of any bloody gang."

"Prove it."

"I've lived alone in that wood for over a year."

"That's what you say. But can you prove it?"

"Angela'll bear me out."

"Angela is in no position to say anything. Sergeant, prepare to charge this man with murder."

"Yes, Sir."

"Now you horrible gypo, you can expect further charges to follow. Like arson, robbery with violence and causing grievous bodily harm."

"But I didn't do any of those things."

"I'm going to prove you were part of that gang, and then you can expect a long stretch in prison."

Jim was stunned and speechless as the sergeant carried out the formalities. Two policemen led him back to the cell and he collapsed on the bunk, this time giving way to tears. A lifetime in a small cell was more than he could contemplate, and he tried to think of a way to end it all.

Inspector Green went back to his office to think about the case, but his deliberations were interrupted by the sergeant.

"I've got the report about the ginger-haired stiff."

"Who was he?"

"Harry Briggs. A small time thief suspected of violence, but it could never be proved. He normally worked with his brother, John."

"I see. You'd better find his brother."

"Yes, Sir. The report says Harry died as a result of a severe battering delivered with superhuman force."

"That'll nail that gypo good and proper."

Inspector Green's men searched the remains of the house and found the safe door open. They searched the forest, finding the lodge containing Jim's possessions, which they listed carefully and then secured the door with a padlock. The inspector visited the scene of the crime and listened to his detectives' reports. A car had been seen leaving the house at high speed during the evening at about the right time, but no clear description was available. The list of items found in the shooting lodge was presented and the inspector read it thoroughly. He was just folding it up when Garry Osborne arrived in his sports car.

"How are your investigations going, Inspector?"

"Quite well, Sir."

"Have you charged that gypo, yet?"

"We're about to, but he denies arson and robbery."

"I bet he does."

"And he insists he's a friend of your sister."

"Absolute rubbish. She would never associate with the likes of him."

"I agree it does seem unlikely."

"Unlikely! Just about impossible. Listen inspector, I want that evil bastard put away forever."

"Don't worry. He'll be put away all right."

"Good. Jail's far too good for him."

"How is your sister?"

"Still in a coma, I'm afraid."

"I'm sorry to hear that, Sir."

"So am I. That gypo's got a lot to answer for."

"Did you know he was living in your wood?"

"No, I didn't. My father couldn't have known either or he'd have thrown him out."

"Well, judging from a list of items found to-day, it seems he's been there for some time."

Garry marched off to see his farm manager, and the inspector sat in his car reading reports, one of which he read twice. A farm worker stated he had seen Grainger leading a horse away from the stables at considerable danger to himself. He read the list of items found in the lodge again, and realised the wild looking man could be telling the truth about having lived in the lodge.

Drink With The Devil

Jim was taken to court and the charge of murder was read out. A lawyer chosen for him said his client would not be applying for bail as he was of no fixed address, and without any means of raising money. The judge ordered him to be detained in custody until further notice.

He was then taken to a remand centre and put in a cell on his own, as he was considered to be dangerous.

Once again a steel door banged behind Jim. He paced up and down the cell like a wild animal. The only release from misery was sleep, which was filled with nightmares of being locked in a small room forever. He was getting thinner and weaker due to continually refusing food, and after a few days when the inspector visited him he was shocked at the change in his appearance. He could only walk slowly. He collapsed in a chair and fixed his eyes on the policeman. "I've already told you all I know. What d'you want now?"

The inspector sat down and said slowly, "I believe your story."

Jim perked up. "Do you really?"

"Yes. You should have told me about the horses."

"What about them?"

"It seems you may have saved their lives."

"I couldn't let them suffer. Especially Gemma."

"Gemma?"

"The horse Angela rides. The other one is an older mare."

"So you really are friendly with Miss Osborne?"

"Yes. Very. How is she?"

"The news is still bad, I'm afraid."

"Oh, my God. That's terrible. I can't stand to think of her lying ill in hospital." Tears came to his eyes, which he managed to hold back. "Did you know she fell off Gemma a few weeks ago and hit her head?" I found her on the bridleway and took her back to the lodge until she felt better."

The inspector made a note in his book and nodded. "It's a pity she's so ill. Her evidence would be very valuable."

"What happens now?"

"We'll change the charge to manslaughter."

"Does that mean a lighter sentence?"

"Yes, but we may need your help to catch the real murderers."

"What can I do?"

"You can try to identify the man you saw looking at Briggs."

"Who's Briggs?"

"Harry Briggs is the man you killed."

Jim shuddered. "I didn't get a very good look at him."

The inspector got up and asked Mike Evans to come in, and the sergeant put a large folder of photographs on the table. Jim looked carefully at hundreds of mug shots, but did not recognise anyone. Tea and cake was brought in, and Jim ate and drank without thinking.

The inspector smiled as he saw the cake disappear. "Well done, Jim."

"But I haven't done anything."

"Yes you have. You've eaten all the cake."

Jim smiled for the first time since the afternoon with Angela. He gave the best description he could, and was taken back to his cell, feeling as though there was some hope left in his life. He ate a meal that evening. Later he fell into an exhausted sleep.

Sergeant Evans spent a week searching for John Briggs. His last known address in Southall was occupied by an Asian family, who had never heard of him. The local police had no information, but were given his description along with that of the other man involved.

The wreckage of the burnt out house was sifted through again for evidence, but the heat had been so intense very little was left. The only certain thing was all the diamonds and other hard-stone jewellery were missing, as they would have survived the fire and should have been found.

The inspector visited the burnt-out house as the search was completed, and was accosted by Garry, who appeared from the farm office and marched across to the police car. Brian Green looked at the tall, dark-haired thin man, who looked older than his twenty-four years. He was frowning and looked angry.

"When'll your men ever get finished here?"

"When we're satisfied there's no further evidence."

"What d'you need it for? You've got your man."

"We've got a man who killed one of the robbers."

"What d'you mean?"

"I don't believe he robbed and killed your parents, or hurt your sister."

Garry nearly exploded. "Who the hell did then?"

"We think it may have been the dead man's brother, and one or more accomplices."

"Have you picked them up yet?"

"No. We can't find them."

"What evidence have you got, then?"

"Very little. Only one eye witness."

"Who's that?"

"Grainger."

Garry let out a mirthless laugh. "So you've no evidence and you've been taken in by that gypo?"

The inspector got out of his car and stood firmly in front of the young man. "You'll have to accept that Grainger knew your sister quite well."

"I'll accept nothing of the sort. You're talking absolute rubbish."

"Mr. Osborne. Did your sister have a fall a few weeks ago?"

"I don't know. I wasn't here."

"Well I think you'll find she did. And Grainger knew about it."

"That doesn't prove anything. You've been taken for a ride by that evil bastard." He was getting very agitated and red in the face.

The inspector stood still, calmly observing the young man's temper rising. "I'm sure there's some jewellery missing. The fire wouldn't have melted diamonds, and that means they were taken by the intruders."

"Ha. It means you can't find them amongst all that debris."

"We've searched very carefully."

"Now, you listen, inspector. I don't care about the jewellery.

I'm only interested in the good name of my family, and my sister in particular."

"The truth'll have to be told."

Garry moved closer and stared into the inspector's eyes. "If you or anyone else suggests my sister was involved with that murdering gypo, I'll sue for slander."

"That's up to you, Sir."

"And now get your men and yourself off my property immediately." Garry turned and stormed off towards the farm office.

The inspector instructed the sergeant to call off the search, and the men gathered in the farmyard. Inspector Green saw a farm worker with a bucket in each hand walking towards them. "Can I have a moment of your time?"

"Only a second Sir, or I'll be in trouble."

"Did Angela Osborne fall off her horse a few weeks ago?"

"Oh, yes, Sir. We were all called out to search for her."

"And where was she found?"

"In the wood. On the bridle way."

"Thank you. I won't keep you any longer."

He watched as the man ran off towards the cowshed and wondered if he had been told not to talk to the police.

Garry watched the police car and van leave and turned to his manager. "I don't want any of the men wasting their time talking to the police."

"Yes Mr. Osborne. You told me before."

"Well, it obviously didn't sink in, did it?"

Peter French was depressed at the thought of having to work for this arrogant young man, and was missing Angela's help in the office. Paperwork was piling up, and he was hoping Garry would go back to London so that he could get on with his job.

The murder of his father and mother occupied Garry's mind, although he had grown apart from them in latter years. The thought of his sister having an affair with a wild man obsessed him, and he was desperate to see the man convicted and imprisoned for life.

Drink With The Devil

Inspector Green and Sergeant Evans drove back to the station together. During the journey Evans broke the silence. "The person to gain most from the fire is Garry Osborne."

"Yes. And he's very obstructive."

"And desperate to blame Grainger."

Chapter Six

The weeks dragged by slowly for Jim, left alone in a small cell. He spent many hours looking out of the small barred window gazing at the clouds in the daytime and the stars at night; wondering about Angela and if she could see the same stars! His thoughts frequently returned to their last day in the forest, imagining he was making love to her over and over again. When reality returned he was pitched into deep depression, certain that Angela would not want to associate with an ex-convict.

At first the prison food made him ill, but slowly he grew accustomed. His fellow inmates kept a respectful distance from him at meal times, knowing he had killed a man, and his appearance did not help as his beard was getting shaggier and his hair even longer. The only visitor he had was his solicitor, gathering information for a trial in which he had agreed to plead guilty to manslaughter, hoping the mitigating circumstances would result in a lighter sentence. The date was eventually set for four months after that fateful night.

After three weeks on the farm, Garry convinced himself his efficiency drive was paying off. He observed the men working harder, and the farm was neat and tidy. He also noticed the men avoiding him as much as they could, with even Peter French having a good excuse for disappearing to the other end of the farm as soon he arrived in the morning.

After another two weeks he announced, "I'll be returning to my flat in the City, and will come down to the farm at weekends."

Peter kept a straight face, whilst secretly heaving a sigh of relief. "I expect you want to catch up with important business," he said as seriously as he could.

"Yes. I've been away too long."

The will was read in a solicitor's office in the City, and Garry was not surprised to learn he had inherited the majority share holding in his father's stockbroking and financial services company, Osborne and Partners. Together with a small holding of shares, he also inherited the farm. His sister inherited a substantial holding of stocks and shares and a large house on the farm, know as Home Farm House, and formerly inhabited by Andrew and Ruth Jones. Garry was delighted to find that death duties would only swallow up his small holding of shares, because the large amount of liquid funds accumulated over the years by his father in various insurance policies would pay the majority of this.

On returning to his London office, Garry was greeted by the senior partners, who offered condolences and commiserations at the passing of his parents. He took over his father's grand office and began to find out how things had progressed since his father's death. Within a couple of days he called the senior members of the company together and announced, "I'm very disappointed with the company's performance. In future I'm to be consulted before any substantial purchases of shares on behalf of clients."

They looked grim faced and a senior employee spoke for them. "Do you want to attend our buying policy meetings?"

"Yes. Of course I do."

"But Sir William rarely attended."

"I'm not Sir William. Besides it's obvious you're not doing a good enough job on behalf of this company."

"We've achieved a steady growth over the years, which your father found satisfactory."

"I can see I'll have to remind you again. I'm not Sir William."

The meeting broke up with his associates leaving the office looking shocked and muttering in low tones. The news that Garry would be a hard master soon filtered through the company, and the staff were nervous and edgy when he walked around the various departments with a frown on his face. Even his old colleagues just nodded and smiled weakly when he approached.

Garry was pleased to be living in his Belgravia flat again. It was well furnished, with one large bedroom, a lounge, kitchen and bathroom. He had lived there, usually alone, for four years, since leaving university with a degree in economics. Several girlfriends had stayed for short periods and left when they could stand his aggressive manner no longer. This detrimental aspect of his character was well known to his father, who had kept him in check at work by placing him in the charge of a strong minded manager. His evenings used to be spent at clubs with old university chums or at home reading, but now he was the boss, he took work home and studied, hoping to find ways to increase the company's profit.

One morning he was drinking coffee in the office whilst glancing at the newspaper, when suddenly he sat bolt upright, spilling coffee into the saucer. "What the hell are the police playing at?" He said aloud to himself. The paper reported that a trial was to take place the next week. The defendant, James Grainger, was charged with the manslaughter of Harry Briggs. The article added that the police were still investigating the murder of Sir William and Lady Osborne, who died on the same night. Garry marched up and down his office getting more and more angry. He shouted at his secretary in the adjoining office. "Carol. Get me our solicitors on the 'phone."

"Yes, Sir," she replied nervously.

A meeting was arranged for that afternoon. Garry tried to stay calm as he explained, "my sister's identity must be kept out of the press in order to preserve the family's good name."

"But, Mr. Osborne, we can't stop the court producing whatever evidence it wants to."

"Then we must sue for libel."

"But that will only make matters worse."

"Why?"

"Because the Sunday newspapers will have a field day."

Garry left the office feeling bitter and angry and returned to his flat to pour a large brandy, followed by several others. Sitting in his favourite leather armchair and thinking about his sister lying in hospital, he imagined her helpless body being ravaged by a hairy giant of a man with bad teeth and ragged clothes. He pictured his parents being burned alive and screaming for help. The more brandy he drank, the worse his fit of depression became, until he finally fell asleep.

The next morning Garry woke up still in the armchair, and tried to think how he could stop any adverse publicity, but his head ached badly as well as his stomach. He decided to stay at home until he felt better and, after a light breakfast, went for a walk in a nearby park to clear his head. He had only walked a hundred yards in the sunshine when he noticed a beautiful blond girl coming towards him, whom he recognised from a party he had attended a few months ago. "Hello Jane. How are you?"

"Garry Osborne. I haven't seen you for ages."

"That's true. I don't go to many parties these days."

"Neither do I."

"Have you got time for coffee and a chat?"

"Yes. That'd be nice."

They walked together through the trees to a small cafe. Garry found he could talk easily to this tall slim girl, whose voice seemed to calm his nerves. They sat and chatted for an hour, and then walked to a park bench.

Jane looked into his eyes and whispered. "I'm very sorry about your parents. It must have been a terrible shock for you."

"Yes it was. And poor Angela's still in a coma, despite all the efforts to revive her. I visit her at weekends, but of course she doesn't recognise me."

"That's terrible." She moved closer and linked her arm with his.

"It's diabolical. And the evil swine who did it looks as if he'll get away with it." His body was tense as he stared at the ground.

Jane squeezed his arm. "Come on, let's go for a walk. I can see you've been under a great strain, but it's no good dwelling on it."

Garry changed the subject as they walked. "How are your parents?"

"Mum's fine, but Dad's feeling the strain of business."

"I bet he is. Trying to run Blakesbuild almost single handed."

"Yes. We've all tried to get him to delegate, but he won't."

They had lunch together and arranged to meet again that evening for a drink. Garry felt light-hearted as he returned to work in the afternoon.

The evening was a success with Jane inviting Garry to her flat for a drink. As they sat chatting on the sofa together, he felt very attracted to her as he gazed into her eyes, whilst she explained how her father's large building contracting company was started. She noticed his expression. "You're not listening, are you?"

"Yes I am. Only I'm distracted by your lovely eyes."

"They're horrible and grey."

"I think they're gorgeous." He ran his hands through her beautiful hair and she moved closer. They kissed and he held her tight, but after a few moments stood up together with Garry looking at his watch and discovering it to be very late. "I must go, but when can I see you again?"

"What about tomorrow night?"

"Okay. I'll look forward to it."

The next day Garry attended a meeting of senior managers, and sat at the head of the table studying the agenda, which he then pushed aside. "I want you to carry on as if I wasn't present."

They looked at each other and one manager said, "Very well, let's proceed."

Garry sat still, watching and listening for an hour, and after the last item had been dealt with he said. "I can see you're all doing what you think is best for our clients, but no one has suggested ways of acquiring new customers."

They all looked aghast and a young manager in a grey suit said, "We always attract new customers by our reputation."

"Not enough, I'm afraid. We need new business."

Another senior manager, a middle aged man, with a large gut added, "What do you suggest?"

Drink With The Devil

"We'll contact an advertising agency."

"I don't approve of advertising and nor did your father."

"I don't care what you or my father approved of. This company needs to bring in new business to cover our rising overheads."

They all sat thinking about this suggestion and Simon Berry, a young manager seated at the far end of the table said, "I think it's a good idea."

Garry looked directly at him. "Good. Then you can help find a suitable agency."

Simon, a man of about his own age of medium height with fair curly hair, was summoned into Garry's office. He looked him up and down, approving of his smart appearance. "Simon, I want you to leave your present duties and concentrate on bringing in new business to this tired old company."

"Yes, Sir. I'd be pleased to have a go."

"That's the spirit. We need a few more enthusiastic people around here."

They discussed the new idea for the remainder of the afternoon.

That evening Garry picked up Jane at her flat, to find her looking tense and her eye make-up smudged. She got into the sports car and Garry kissed her cheek. "What's the matter, Jane?"

"I'm fine, but Dad's been taken to hospital. He collapsed at work."

"Oh, that's pretty serious. Is there anything I can do?"

"No. I've been visiting the hospital on and off all day."

"What do they think is wrong with him?"

"A heart attack, I'm afraid."

"I'm sorry to hear that. Is he stable now?"

"Yes, so they say."

"He's tough and sure to get over it."

"I do hope so, but he was very run down."

They went to a restaurant and Jane picked at her food. Garry found himself worried about a girl for the first time in his life. They visited the hospital together after dinner, but Jane was told there was no change in her father's condition. She introduced Garry to her mother, who would not budge from the waiting room despite Garry offering to take her home. They went back to Jane's flat and drank coffee, and although Garry tried to talk about light-hearted matters, she was inconsolable.

The next morning Garry rang the hospital to find Roland Blake was out of danger. He felt relieved, and worked hard reviewing the performance of each key member of staff and their cost to the company. He finished late and was about to leave when Jane rang. She sounded cheerful. "I'm sorry for being so dull last night."

"Think nothing of it. It was only to be expected."

"Will you be taking me out to dinner tonight?"

"Yes. I'll pick you up later." Garry felt very happy, as having forgotten to ask her out the previous night, he was worried that she would not want to see him again.

Jane climbed into the car and spoke before Garry could welcome her. "Dad's a lot better."

"That's marvellous news." Garry smiled as he asked, "d'you think he'll delegate a little more now?"

"He'll have to. I'll make sure of it."

"D'you work near to him?"

"Yes. In the adjoining office."

"That's useful."

They were a little merry as they walked back to Jane's flat, where she immediately rang the hospital to find her father's condition was still improving. They had a drink and cuddled on the sofa, Garry feeling very happy to be with her. Their kisses became more intense and they clung to each other, lying back on the wide surface. Clothes were soon loosened and Garry untied her hair, letting it cascade down over her shoulders. As he felt the silky blond strands between his fingers, he became aroused. They undressed each other slowly, stopping to kiss deeply. Garry was quivering with excitement at the beauty of her body and stammered. "I-I love you, Jane."

She said nothing, but felt different than ever before as she clung to his slim body, and their kisses became more and more passionate. After they had made love they lay still for a few minutes and Jane whispered, "I've never felt like that before. I think I love you, too."

The following day was Saturday, and Garry had arranged to see Peter French at the farm office. Jane brought him breakfast in bed early and they discussed their plans for the day. "I want to go to the hospital to see Dad."

"Okay. Why don't I take you, and then we could go on to the farm together, returning here tonight."

"That's a good idea. I'd like to see your farm."

Jane went into the private ward on her own and found her father sitting up and looking cheerful.

"Hello my dear. When are you going to bring that young man to see me?"

"You're only allowed one visitor at a time, so you'll have to wait."

"Not for too long. I'll be out of here in no time."

Jane studied her father's face which seemed to have got thinner. His white hair was combed back, revealing his bald head, and his pyjamas were pulled tightly around his slender frame. She thought how fragile he looked. When she left an hour later she was replaced in the ward by her mother.

Garry drove fast along the country lane to the farm, and pulled up outside the office. Peter looked out of the window and spoke to his wife, who was helping with some filing.

"Good God. I believe he might just be human after all."

"What d'you mean?"

"He's got a girl with him."

"Perhaps she's just an ornament to be shown off."

"Maybe. But she's beautiful."

"That's what I mean."

Whilst the meeting in the farm office was taking place Jane wandered around the farm buildings, looking at the new born calves and trying to make a fuss of them. Garry found her talking to a farm worker, who almost ran as he approached.

"Why did he go off like that?"

"I don't know. Perhaps he's frightened of me!"

"D'you give your employees a hard time then?"

"I chase them every now and then."

Jane gave him a strange look. "You won't start getting nasty with me, will you?"

"Of course not. Don't be silly."

They walked around the farm for a couple of hours and then drove back to London, so that Jane could visit her father again. She looked happy when the visit was over. "If the improvement continues he'll be home on Monday."

"That's certainly good news."

She looked at him with loving eyes. "What now?"

"Dinner. Then back to my flat for a change."

"That sounds good."

The evening passed quickly and Jane walked around the flat looking at his furniture and pictures. "I can see this is a man's flat."

"Yes. Perhaps it needs a woman's touch."

"Are you asking me to stay?"

"Yes. That would be nice."

"We could give it a try."

On Monday morning Garry rang his secretary to say he would be late, and then took Jane to the hospital to collect her father. They were greeted in the waiting room by Jane's distraught mother sobbing uncontrollably. Jane ran up to her. "What's the matter?"

"Dad's gone."

"He can't have. I don't believe it!" she screamed.

A white-coated doctor came in, looking serious. "I'm sorry, Miss Blake. Your father had a massive heart attack an hour ago and we couldn't save him."

Jane and her mother clung to each other, their bodies shaking as they cried and sobbed. Garry felt uncomfortable and stunned. He looked at the two women and, not wishing to intrude on their grief, moved to the corner of the room and sat down

Drink With The Devil

quietly. Remembering how he had reacted when given similar bad news, he realised he was not affected so badly. He could only remember being sad, but not bad enough to cry, and he felt jealous of Jane's feelings towards her parents. Both Jane and her mother sat down continuing to sob. A nurse come in, looked at them and walked away.

After about ten minutes Marian stopped crying and said quietly, "We'll have to be brave and face the future without him." This statement made Jane cry even harder. The nurse returned with cups of tea, which had a calming effect, and Garry arranged for a taxi to take both ladies to the Blake's large house on Hampstead Heath.

Jane looked at Garry with bloodshot eyes. "I must stay with my mother. Can you fetch my things?"

"Yes. Of course."

On arriving back at his flat, he quickly packed her clothes and drove back to Hampstead to be let in by Jane's mother. She was a tall white-haired trim lady and trying her best to cope with her grief. They had another cup of tea and Garry left, feeling depressed and sad for the two distraught ladies.

Jane followed him out to his car. "I'm going to be busy trying to help run the business, and I won't have time to go out with you for a while," she said.

Garry went home depressed, thinking that was the end of another brief encounter.

Chapter Seven

Judge Edwin Thomas presided over the court as Jim stood nervously in the dock. The judge looked hard at the wild-looking man in prison clothing, and wondered why anyone would want to look that way. Jim glanced around the large room and noticed his barrister checking a pile of papers. In the public gallery several reporters were sitting with note pads ready, but his eyes suddenly focused on a tall, slim dark-haired man dressed in a grey suit, who was staring at him with a stony-faced expression. Jim looked away, wondering who he was.

The trial did not last long with Jim pleading guilty, and his young barrister reading out the mitigating circumstances with such eloquence and passion that the judge was noticeably moved, nodding his head in approval. He sentenced Jim to twelve months in prison, after giving him a lecture on self-control and telling him not to take the law into his own hands again.

He felt relieved and happy to know at last how long he would have to wait for his freedom. His lawyer met him after the trial. "With any luck you'll be out in four months. You've already done four, so keep your nose clean and all will be well."

"I'll do that I can assure you."

"I know you will."

Jim was taken to Wormwood Scrubs and subjected to the usual degrading strip search, then a bath and on to the barber's. The prison barber, an elderly man with white hair, looked at his client as he entered and groaned. "What 'ave we got 'ere, then?" A bloody monkey?"

Jim did not answer. He sat down and watched as the man removed his "wild man gypo" identity. He smiled when the job was done and turned to the old man. "Thanks very much. I've wanted to get rid of that for months."

Drink With The Devil

"My God. You do look different."

Jim looked again at his clean-shaven face and stroked his white chin. He even liked the short back and sides.

The small cell had two bunks, and when Jim sat down to test the mattress, it was hard and just how he liked it to be. The man lying on the other bunk stood up and extended his hand. "How do you do?" He said in a cultured public school voice.

Jim was surprised to be greeted in such a manner. "My name's Jim Grainger." He towered over the other man, a middle aged short chap with grey-streaked dark hair.

"Hello, Jim. I'm Oliver Smythe."

Jim sat down again. "Well, Oliver, what are you in for?"

"Oh, only a trivial matter of company fraud. I was quietly running my own business. Not hurting a soul. Just selling the odd bit of stock and placing the proceeds in an offshore account in my own name, when the taxman pounced."

"Oh, that was bad luck."

"Not so much bad luck as a bad choice of stockbrokers."

Jim was intrigued. "How did they cause a problem?"

"I needed to raise money in the City, so I contacted a firm of stockbrokers who agreed to find an investor for me. What I didn't bargain for was their own investigators unearthing my private business, and blowing the whistle on me."

"That's terrible. How long did you get?"

"Eighteen months and a fine. What are you in for?"

"I killed a man." Jim said quietly.

Oliver looked shocked.

"It wasn't intentional."

"Good. You don't look like a killer."

"Don't you think so? I reckon I might have done this morning." He told his story and Oliver sat wide-eyed in amazement, listening to Jim's deep husky voice giving a graphic account of his life.

"So now you know all about me."

Oliver smiled. "You and I have one thing in common."

"What's that?"

"We've both fallen foul of the Osbornes."

"How d'you mean? Both of us."

"The firm who let me down was Osbornes. And the investigator who took a great deal of delight in calling the fraud squad was young Garry Osborne."

"Angela's brother. She told me about him, but I've never seen him."

"I have. A nasty piece of work."

Suddenly recalling the stony-faced man in the court room, Jim said, "What does Garry look like?"

"Tall, slim, dark-haired. Bit of a womaniser they say. Matter of fact he's about your height, but not so well built."

Jim told him about the man he had seen staring at him at the trial.

"That was probably him. I expect he's gloating over your incarceration."

"Could be," agreed Jim.

The two men talked for hours. Oliver told him all he knew about the Osbornes and their company. He listened intently and asked questions until he had learned all that Oliver knew.

The next morning Jim was in the washroom having a shave for the first time in over a year. He stroked his chin, appreciating the feel of a close shave, and then washed. Just as he was about to leave he heard a gruff voice behind him.

"So you're the evil bastard who killed my mate 'arry Briggs?"

Jim turned around and received a powerful punch in the stomach, which doubled him up, and then felt a stinging blow in the back. He was on the floor receiving kicks and blows to his body, which seemed to go on forever, but suddenly the onslaught stopped as he passed out. The next thing he remembered was someone splashing water on his face. Two men helped him up, his body ached all over and he felt sick. He opened his eyes to be confronted by a thick-set man, with a neck like a bull and as tall as himself, who looked him squarely in the eye. "That was for my mate 'arry. And when you get out his brother'll be waiting to finish the job."

Drink With The Devil

The two men let go and Jim staggered backward, propping himself up against a wall. The washroom was empty and he slowly gathered his towel and shaving things up, feeling dizzy and in severe pain. After splashing more water on his face, he walked unsteadily back to his cell. A prison officer spotted him and shouted. "Are you all right?"

Jim just nodded. "I'm okay, thanks."

Oliver looked at him. "Good God, man. What happened to you?"

"Someone doesn't like me."

It was a week before Jim felt fit again. He kept a wary eye out for the thick-set man and his henchmen, but they seemed to ignore him. After getting over his beating and, in an effort to get fitter, he exercised in his cell until he was exhausted. This made him hungry and he ate all he could. Slowly his self-confidence returned and his muscles got larger.

During their long hours locked up, Jim and Oliver talked a great deal. Oliver told him how he had started his own company, a small shop that became a chain of grocery stores. He was very interested and asked many questions about running a business. With Oliver pleased to pass on his considerable knowledge, every evening became a lesson for Jim and he was the most intensely interested student a lecturer ever had.

This mental activity made time pass quickly for both of them, but during the dark hours of night Jim still dreamed of being with Angela. He could still visualise her beautiful face smiling at him, and the enjoyable time they spent together. His forest home seemed a lifetime away. Life in prison was so different and alien to him, and freedom was uppermost in his dreams - being able to walk with the wind in his face, to smell the perfume of the countryside and the sight of trees and animals. He spent a lot of time thinking about what he should do when released, as it was quite obvious he could not return to living in a wood.

Oliver had made him interested in starting a business, but how could he start with no money at all? He churned this question over and over in his mind, and one evening asked Oliver what his advice would be.

Oliver frowned and thought for a while. "It's always more difficult for an ex-con to get started."

"Yes, I can imagine."

"I think if I were a young, strong and fit man, I would go into the building industry."

"Why building?"

"Well, this is 1959 and I can foresee a boom throughout the sixties in house and local authority building."

"But I don't know a thing about the trade."

"You'd soon learn. It's well worth considering."

* * *

Garry attended the trial and sat in the public gallery as close as possible to the dock, so he could study the accused. He felt tense and nervous at the thought of his family's name being ridiculed by the press, which was well represented on the benches beside him. Some of them had done their homework well and recognised him. "Can we have your comments on the trial, Mr. Osborne?"

"No comment," was all the response they received.

Garry watched as Jim appeared in the dock. His stomach twisted and he felt weak as he realised the man looked every bit as bad as he had been led to believe. How could Angela associate with that man? It just could not be true. He kept telling himself over and over again it was impossible. He wanted to cry out "murderer," but just managed to stop himself. The more he studied the man, the more he was convinced this was the murderer of his parents and the animal that hurt his sister, still lying in a coma. He looked around the public gallery and noticed an artist drawing a portrait of the prisoner.

The Court was suddenly brought to order, and Garry stayed throughout the proceedings, horrified at the defence council's speech advocating mitigating circumstances. He felt like leaping over the balcony and throttling the man. As his sister's friendship with Grainger was described, he nervously looked around at

Drink With The Devil

the reporters all scribbling frantically in their notebooks, and groaned. There was nothing he could do to stop them, and it was so frustrating not being able to do anything about it, but the worst part was to come. The judge announced the sentence, and Garry gasped, choked and ran from the gallery, scattering the reporters. He was livid. Only twelve months! Nearly half of which the man had already served!

A taxi took Garry back to his office, where he sat and brooded until Carol, his secretary, announced, "Inspector Green from the police to see you."

"Send him in."

The inspector strode in and stood in front of Garry's desk.

Garry stood up. "Well inspector, have you found your murderer and arsonist yet?"

"No, Sir, we haven't, but our enquiries are continuing."

"What for? You have the right man locked up in prison."

"Grainger did not kill your parents, and I didn't come here to discuss him."

"What are you here for then?"

"To ask you how well you know the Briggs Brothers."

Garry went very red. "I told you before I've never seen Harry Briggs. What are you trying to prove, inspector?"

"Just routine enquiries."

"You're trying to pin it on me because you can't find anyone else. Is that it?"

"That's all I had to ask. Goodbye, Sir."

Garry left his office late and had a solitary meal in a pub. He drank too much and went to bed in a drunken stupor, where he dreamed about a hairy beast of a man chasing him into a house and then setting fire to it. He saw flames leaping up all around him, and the hairy man watching from a safe distance. He awoke in a sweat and shouted out loud. "That bastard, Grainger. I'll kill him." After a while he slept again, this time dreaming about Angela being attacked by that hairy monster. Again, he woke up in a sweat, but this time he got up and had another drink and collapsed on the sofa, and slept unconscious until dawn.

He arrived at work on time the next day but looking dreadful. Carol took one look at his face and bloodshot eyes and groaned, knowing he would be hell to work for all day. Even Simon Berry approached with caution. The morning papers carried the story, telling how a fairy tale romance between a beautiful rich girl and a wild man living in a wood went sour. They defended his action of trying to save the girl and expressed sympathy at his bad luck having killed the man in a moment of anger. One of the more sensational papers Garry read went on to speculate as to the lurid details of the romance, making him turn pink with anger. He rang his solicitor. "Mr. Vine, I want you to sue that cheap rag for libel."

"As you wish, Mr. Osborne. But it may not be wise."

"Why not?" He nearly exploded with rage.

"Because you'll have to prove your sister didn't associate with the defendant."

"She couldn't have."

"I'm sure that is so, but can you prove it?"

Garry slammed the telephone down and fumed for a while, but then tried to put the previous day out of his mind; telling himself he had got months to think of a plan, and in the meantime at least Grainger was where he belonged, in jail.

That evening Garry visited Jane, surprised that she still wanted to see him. They talked for some time about the problem her father's death had caused at work. Obviously she was coping very well, but Garry could see she was tired.

* * *

The funeral took place the following Monday, Garry doing his best to comfort his girlfriend, who wept uncontrollably as her father's body disappeared behind the crematorium curtain. Garry visited her every night for the next week and felt very close to her, having shared her grief, and felt their love for each other was now much stronger.

Drink With The Devil

Marian noticed the way the couple looked at each other, and one night as they sat together drinking coffee said, "If you want to get together you must go ahead. I've got to learn to live on my own."

Jane protested. "But I couldn't leave you so soon."

"Nonsense. You've got your own life to lead."

"Are you sure you'll be able to cope?"

"Yes. Of course."

Jane moved into Garry's flat that weekend and they made love for the first time since that tragic Sunday afternoon. She felt overwhelmed with love for him. She wanted to return all the love and understanding he had shown, she wanted to be part of him and clung desperately, hoping their bodies would be fused together in love for ever. Garry was equally desperate to make love after so long, and was delighted at her passionate response. He had never made love with a girl in such a sexual frenzy. Her arms and legs enveloped him, firing him with a tremendous passion, and just before he reached his height of ecstasy he blurted out, "Please marry me."

The answer was instant. "Yes."

Their spasms of ecstasy died down, and as they lay in each other's arms Jane whispered. "Do you really want to marry me?"

"Yes. Very much."

After a light meal Garry sat in his armchair reflecting on his impulsive decision. Then he thought about Blakesbuild, a large construction company worth several million pounds and this alone made it worthwhile for him to go ahead with the marriage. He smiled to himself when he realised how much he would be worth in the future.

Jane sat opposite him. "When are we getting married?"

"As soon as possible."

"Really? Do you mean that?"

"Yes. Why not? Once a decision is made, one should always act without delay."

"Yes. But we ought to talk to Mother."

"Okay. Then we'll be officially engaged."

That evening the couple drove to Hampstead. Marian was delighted to hear the news. "Congratulations. You'll let me make all the arrangements, won't you?"

"That would be wonderful."

Jane returned to work the next day to find the vital decisions her father used to make were being put off and, despite meetings with her key staff, none of them were sure what to do. Trying to imagine what her father would have done, she nervously went ahead with some minor contract tenders. She was getting desperately worried about the major contracts lying on her father's desk, awaiting approval before being sent off and committing the company to large building projects. She studied the small print and noticed the penalty clauses, fixed priced items and other details that made her nervous. In sheer desperation she took one of them home to the flat and, after they had eaten and Garry was studying his own paperwork, she said casually, "Be a dear and have a look at this contract for me."

"Good God, woman. I've got enough of my own work to do."

"Please have a look."

"Oh, all right, if I must." He picked up the folder and began reading the documents, getting excited over the details. After an hour he put the folder down and spoke slowly. "You've got to make a decision in two days time or lose the contract."

"Yes I know. That's why I need your advice."

"But I can't just give advice without knowing any of the background."

Jane groaned. "I suppose not."

"I'll offer you a business proposition though."

"Go on, then."

"I'm prepared to spend one day a week at your office in exchange for a small shareholding in the company."

"Agreed. To be transferred after we get married, but are you sure you can spare the time?"

"I'll make time. You must arrange a meeting with your

Drink With The Devil

estimators and any other parties involved with the contract at 10 a.m. tomorrow."

"That's no problem. They'll be in the office."

"Good." Garry was feeling pleased with himself. They had only been engaged a week and he had already made his first move.

He studied the contract the next morning and wrote down all the questions he could think of. At 10 a.m. precisely he swept into the company's foyer, walking straight past the receptionist and upstairs to the office, easily finding the boardroom. Jane greeted him with a brief kiss and then introduced her team of estimators, surveyors and financial staff. All of them were men in their fifties. He was welcomed warmly and they sat down with Garry at the head of the table and Jane on his right-hand side. He glanced down the table and noticed they each had notepads and a copy of the contract for the building of a new school in South London. He got down to business immediately and went through the contract, line by line, stopping to ask the person concerned searching questions.

By lunchtime they were only half way through, so he turned to Jane and whispered,

"We can't stop now. How about getting someone to go out for sandwiches?"

"Good idea."

They worked on until seven in the evening, when Garry had grasped a clear picture of the contract and said. "Right, I've studied every point in detail. The question is, do we complete the tender form with a slightly increased price, or increase it more and risk losing the deal?"

They all looked stony-faced for a moment and Garry went on, "I think we should sign as it is. Right. We're all agreed."

"I'll sign on behalf of the Company." Jane added.

They all shook hands and thanked Garry for his help. Jane felt proud to be engaged to him. She was amazed at the way he handled the meeting, impressing her and her colleagues with his clear thinking and leadership. When the men had gone she cuddled him. "You were fantastic. I'm going to marry the finest man in the world."

"You exaggerate, my dear."

"No, I mean it. You're the best."

He kissed her forehead and whispered. "Let's go home. I'm shattered."

They stopped for a meal on the way home, which Jane insisted on paying for.

The following day Garry went to his own office and was pleased to find his advertising campaign had started to pay off with new customers applying to the company, asking for help with their portfolios.

Simon Berry was moved to a new office next to Garry, and was briefed to handle things in his absence. He was delighted, but the older staff were upset and Simon spoke to Garry about it. "The old boys don't like it."

Garry grinned. "Too bad. They'll have to get used to the idea."

In the following weeks Garry settled into his new routine, spending each Monday, which sometimes stretched into Tuesday, at Blakesbuild, mostly because he enjoyed the work more than stockbroking. The staff saw him as a saviour, and he was even more popular when they landed the school contract. All the contracts were thrashed out in the same way as the first, with Garry acting as company chairman.

Jane relied on his judgement more and more and did not mind when he snapped at her, but just attributed it to pressure of work. He felt happy in his new role, finding it a pleasant change to be wanted. Jane still treated him like a god, making sure he had everything he wanted, both at home and at work. All thoughts of avenging his parents' death seemed to have evaporated.

The only remaining dark cloud in his life was Angela still being in a coma. He and Jane visited her every Sunday. The doctors said she needed something to bring her back to life, so her favourite music was played, and her friends visited and talked to her. Every kind of inducement and stimulus was tried, but to no avail.

A serious faced doctor said, "We're running out of ideas, I'm afraid."

"How long can she go on like this?" Garry said quietly.

"Impossible to tell, but you must be prepared for the worst."

"Oh my God. What'll happen?"

"She could just slip away."

Garry was stunned, and sat with his head lowered and supported by his hands.

Chapter Eight

The two-month engagement was over in a flash. Jane had inherited the entire company of Blakesbuild, formerly owned by Roland Blake, who had raised the money to start the company and kept all the shares himself until his death.

The wedding was a grand affair with the men in morning suits and toppers, and the ladies in outfits of the latest fashion crowned with hats of all shapes and sizes. The church was filled with flowers. The bride wore a white dress with a long train, held by four bridesmaids. Garry invited the few members of his family he could remember, supplemented by his university friends. His side of the church was sparsely occupied compared with Jane's, who seemed to have an endless amount of relations and lots of friends. Garry insisted the front pew on his side of the church be left empty in honour of his parents and Angela.

The reception was held in a marquee erected on the lawn behind the family house in Hampstead. Garry spent most of the time drinking with his friends, becoming more and more unsteady on his feet, which rather alarmed Jane who broke away from her friends at the sight of him staggering towards the bar. "Come on. You've had enough."

"Who the hell d'you think you are, telling me I've had enough?"

Jane was shocked at his response. "I'm your wife, dear. Now, please be nice and stop drinking."

Garry looked wildly around to see that many eyes were fixed on him. "Sorry, dear." He gave her a drink-laden kiss, smudging her make-up, and she wanted to cringe away from the brandy fumes, but thought it would be better to support him. She led him to a chair and someone arrived with black coffee. Garry sneered. "Do I have to drink that?"

"Yes dear, and then I've a surprise for you."

He drank the offending liquid quickly, trying to clear his mind as she handed him a large buff envelope, which he tore open with gusto. A note was pinned to a large share certificate — To my dearest Garry, a 50% share holding in Blakesbuild. He nearly wept with joy. He stood up and hugged his wife.

Marian called the couple to one side. "I've come to a decision. The house is far too big for me, so I'm moving to my cottage in Wiltshire. You'll need a large house, so when you return from honeymoon I want you to move in here permanently."

Jane was not surprised at this announcement. "But are you sure?"

"Yes of course. Besides, I've friends in Wiltshire as you know."

Garry was delighted. "This is very kind of you, Mother. We do appreciate it." He could not believe things were going so well and his euphoria was hard to contain — in three months he had met a beautiful blond, married her and was in control of a large construction business. His own company was doing well, he had the farm as well and now a very valuable property was being handed to him on a plate. He felt like celebrating with a large brandy, but one look at Jane talking seriously with her mother stopped him.

The couple arrived at a luxury hotel in Cannes for their honeymoon, having agreed to stay away for just one week because of business commitments. Their time was spent sailing along the coast, water skiing and sun bathing. They looked the perfect couple as they walked along the long promenade after dinner — a beautiful blond in a white dress accompanied by a tall dark-haired man. Jane took a deep breath of warm evening air and whispered, "Could we do this more often? After all, we can afford it."

"It's very nice here, but our businesses have to be run."

"Yes, but we're so happy away from work."

"I doubt it would last. We'd get bored."

"I wouldn't. Especially if you were as nice to me as you have been."

The week passed very quickly and they flew home, immediately moving into the large house on Hampstead Heath.

Garry spent three days a week at Blakesbuild and two at Osbornes, mainly because Simon Berry was doing such a good job running the business. Some of the older partners had left and younger people replaced them, Garry choosing them carefully and making sure they agreed with his point of view. The construction business was booming and Garry, having taken over Roland Blake's office, was enjoying running the company. Jane still worked with him, making sure he had everything he needed, but he gradually became more aggressive with the staff and she saw the mean streak in him for the first time at work. She brought him coffee one morning and sat opposite him in an easy chair, sipping nervously.

"Garry."

"Yes."

"Why d'you get so angry with the staff?"

"I don't get angry. I'm trying to run the company properly."

"But there's no need to be so aggressive."

He gave her a steely look. "Look, if you don't like the way I run things, then do it yourself."

"I didn't mean to upset you."

"You haven't. I've got a lot to do."

"Why can't we talk like we used to?"

"Because there's no time."

Jane got up and walked out with tears in her eyes. Later that afternoon she brought him tea, and as she put it in front of him whispered, "I'm sorry if I upset you this morning."

"I told you I wasn't upset."

"Can we try to talk this evening?"

"If you like. What about?"

"Anything." She fled the room again.

That evening after dinner Garry was sitting in his favourite

Drink With The Devil

chair, nursing a large brandy. Jane looked at him and thought he might be in a good mood.

"Garry, are you happy with everything?"

"Yes. Why d'you ask?"

"Well, you seem in a bad mood at work these days."

"Oh, do I?"

"Yes, you do. And there's no need to be aggressive with the staff."

"I'm only trying to get some work done."

"But you're creating a bad atmosphere."

Garry gulped his drink and said in a high pitched tone. "That's rubbish. The staff respect a firm boss."

"I'm just saying you may be trying too hard."

Garry poured another large brandy. "You're saying I'm rude?"

"Not exactly."

He swallowed the drink in one large gulp. "If that's what you think, you can run the bloody place on your own."

"Oh, Garry. Don't be silly."

He filled his glass again and his eyes were blazing. "Now you listen to me, you bloody silly woman. I'm not silly or rude, and I've done my best for that damn company of yours." He drained his glass.

Jane got up and tried to prevent him filling it again. "Please don't drink any more."

"Christ. Now I drink too much." He pushed her away and poured a large full glass.

She sank to her knees in front of him. "Oh, Garry, I'm so sorry. I didn't mean to upset you."

He sneered at her and spoke again in a high pitched tone. "Get up, you stupid cow."

She rose slowly. "Please forgive me, but I don't like to see you drunk."

"I'm not drunk." He sank the glassful and Jane went to take the glass from him. "What are you doing? I want another drink."

"You've had enough."

He tried to grab the glass and stumbled forward. "You bloody woman, give me that glass." He lunged at her, striking her face with his fist. She screamed and fell on to the settee, blood trickling down her chin from a split lip, and she was stunned into silence.

Garry leered at her and then grinned, his face red. "I'll teach you who's boss. Now get up and pour me a drink."

Jane was very frightened. She got up, wiping her mouth and poured the brandy, giving it to him before retreating to an armchair.

He stood unsteadily drinking while she watched nervously. Having drained the glass, he sat on the settee. "Come and sit here."

Jane said nothing, but got up and slowly sat beside him.

His voice was a slurred whisper. "Now be nice to me." He put his arm around her shoulder, his other hand fondling her breast, and leaned towards her, kissing her mouth. She was filled with disgust as his saliva trickled down her chin mingling with blood from her painful lip, and wrenched herself free before running from the room. Garry shouted after her and then collapsing forward on to his face passed out, staying there until morning. When he awoke he was cold and felt ill, just managing to reach the bathroom before being sick. Looking at himself in the mirror, he shuddered when he remembered his behaviour the night before.

Jane was awake when he brought in a cup of tea and eyed him nervously as he approached. He smiled weakly as his unsteady hand spilled the liquid into the saucer. "I'm very sorry about last night, and I promise not to hurt you again."

"So I should think. I've never been so frightened in all my life."

"Please forgive me. I'll do my best to be nice to you and the staff."

"Very well. If you're really going to try."

"I'll try. Just for you."

He tried to be reasonable to the staff the next day, and was polite without overdoing it. In the evening he was about to pour a glass of brandy, but checked himself just in time. Jane was still nervous and sat on her own, but soon responded when he made an attempt at conversation. After an hour she cuddled up to him on the settee and whispered,

"Why can't you always be nice to me?"

"I don't know, but I promise to try."

* * *

Jim walked away from the cell that had been home for the last four months, shaking hands with Oliver and promising to contact him on his release in a few months time. The outer door clanged shut and he stood for a moment looking up at the sky. His gaze was interrupted by a shout from a parked car. Jean Wilks was a voluntary prison visitor who had promised to help him find lodgings and work; a married woman in her mid thirties with a nice kind face and mousy hair, and with a husband who worked in the City. She was left at home and bored, but had a small car and enjoyed visiting prisoners who needed help. Jim ran across to the car. "Hello Jean. This is very good of you."

"My pleasure. I wondered if you'd look different outside."

"It feels really good to be out."

They drove through the traffic with Jean telling him how things had changed in the last eight months, and Jim feeling on top of the world and chatting about what he would like to do in the future. When they pulled up outside a terraced house in Kingston-upon-Thames, Jim jumped out with his small bag of old clothes. He was introduced to a short round-looking lady with a red face and broken teeth, which she displayed when she smiled at the sight of him.

"Hello. You must be Jim. My name's Rosie."

Jim towered over her and shook her podgy hand. "Hello, Rosie. It's very kind of you to put me up."

"It'll be a pleasure to have someone to cook for. My old man died four years ago and my kids never bother to visit." She showed him a small room at the back of the house, which was neat and tidy with a single bed, dressing table and wardrobe.

Jean waved goodbye. "I'll come and see you in a few days."

"Okay. And thanks for all your help."

"You're welcome."

Rosie cooked a huge meal that evening and, just seeing the mountain of food on his plate made Jim's eyes water. He had never tasted such good food in his life.

The next morning he was up at dawn and ate a cooked breakfast, which Rosie had waiting for him. He ran down the street following Jean's instructions and ten minutes later walked on to a large construction site. He waited outside the empty site office for five minutes until a burly looking man wearing a trilby hat arrived and stared at him.

"Blimey mate, you're keen, ain't yer?"

"Well, I'd really like a job."

"The office don't open for another 'alf hour."

"I'll wait."

"Better come in and sit down, then."

Jim waited and saw workers arrive, and a small queue formed outside. When the trilby-hatted man returned he looked at him.

"What d'you want to do?"

"Labouring, please." Jim said politely.

"Stand up."

Jim stood with his head just short of the low ceiling. The man grunted. "You fancy 'od carrying?"

"What's that?"

"Well, you fill a 'od full of bricks and carry them up a ladder to the brickies."

"Yes. That sounds fine."

"Right. You can start straight away."

Another man showed him where to work and handed him a hod, a pole with a three-cornered wooden box on the top.

A bricklayer shouted down from the scaffolding. "Come on. Get some bricks up 'ere."

Jim grabbed the hod, filled it with bricks and almost ran up

Drink With The Devil

the ladder. The man, a short ruddy faced character, snatched a brick from the pile and said, "What's yer name, mate?"

"Jim. What's yours?"

"Ian. But yer won't be 'ere long enough to get to know me."

"Why's that?"

"Cause after a week of 'od carrying, you'll be off."

"We'll see."

"I bet you a quid you won't last more than a week."

"You're on, mate."

By lunchtime Jim was tired and his limbs ached. Ian kept shouting down to him, "For Christ's sake get a move on."

By the time he had finished that evening Jim was in a bad way, with hands nearly raw, legs feeling like lead and his arms and shoulder aching badly. Rosie took one look at him. "Oh my God, Jim, you need a bath."

The bathroom was an outside extension of the kitchen and Jim soaked while his meal was being cooked. Blisters had formed on his feet and they hurt, but the bath soothed the aching and he managed a large meal before collapsing in an armchair. Rosie found a pair of thick gardening gloves and socks, which he wore the next morning.

Ian looked at Jim's pale features. "You won't last the day out."

"Oh yes I will."

"Right, get those bricks up on that scaffold."

He worked hard all day, just managing to keep the bricklayer supplied with bricks and mortar. He limped home to discover the blisters had burst and he felt even worse than the first day. Rosie's gloves had saved his hands, but his arms and legs still ached badly.

The next three days were similar to the first two and, when he collected his wage packet on Friday night, he was relieved to have two days off.

As soon as he got home he said to Rosie. "Now, how much do I owe you?"

"Nothing. The first week's on the house."

"That's very generous. But I must pay you."

"I want you to go out tomorrow and buy some clothes."

"You're very kind."

She grinned. "It's a pleasure to have you here."

He walked the short distance to the shops, buying a pair of heavy boots and working clothes, and then spent the rest of the day doing odd jobs around the house.

On Sunday morning Jean Wilks called in to see him and found Rosie in the kitchen.

"Hello. Where's Jim?"

"In the bathroom, fitting a new tap washer."

"How's he settling in?"

"Very well, my dear."

Jim came in and they drank coffee together. Jean looked at him. "I must say you do look tired."

"I haven't worked for so long. I'm bound to find it tiring at first."

"Is there anything I can do?"

"Well, I know it's a bit of a cheek, but will you take me to the hospital?"

"Good heavens. Are you feeling that bad?"

Jim laughed. "It's not for me. I want to visit someone."

"I'm not busy at the moment. Let's go."

The private hospital was not far away, just outside of town, and Jim had been looking forward to seeing Angela for so long. He knew she was still in a coma, but the thought of seeing her face again filled him with excitement and love for her. Jean looked at his beaming face. "Well, who's the lucky lady?"

"Angela. But she's very ill." He gave her a brief account of what had happened, leaving out the part about killing a man.

Jean just smiled, knowing the full story anyway.

They pulled up outside a large house which had been converted to a hospital. Jim went in dressed in his new working clothes and large boots, which made him look even taller. A young nurse smiled. "What can I do for you?"

"I've come to see Angela Osborne."

"Are you a relative?"

"No. A friend."

She walked away and spoke to someone in an adjoining room. Jim's heart sank, thinking they would not let him see her, but the nurse returned smiling. "I'll come with you," she said.

He heaved a sigh of relief and followed the slightly built girl, who opened a door to a room with one bed in the centre. There was an abundance of floral displays from both relatives and friends. When Jim saw Angela's white face, a lump appeared in his throat, and tears came to his eyes. "Can I sit with her?" he croaked.

The nurse saw his reaction and quickly placed a chair as close to the bed as possible. He could not take his eyes off her face as he sat down slowly. "Oh my poor Angela." His voice shook as he held her lifeless hand, oblivious to all else around him. Tears ran down his cheeks as he said: "My dearest Angela, I love you so much." He stopped to wipe his face and then spoke more clearly, his deep husky voice recalling every detail of their last meeting in the wood, and then telling her over and over again how much he loved her.

The nurse sat in one corner, spellbound by this display of uninhibited emotion and love. She clasped her handkerchief to her mouth to stop herself making a noise, as she could not stop tears coming to her eyes. She wanted to get up and kiss him, but did not want to break the spell. It was as if a god of love was sitting there, pouring out his heart to a lifeless girl. Suddenly they both gasped as Angela's eye lids flickered. Jim felt her hand gently squeeze his, and then relax but he carried on talking.

"Come on my love, wake up for me."

Her eyelids moved again and her lips parted, but neither Jim nor the nurse could understand what she uttered.

There was silence for a second, the door opened and a man wearing a white coat came in. The nurse looked up and whispered. "Doctor, look at Angela."

He looked at her eyes and then at Jim. "Please carry on talking."

He stood back as Jim talked to her for another five minutes. Angela moved her head towards him slightly and whispered very faintly, "Jim?"

He nearly choked with emotion and croaked. "Yes, my love. It's me." The doctor spoke quietly. "Be careful. Don't rush her."

Jim kissed her hand and got up slowly. He left the room but glanced back as he shut the door to see her staring at the window. His whole body shook as he tore himself away from the room. He had decided long ago it would not be fair to expect her to love him, but after what had transpired he left with mixed feelings. He was approaching the car when he heard footsteps running after him. The nurse grabbed his arm and when he turned to face her, he saw tears still running down her mascara-smudged face. She hugged him and then stood back. Jim was bewildered. "Are you quite all right?"

She spluttered. "I've never seen or heard anything so beautiful." Jim was stuck for words.

She dried her face and spoke again. "You can't just leave. After all you may have saved her life."

"I owed her that and now it would be best if I went."

"Why? I don't understand."

"Because I think she would regret it if I stayed."

"Fair enough. But please tell me your name."

"Sorry. I must go."

The nurse watched as Jim and Jean drove away. Jean had watched the nurse pounce on Jim and was laughing. "Well Jim. You certainly made an impression on that pretty nurse."

"She was a bit overwhelming."

"I could see you were getting on well with her. How long have you known her?"

"I don't know her."

"You're kidding?"

"No, I'm not. I never saw her before to-day."

Jean gave him a look of disbelief. "Oh. How was Angela?"

Drink With The Devil

"Much better. I think she has a chance of recovery."

"I thought you were going to be in there all day."

"I'm sorry to have kept you waiting so long."

"It was worth it, seeing you have a cuddle with that nurse."

On Monday morning Jim arrived at work feeling refreshed and energetic. He shot up the ladder with a load of bricks, his legs feeling much fitter as the boots cushioned the bite of the rungs. He had a large pile of bricks waiting when Ian arrived and grinned at him.

"You owe me a quid."

"I give in. You win. Here you are." He handed over a grubby pound note.

"Thanks. Now you can lay bricks as fast as you like."

"Right. I bloody well will."

That evening, straight after work, Jim rang the hospital and was told there was a slight improvement, but that a full recovery could not be certain.

Chapter Nine

The telephone rang in the hall as Garry burst through the front door with Jane, following an evening meal at a local hotel. "Who the hell's that at this time of night?" He snatched up the receiver. "Hello."

"Is that Mr. Osborne?"

"Who wants me at this hour of the night?"

"Doctor Riley here."

"But we only visited the hospital yesterday."

"Yes I know. But I've got good news for you. Angela has recovered consciousness."

"Good heavens. That's fantastic. How did it happen?"

"She had a visitor, who talked to her and she responded."

"Who was the visitor?"

"A man who didn't leave his name."

"Really. That's funny."

"Yes. Will you be coming to see her?"

"Yes, of course. Straightaway." He put the receiver down and shouted to Jane,

"Angela's recovered. We must go to the hospital."

"That's wonderful. But I think you should go by yourself at this stage."

"Okay. Don't wait up." He ran out to the car and drove away, puzzled as to who supplied the miracle cure.

The doctor met him outside the private ward, and warned him not to expect her to recognise him instantly. "Her memory will be hazy for a while, so be patient."

"Okay. I'm just so pleased she's recovering." He went in to find his sister sitting up in bed looking at all the flowers surrounding her, but when she saw him she looked away, without any signs of recognition. He sat down. "Hello Angela. How are you feeling?"

"I don't know how I feel. D'you like my flowers?"

"They're beautiful."

"They are nice, aren't they?"

"Angela, this is your brother, Garry," said the nurse sitting the other side of the bed.

"Garry. My brother? I can't remember my brother."

Garry smiled at her. "Never mind. I expect it'll come back to you soon enough."

"Yes. I suppose so. The doctors say I've been asleep for a long time."

"That's true. Far too long." He stayed for half an hour trying to communicate with her, but found it hard going with her vague responses. He said goodbye and left to find the doctor in charge waiting for him in the reception area.

"Doctor, who was the man who visited my sister?"

"I don't know."

"What d'you mean, you don't know?"

"What I said. He wouldn't tell us his name."

"D'you let any Tom, Dick or Harry in here to see her?"

"If they satisfy us they're friends, we do."

"That's a pretty poor way of going on."

"Why are you so upset? He probably saved Angela's life."

Garry calmed down. "Yes, I suppose you're right. What did he look like?"

"He was a big man, in his twenties, with a deep husky voice."

"Was he fat or thin? And how was he dressed?"

"He was tall, well built and not at all fat. He was wearing manual working clothes, and I noticed he had a pair of huge new boots on."

Garry thought for a moment, and then went pale as his heart sank.

The doctor noticed his change of colour and look of dismay. "What's the matter, Mr. Osborne?"

"Did he have a black beard and long hair?"

"No. On the contrary, his hair was fairly short and he was clean shaven."

"What colour was his hair?"

"I'd say it was dark."

Garry turned on his heels and walked out, his hands thrust deep in his pockets as he stared at the ground in front of him. The doctor turned to the receptionist. "What a strange man. His sister's life has just been saved and he acts as if she's just died!"

The nurse behind the desk nodded. "Yes, I can't understand it either. Nurse Bowen said the chap who saved her life was wonderful."

"Yes. He certainly was."

Garry proceeded slowly home, thinking about Angela's response to him, certain it was Jim Grainger who called at the hospital to deliver the magic cure. He was determined to be proved right. He was pleased about Angela's recovery, and convinced it would only be a matter of time before her memory returned — but the man he had managed to put out of his mind for so long had entered it again.

Jane was waiting for him. "How was she?"

"She looks good, but her memory's gone."

"I suppose it's to be expected after all this time."

"The doctor said she should make a full recovery."

"Oh good. But then she'll have to face the loss of her mother and father."

"Yes. That'll be a nasty shock."

"Were they very close?"

"Yes. Very."

"Oh dear. But how did she suddenly recover?"

"Some bloke turned up, talked to her for a while, and that was it."

"Who was he?"

"No idea. Neither has anyone else."

Garry walked away, sat alone in his study and churned the day's events over in his mind. Nagging doubts about his sister's relationship with Grainger worried him. Could she really have

Drink With The Devil

had an affair with him? No surely not - he was just not her type. He slowly convinced himself that the man who called at the hospital was an old friend with a special gift of penetrating speech.

The next evening Jane handed him a brandy; she found it a good idea to give him his drink, which usually started a conversation and tended to stop him drinking any more. She looked at him deep in thought.

"Funny the hospital didn't take the man's name."

"Yes," he growled. "That's what I said."

"He must be a remarkable chap to get through to her, after so many others had failed."

"Remarkable, yes. But who the hell was he?"

Garry poured another large drink, gulping it down as he stared at the floor. Jane quietly slipped out of the room and up to bed. Another hour went by and she suddenly sat up in bed as a crash of glass from downstairs awoke her. She began to worry about what damage he was doing when the door burst open, and he lurched into the room, stumbling on the loose carpet. "Jane. Why did you clear off?" He fell on to the bed and she cringed away from him in terror. "What's the matter? Don't you want me anymore?"

She stayed silent and the colour left her face. He lunged forward and tore her nightie from top to bottom. She screamed, but was pinned down as he smothered her with drunken kisses, one hand gripping her breast tightly. The shock of the pain filled her with strength and she pushed, wriggled and eventually fell off the bed, leaving him swearing at her. The torn nightie fell off as she ran towards the bathroom, locked the door and draped a towel around her naked body. Within half an hour it was quiet and she guessed he must have fallen asleep, so she made her way to a spare room where she had a bed already made up for such an eventuality. She locked the door and lay awake shivering and sobbing, finally realising her husband had turned out to be a drunken beast. Although she knew she still loved him, she did not know how long she could put up with his nasty ways, and kept trying to think of a way to reform him.

The next morning he was his usual repentant self. "I promise I'll never do that again."

But this time Jane did not believe him. She just looked at him sternly and said, "If you do, I'll leave you."

Garry was shocked and thought quickly about how much he could lose.

"This time I really will stop myself drinking too much."

"We'll see."

They went to work together and he made an effort to be civil with everyone.

* * *

Garry's enquiries regarding Jim Grainger's whereabouts came to nothing. All he could find out was that Grainger had been released a couple of weeks previous, but neither the police nor the prison authorities would divulge his present address. Garry soon gave up and concentrated on running the construction company.

Later that week Jane announced she was pregnant. She told her mother first, tearfully pouring out her problems with Garry. "Now I'm trapped with a man who turns into a drunken beast at the slightest excuse."

Marian was sympathetic. "I'm sure he'll change when he knows about the baby."

"I do hope so. But how long will it last?"

Garry was delighted with the news. "We'll have a son to carry on the Osborne name and business." He even had a large bouquet of flowers delivered.

On Sunday morning his concern was suddenly overwhelming. "My dear. You must stay at home and look after yourself."

"But I want to carry on working as long as possible."

"Do you really? Why not come in part time for a while?"

"Only part time?"

"Yes. I insist that you rest as much as possible." He was even more delighted at the prospect of having the entire company to himself, without his wife checking up on him. Jane was pleased with this display of affection and poured him a drink.

"I promise to drink just one brandy a night until our son is born."

"Oh, yes. But it might be a girl."

"No chance of that happening." Their relationship improved somewhat, as he tried desperately to keep his promise.

* * *

Angela's memory did not improve and she stayed at the hospital receiving treatment, Garry and Jane visiting at weekends. She liked Jane and they talked whilst Garry sat listening. Eventually she was allowed an outing from the hospital. After a couple of weeks he took them both to the farm. The burned-out shell of the house had been flattened, and a digger was working on the new foundations. Gemma was pleased to see Angela and nuzzled her affectionately, whinnied with excitement, and this was the first time any of her past life returned to her memory. The smell of the warm breath and sound of the horse sparked a cord in her mind and she said, "Gemma, it's nice to see you."

Garry was pleased to see his sister's reaction. "You remembered her name?"

"Yes. Maybe I'll remember other things now."

They returned to the hospital and the doctor said to Garry. "Angela's mind may be blocking out those things which she can't accept — like her parents' death. I would recommend she stays near the farm for a while to try and remember her old surroundings."

"Fine. She can stay with Peter French, the farm manager."

Jane took her sister-in-law to London for a day's shopping to replace clothes destroyed in the fire, but the day turned into two days. They managed to buy a car full of clothes for both of them, including two maternity dresses for Jane. The outing breathed new life into Angela, who was looking forward to riding Gemma again.

* * *

The site manager walked around the huge site checking on the progress of bricklayers and carpenters, as he was under pressure from his bosses to complete the new school on time. The company was suffering from a shortage of labourers to keep the skilled men working at full capacity.

Jim saw him approach and grinned. "Good morning, governor. How are you this morning?"

"Under pressure and fed up."

"What, still short of labour?"

"Yeah. Bloody short."

"I'll make you a proposition."

"Go on, then."

"If I keep two brickies going, will you pay me double?"

"How are you going to do that?"

"If you can make a hod to carry double the amount, it'll be no trouble."

"All right. I'll arrange for that." He looked at Jim's heavily built frame and knew it was a possibility. "We'll give it a try and if it's successful you'll be earning more than me."

Jim smiled. "I'll look forward to that."

The huge hod carrier was made up with strong bracing at the corners and Jim started using it on the following Monday morning. It was hard work but he managed to keep two fast bricklayers going, and even worked on into the evening for overtime. Rosie piled mountains of food on his plate to satisfy his enormous appetite, and always had second helpings ready if needed. How different he looked since he first arrived. He had become tanned as a result of being constantly exposed to the elements and his body was bursting out of his new clothes, which Rosie spent a lot of time mending.

Jim thought a lot about Angela, and wondered if she had fully recovered. He could still see the vision of her beautiful face vividly in his mind, and ached to see her again, but was still convinced she would be unhappy with a labourer and ex-convict. He pitched himself into his work to keep his mind occupied.

He saved a great deal of money in the next few weeks, and began to think of ways to start a business. The construction of the new school was still behind schedule and he talked to the site manager again. "If I produce extra labourers and deliver them to site, will you pay me their wages plus 20%? And I'll pay them."

"Sounds like a fair idea. But how'll you produce these men, when I can't?"

"I'll collect them from the surrounding area and deliver them in a van."

"I'll let you know if it's on."

Jim bought a second-hand van and worked on the engine and, after spending all day Sunday working on it as well, it ran properly. When he arrived for work on Monday morning the site manager called him. "My boss is agreeable to your proposition."

Jim was delighted, and spent several evenings fitting seats purchased from a local scrap yard into his van. The local paper carried an advertisement offering labouring jobs with free transport to the site, and interviews were held in the local pub. The landlord had agreed to let him use a corner table, and Jim sat nursing a pint of bitter, hoping someone would apply.

An hour passed but no one arrived, and just as he was beginning to get despondent two men walked in together. He could tell they were construction workers from their build and dress. They ordered pints and the landlord directed them to Jim, who shook hands with both of them. They sat down and explained they already had jobs but had to use their own transport, so if the money was right they would be interested. When Jim quickly explained the terms, they agreed to join straightaway, and he bought them two more pints. Other men arrived and, by the end of the evening he had recruited eight, all of them heavily built with existing jobs, but wanting the overtime and free transport. Only one, after listening to Jim's proposition, left saying he would think it over.

Jim wondered about this particular man for some time after. He was a small chap with slender clean hands, not at all used to manual work, and he had asked a lot of questions about the site and even wanted to know where Jim lived, to which Jim replied, "Not far from here."

The other chaps were still in the bar drinking and one of them said to Jim as he was leaving. "Did you take him on?"

"No. He didn't want the job."

"That's just as well. He couldn't do a day's work if he tried."

"D'you know him, then?"

"No. But I've seen him about."

"D'you know what he does for a living?"

"No idea. Nothing, if the truth be known."

Jim forgot about the small man, and the following Monday he got up early and set off in the van. All the men were waiting as arranged, and the site manager was delighted with the extra help, thanking Jim warmly. They all worked on until eight in the evening, with Jim still doing two men's work.

The new arrangement worked very well and two more men joined the team the next weekend. The old van was loaded down, and Jim wondered if he should have bought a bigger vehicle.

The following Monday, when all the men were packing up to go home, Jim was still taking loads of bricks up twenty feet on to a scaffold attached to a short end wall. He wanted to be ready for the next morning's rush with bricks in hand, so he stacked a load at each end of the thirty feet run of boards. He stood up and stretched, feeling tired and looking forward to a good meal. When he looked around, the site was empty apart from four men, two with ladders on their shoulders.

He was about to climb down to catch up with the other workers who would be waiting by the van, when he noticed the

Drink With The Devil

approaching men were all carrying short lengths of heavy chain. The two men with ladders placed them at each end of the scaffolding and started climbing, whilst the other two followed up behind. Jim was about to descend, but the sight of these rough looking men filled him with alarm. He stood nervously and watched as the first man reached the top of the ladder and peered over the scaffold boards. His heart sank when he saw the familiar face, and the dreadful scene on the night of the fire flashed through his mind.

Chapter Ten

A man with ginger hair and a deep scar on the side of his head approached, rattling his chain and laughing when he saw Jim's nervous expression. "So you're the gypo bastard that killed my brother?"

Jim glanced along the scaffold to see the two other men approaching with grim expressions. The fourth man, who was taller than the others, stood behind the ginger-haired man, who spoke slowly. "You're a stupid bastard advertising yourself in the paper. Now you're going to pay with your life."

All four men laughed as Jim crouched ready to defend himself. "You don't stand a chance," the tall man growled.

Jim grabbed a recently laid brick and hurled it at the nearest two men, and it landed with a thud in the big man's stomach. When the ginger-haired man ducked, this action spurred the other three men forward, whirling their chains round above their heads. Jim could see there was no escape, so he hurled more bricks, making them retreat for a few seconds. Then he turned, sat down on the planks, placed his feet against the new wall and pushed, gripping a supporting scaffold pole under him. He strained and heard the sound of metal tearing away from brickwork, and the four men shouted in horror as the entire structure started lurching over. Jim got up, grabbed a concrete lintel, pushed with his feet, and then hung on as the steel pole and wooden board structure crashed to the ground. The men screamed as they hurtled downwards, but fortunately for them the ground was soft and muddy, which cushioned their fall. All four men lay still for a few seconds and then got up slowly. Jim was pleased to see none of them was seriously injured or worse.

Drink With The Devil

The other workers ran towards the broken scaffolding when they heard the crash, and one of them leaned a ladder up against the wall so Jim could climb down. The four attackers walked away unsteadily, covered in mud and saying nothing when asked if they were injured.

While Jim was standing looking at the damage, one of his workers said, "What happened, Jim?"

"Those four blokes came to see me and the whole thing came down."

One of them picked up a length of chain. "Well, they didn't come for a chat."

Jim nodded. "That's true."

"What 'ave they got against you then, Jim?"

"It seems I upset one of them years ago."

The men looked at each other and nodded. "We won't ask any more questions, but we don't like our new boss being got at." They all laughed as they walked towards the van.

Jim watched the four muddy looking figures disappear in the other direction and wondered when they would return. The last man to be dropped off that evening sat next to the driver's seat and broke the silence. "You know any of those men, Jim?"

"Never seen them before in my life."

"Well, I've seen the ginger headed fellow with the scar on the side of his head."

"Where?"

"In the King's Head."

"Does he drink there regularly.?"

"He might. I've seen him in there at least twice."

Jim thought about it for a minute. "Thanks, mate." He parked the van farther away from the terraced house than usual and walked home deep in thought. Rosie had a meal ready, which he sat down and ate in silence and after he had finished she looked him straight in the eye. "What's the matter? You look worried."

"Oh, it's nothing. Just a small problem at work to-day."

"Come on, then. Tell me about it."

He thought for a moment and realised she could be in danger, so he told her the full story.

She looked horrified. "Blimey, you said a small problem. They'd 'ave killed yer."

"Yes. I suppose they would."

"You ought to tell the police."

"They won't believe an ex-con."

"But the police should be looking for them."

"Yes but my main worry is your safety. If they find out where I live you could get hurt."

"I'm not afraid of them bastards. Adolf 'itler didn't make me leave this house, so a few ruffians certainly won't."

"It would be better if I left until this is over."

"Don't you even think about it."

"In that case I'd better think of a way of sorting things out away from here."

"What d'you mean?"

"Well, if I could meet this man and talk to him."

"He won't talk to you. All he wants is you dead. Just 'cause you killed his rotten brother, who deserved all he got."

Jim thought about the problem for a while and, even though it was a warm summer evening, he made sure all the windows were secure, and checked the front and back door locks.

Rosie watched him shutting the kitchen window. "How long d'you think a bolted window'll stop them?"

"Well it'll be better to hear them coming."

"I suppppose that's right."

They sat and talked the matter over for a while. "I'll ring the police in the morning," said Jim.

Rosie was relieved. "I'm sure they'll take some action."

"I certainly hope so."

* * *

Inspector Green was about to go out for lunch when the telephone rang. "Yes," he barked.

"It's a man called Jim Grainger. Will you talk to him?"

He thought for a moment. "Yes, of course I will. Jim. How are you?"

"I'm fine, but a little worried."

"Why's that?"

"I had a visit from a very angry ginger haired man, who seems to want to kill me."

"Are you hurt?"

"No. He was interrupted and left in a hurry."

"That'll be John Briggs. I'd like to find him."

"They say he drinks in the King's Head."

"I think we tried there before."

"You'll have no problem recognising him with that scar on the side of his head."

"Oh, that's interesting. I wonder how he got it. Right, Jim, don't do anything drastic and don't go anywhere on your own. Meanwhile I'll see what I can do."

"Thanks."

The inspector made arrangements to have the pub visited for a few nights by CID men, who also went to the other pubs in the neighbourhood.

The second night a tall man sat down by the bar, drinking a pint of beer, and studying a stranger sitting at a table in the corner. He drained his glass and sat opposite him. "Hello, mate. Haven't seen you around here before."

"Just moved into the area."

"Where d'you live then?"

The detective mentioned a street name. The tall man got up and walked to the bar, slamming down his glass, and the barman said, "Another pint, mate?"

"No thanks. It's beginning to smell in 'ere."

The barman looked across at the man in the corner and nodded. "What are they back in 'ere for?"

"Dunno. You'd better find out."

The tall man walked out, leaving the bar empty, and the

barman walked across to the corner table. "Who yer looking for this time?"

"What d'you mean? I've just come in for a quiet pint."

"Load of balls. You're waiting for someone and scaring my customers away."

The detective sighed. "Very well. I want to see a ginger-haired man called John Briggs."

The barman laughed. "Still looking for 'im after all this time. Why don't yer give up?"

"We never give up. I understand he comes in here."

"Never seen 'im, mate."

"But he's been seen in this pub."

"Listen. Lots of ginger-haired men come in 'ere."

"Yes, but not many have a scar on the side of their head, do they?"

The barman, a bald-headed thick-set individual, looked down at the empty glass on the table. "You goin' to 'ave another drink?"

"No. I'm not thirsty. Now, you can tell me when you last saw John Briggs."

"I don't know the man, guv."

"You're afraid to tell me, aren't you?"

The barman looked nervous and walked back to the bar. The detective knew it was no good continuing with the questioning and walked out. All other attempts at finding Briggs were fruitless.

Jim continued to work as hard as ever, but keeping a lookout for Briggs and his gang. He had telephoned Inspector Green again, but was told they were continuing their search. He was getting depressed and edgy, not knowing when the gang would strike again.

Rosie remarked. "They must have given up by now."

"I do hope so." But her arguments only made him more worried about her safety.

One evening he dropped off the last of his men and started driving home, feeling tired and hungry, when suddenly a large black car swerved in front of the van, blocking the narrow

Drink With The Devil

street. Jim slammed on the brakes and stopped inches away from the car, from which four men jumped out carrying pickaxe handles. Jim thrust the gear lever into reverse and drove backwards, whilst a man clung to the door handle shouting abuse. He let go and fell in a heap on the pavement as Jim backed into a garage entrance before driving forward again.

Keeping up a fast speed through unfamiliar streets, Jim looked into his mirror to find the black car was gaining on him. He racked his brains for good ideas but none came so he kept going, with the black car close to his rear bumper, until he reached the town centre. He thought this cannot go on and pulled over to the side of the road, where evening strollers were window shopping and generally ambling along the pavement. He jumped out and ran back to the black car parked behind.

The door was opening so he stood back and waited for the ginger-haired man, who was wearing a peaked cap to cover his scar, to get out. Jim spoke first. "If you want to kill me, do it right here."

"I'll kill you when I'm ready. And it'll be no good you goin' to the cops again."

Jim was tense and angry. "This is bloody stupid. Why can't you get on with your life and let me alone."

"Because you killed my brother."

"Killing me won't bring him back."

"No. But I'll feel better about it."

"You're a complete nutcase and deserve to be locked up."

The other men jumped out of the car at this provocation. Briggs turned to them. "Not 'ere, you bloody idiots."

The spectacle was being watched by several passers by. Briggs looked at them and then back at Jim. "Right you bastard. You've got away with it this time, but we'll be back." He slammed the door and drove away with screaming tyres, leaving Jim standing there feeling extremely angry. He drove home slowly and told Rosie what had happened.

Rosie was sympathetic. "When will it all stop? You can't look over your shoulder for ever."

"I know. The police are useless, and don't know what to do."

"You'll have to think of a way to bring it to a head on your terms."

"Yes I agree, but how?" They discussed different ideas for a while until Jim was so tired he could not stay awake any longer.

The next day, following his usual routine, Jim regularly looked in his mirror as he drove along.

His fellow workers noticed his nervy silence and one asked, "What's up, Jim?"

"I'm okay, thanks," was his brief response.

One of them laboured the point. "Look Jim, if you need any help with those evil bastards, just say the word."

"It's very kind of you to offer, but I'll manage."

The rest of the week dragged by slowly, and he collapsed in an armchair on Friday night, looking forward to two days rest. Rosie gave him a cup of cocoa and they sat and chatted, but their conversation was halted abruptly by a crash and splintering of wood coming from the back door. They both jumped to their feet and froze, as four masked men entered carrying cudgels and long knives.

Chapter Eleven

There was a brief silence and then Jim, recognising the first man's voice, stepped forward in front of Rosie.

"Right gypo, you'll do exactly as I say or the old dear gets cut up."

"Ok, but if you lay a finger on her, I'll kill you."

"Don't be bloody stupid. You won't get the chance."

Jim stayed silent as Briggs held a knife to Rosie's throat and growled in her ear. "If you report this to the cops you'll be dead as well. Now say goodbye and we'll leave you in peace."

Rosie was so shocked she could not say anything. Jim said calmly. "Don't worry, I'll be back."

One of the men tied Jim's hands behind his back, then blindfolded him, and the last thing he saw was Rosie's pale frightened face with the knife at her throat. He wanted to fight but could not endanger her life. Someone poked him in the back with a knife. "Come on, you big useless gypo, start walking."

He walked forward, bumping into the door, but someone grabbed his shirt and pulled him forward. He stumbled over the remains of the back door out into the night, and a voice from behind said gruffly, "Don't say a word or you'll die right here."

The car was parked by the back garden gate and they shoved him inside with a man either side of him. The car started up and accelerated away, forcing him back against his hands that were trapped behind him, which was uncomfortable and reminded him of the trip in the police car after the fire. He tried to think of an escape plan but no inspiration was forthcoming, just the thought of knowing he would probably be dead in a short time filled him with fear. The men in the car stayed silent, and all he could hear was the soft drone of the engine. He tried to work out where he was going but soon gave up, and thoughts of impending doom were interrupted by Briggs' voice. "Well, you 'orrible bastard. How does it feel to know you're about to die? And slowly."

Jim swallowed and stayed silent, trying to loosen the rope bound tightly around his wrists, but his efforts chafed his skin painfully. After about fifteen minutes they pulled up sharply, and Jim lurched forward as a hand grabbed the shoulder of his shirt and pulled. "Come on, gypo. Get out slowly and don't try anything clever."

He stumbled out on to a hard pavement, rough hands grabbing and pushing him forward. His hair brushed a low doorway and he felt bare floorboards under his slippered feet, but was pushed forward again and shuffled along with only the sound of boots on wooden boards to be heard. A door slammed and Briggs said, "Stay there. I've someone who wants to see you." Jim stood nervously wondering what he meant and another door slammed.

" 'ere he is Vi. That gypo bastard that killed your 'arry."

"He don't look like a gypo, but I'll take your word for it."

"Well, what d'you want done with 'im?"

"I want 'im dead," she screamed, and launched a verbal tirade of abuse at him.

Jim just stood numbed by the outburst. He had never heard such bad language from a woman before. Her high pitched voice got more and more excited and angry and she suddenly started punching him, but he just stood still absorbing the blows to his chest and stomach. His composure only made her more angry and she screamed at him again. "You bloody animal. I'll kill you myself."

He felt a stinging blow as she kicked him in the crotch. The pain shot up through his stomach doubling him up and he sank to his knees, bending forward to bring some relief to his tender parts. She laughed and kicked his lowered face, the blow to his mouth making his lip numb, and as he swallowed he could taste his own blood. All the men were laughing as Vi said, "I feel much better for doing that."

Briggs said, "I think we should throw him down the cellar to contemplate his doom."

Vi laughed again. "Yeah. Let 'im sweat on it for a while."

Jim felt hands pulling him up and he rose slowly and painfully before being pushed forward. He heard a creaking sound and Briggs' voice. "Right, poke 'im down there."

"Okay, guv. When'll you kill 'im?"

"When we get back from our rounds later on."

Jim felt a violent shove from behind, fell down a short flight of wooden stairs and hit his head against the floor at the bottom, seeing stars despite being blindfolded. His body ached as he lay still for five minutes after the hatch above was slammed shut. Lying on his side and getting cold, he then realised the floor of the cellar was covered in water. The smell of sewage filled his nostrils as he rolled over, soaking the rest of his body. He groaned with discomfort, feeling the slimy water between his fingers and his clothes sticking to his body. His mind was frantically trying to think of a means of escape. His hands, partly submerged in slime, were getting colder and his wrists slippery, so he concentrated on the rope.

Within five minutes of trying the rope slipped off, he massaged his numbed fingers and then undid the blindfold. It was pitch black in the smelly cellar, except for a little light coming through the crack of the wooden hatch in the ceiling above. He stood up slowly but felt dreadful. His stomach and sides ached, his head throbbed and his legs felt wobbly, so he sat on the stairs and listened as voices from above filtered through the crack. He heard a woman's high pitched voice.

"I 'ope to Christ we get that bloody stinking cellar cleaned out soon."

A man's voice answered. "We'll clean it up after that bastard down there's been buried."

"What'll it be this time? A concrete boot?"

"Yeah. The arrangements 'ave already bin made."

"Good. I'm looking forward to seeing 'im die." The man grunted.

This chilling conversation reminded Jim of the perilous situation he was in. A telephone rang and the woman answered giving the number.

There was a silence followed by "It's okay. Everything's quiet 'ere." Then there was the sound of the receiver being replaced. "He'll be 'ere in 'alf an 'our." She said to her companion.

"Good. I'll tell 'im down there he's only got 'alf an 'our to live."

Jim quickly lay on the floor, giving the impression he was still tied up. The blindfold was on the step beside him so he tied it on just in time as the man shouted down. "Only 'alf an 'our to live, so make the most of it."

The woman joined in. "Yeah. Why not pray for a while." They both laughed and slammed the hatch down.

Jim got up quietly and started moving his painful limbs slowly, and after a while managed to climb the stairs and listen to see if the couple were still there. He heard the woman say. "Only five minutes. I 'ope he's managed to collect from all of them."

The man replied gruffly. "He will, or we'll do a demolition job on their clubs." They both laughed.

Jim moved closer to the hatch, placing his shoulder against the latch end, and his feet firmly on two steps. He drew a deep breath and pushed hard, and heard the splintering of wood as the latch tore away from the floorboards. The hatch sprang open, the woman screamed and Jim jumped out of the cellar. The man ran at him with fists clenched, but Jim weaved out of his path and turned to face him, receiving a blow to the stomach which he hardly felt. He grabbed the man by his shirt and lifted him off his feet and then shoved him down the cellar stairs with a mighty push. Jim heard the thud and splash as the woman launched herself at him, but he grabbed her arms and shoved her down as well. She screamed as she fell on top of the man just trying to get up, and they both rolled over in the slime.

Jim slammed down the broken hatch and pulled a table

Drink With The Devil

over to hold it down, but at that moment the door burst open and a man shouted. Jim looked around and saw a flight of wooden stairs. He ran up them and through a door at the top, which led to a carpeted and well decorated corridor with soft lighting. The room was well lit, had expensive furnishings and Jim was astounded to see a naked man laying spread-eagled on a double bed with his legs and arms tied to the corner bed legs. A naked girl stood by the bed with a horsewhip in her hand. She looked at Jim and sneered. "Piss off mate. And come back later."

The man on the bed looked embarrassed and tried to bury his face in the pillow, but the girl just stood there unashamed with her hands on her ample hips. Jim heard footsteps climbing the wooden stairs and grabbed the bed, dragging it towards the door. He lifted one side up so it leaned against the door heavily at forty-five degrees, while the man struggled and whimpered, but could not move. The girl started thrashing Jim with the whip, but he grabbed it and broke it in two. The girl screamed and came at him like a possessed demon, with arms and legs thrashing out at him. He grabbed a rising leg and pulled. She fell back stunned and he rolled her up in a loose carpet.

The bed began to move as men were pushing from the other side, and Jim ran across to look out of the window. A big black car was directly underneath, so he lifted the window open and, when he looked back into the room, saw the bed toppling over with the man looking horrified as he fell face down on to the floor. Jim jumped, landing on the roof of the car, which sagged under his weight, and as he jumped off he saw figures emerging from the house.

Jim grabbed the driver's door and wrenched it open, finding a man sitting petrified inside. He grabbed him and pulled him out, shoving him across the road. After getting in the car he found the ignition keys were in position so he started up and crashed it into first gear.

A man was pulling on the door as Jim lurched away amid shouts and running feet. The man let go and ran alongside, but was soon left behind as Jim found second gear. He gripped the wheel so hard his knuckles went white, and was so tensed up that it was quite a while before he relaxed a little and found the light switch along with other controls. He drove slowly, trying to ascertain his location. Another few minutes passed before he found a road he recognised and set off in the direction of home.

A set of traffic lights delayed him, giving him an opportunity to look around inside the car and, to his horror, there was a sawn off shotgun on the front passenger seat. He tossed it on to the floor before anyone could look through the window and spot it. On the floor was a large bag of the type doctors use and, as the traffic lights were still red, he bent over and opened it to find it stuffed full of money. He closed it quickly and moved off through the green lights.

These discoveries made Jim realise how much danger he was still in — the men back at the house would want the car and money back and would be even more desperate to kill him. The big car purred reassuringly as he pondered over his next move, but suddenly a green car flashed by and braked hard, sliding itself across the road and blocking the way.

Drink With The Devil

Chapter Twelve

The breeze sent wisps of straw scurrying around the floor of the empty stable, the brood mare having been sold soon after the fire. Garry decided the farm staff would be too busy to deal with her properly, so Gemma was alone in the adjoining stable and had pined for her companion and Angela, who had been away so long.

The day arrived when Angela decided to go out for her first ride since leaving hospital but after about half an hour she began to feel tired and headed back to the stable. Gemma let out a whinny of disappointment as they entered the stable yard. As Angela got off her legs felt like jelly, so she led the mare back into her box and then sat down on a bale of straw in the adjoining stable. She smelt the sweet aroma of the hay piled high around her and as she moved back to rest her head against a bale, she felt a lump under the palm of her hand. She picked up a button and studied it. The coat button was large and brown with a fleck of yellow in its texture, and seemed familiar to her. She turned it over in her hand, trying to think where she had seen it before. Somehow it seemed important, so she put it in her pocket and went back to Gemma who was waiting to have her saddle taken off.

Another week had passed, and as she prepared an excited Gemma for a long ride, she felt much stronger than on the previous occasion. They set off on a warm sunny day with only a few puffy clouds in the clear blue sky as they rode away.

Gemma seemed content to walk in the heat of the afternoon, and they followed hedgerows around wheat and barley fields until they reached a bridleway where they stopped. Angela wondered in which direction to proceed. Gemma chose for her and walked off at a brisk pace. Angela looked back at the disappearing farm buildings and wondered why her mare was so keen to go down this particular path and hoped she would remember the way back. She patted Gemma's neck and said, "You'd better not get me lost."

When they reached the edge of a wood, the bridleway ahead was overgrown with a narrow track just passable down the centre. Angela pulled back on the reins. "That's as far as we're going." They stopped and Gemma whinnied, her ears pricked as she stared at the trees. "What's the matter with you? We can't go in there." She felt the need to walk a little so she got off and stretched her legs, which were still not used to riding. Gemma nibbled at a tuft of grass and moved slowly towards the wood, eating grass as she went. Angela watched and thought how peaceful it was and pleasing to see the horse content in finding the best tufts of grass to eat.

Suddenly Gemma lifted her head, whinnied and walked forward along the bridleway with Angela hanging on to the reins.

"Hey, come back. Where d'you think you're going?"

The mare took no notice and turned right between two trees and, once under the canopy of old hardwood trees, Angela felt at home and happily walked beside the horse.

"Gemma, where are you taking me?" She giggled.

Gemma just carried on walking, picking her way between oak and beech trees, and sometimes just brushing against their thick lower branches. Angela was out of breath by the time they had climbed up the side of the hill, and then Gemma suddenly stopped and whinnied again.

When Angela looked around she saw large rhododendron bushes, some flowers blooming on their top branches.

"Well. Why have we stopped here?"

Gemma just stood still, staring at the bushes with her ears pricked. Angela followed her stare and saw a gap between the bushes. She walked through and when she emerged the other

Drink With The Devil

side the lodge came into view, and she knew she had been there before.

Trembling with excitement she tried the door but found it was locked. The windows were covered in cobwebs and dirt, but she could see a table inside and a pile of what looked like rubbish against one wall. She stood back and felt a warm glow come over her as she realised this was a happy part of her former life. She walked back slowly to Gemma.

"I know why you brought me here. This place is special, isn't it?"

Gemma nuzzled up to her and whinnied softly. After a little while Angela broke away and studied her surroundings, finding it all very familiar as the breeze rustled the leaves and branches above, letting sunlight through in dancing shafts of light.

She was mesmerised by the scene and started walking along a faint path where bluebell leaves were shorter and stunted. As she looked back, Gemma was just standing still watching her, and Angela moved farther away along the side of the hill as if drawn by a magnet, until she reached the pool. She stood staring at the crystal clear water, listening to it splashing as it flowed over the rocks and on to the stream down the hill. Her reflection was clear in the pool, and she studied it for a minute before looking around, suddenly feeling weak as she sat down on a rock.

A weight seemed to be lifting from her mind as she remembered the last time she was at the rock pool. She stared again at the water, trembling as the memory of that afternoon and making love came back to her, and she closed her eyes to re-live the wonderful time they had in that beautiful pool. "Oh Jim," she muttered over and over again.

She walked slowly through the wood, finding the spot where they had eaten lunch and made love, and a shaft of brilliant sunlight marked the clearing not far from where Gemma was still patiently waiting. Angela looked at the lodge again and peered through the windows. The bed was still there on the floor with its bedclothes in a pile covered with cobwebs, and the cooking utensils were stacked neatly by the blackened fireplace. The old motorbike, covered in dust, was still leaning against the wall. She walked back to Gemma and hugged her warmly.

"Thank you for bringing me here, you wonderful horse."

Gemma twitched her muzzle from side to side and pressed it against Angela's face.

After a few more minutes of looking around they left, walking down the hill slowly to the bridleway. Angela remembered the way and went first, and they arrived back at the stable just as Peter was organising a search party.

"Angela!" he exclaimed. "Are you sure you're well enough to ride?"

"Yes, thank you. I feel marvellous."

"Oh, good. I thought you'd got lost."

"So did I. But then I began to remember!"

"You remembered?"

"Yes, the lodge! I've been there before!"

"That's splendid news. How did it happen?"

She told him briefly, leaving out the intimate details.

"Good heavens. So you really did know Grainger?"

"Yes, I certainly did."

They unsaddled and brushed Gemma down together, and went in for a meal. Peter related the good news to his wife, Sue, while Angela, who was ravenous, sat and ate.

* * *

Jim gripped the wheel and drove up on to the empty pavement, passing the car with the four men inside. With the other car on his tail, he drove hard through the town and out into the country. A glance at the fuel gauge indicated a nearly full tank, the car clock was at 1 a.m. and the roads were empty, but no matter how fast he drove the pursuing car stuck close behind with its headlamps on main beam.

Jim was beginning to get used to driving the big car, resisting all attempts by the following car to get in front, and once out into the country lanes in familiar surroundings he felt more at home. Gradually he got ahead of the green car and the lanes were very narrow with high banks either side, and he took each corner at breakneck speed using the banking to good affect. A glance in his mirror told him the following car had fallen back several hundred yards, so he took two sharp left turns and then went into a farm entrance, turning off his lights.

As he drove by moonlight into the farmyard, he looked behind and saw the other car flash by the entrance, so he sat and waited for a while. As he got out of the car, his heart was beating almost painfully against his chest, but he took a deep breath of cool night air and started to relax. The Home Farm buildings were just as he remembered them, but now they were strangely silent — no cows could be heard munching away in the cowshed. He stood for a few minutes appreciating the calmness and silence, comparing it with the frantic chase he had just abandoned. An owl hooted nearby and he watched its distinctive flight, as it disappeared across the fields in search of prey.

He walked around in the moonlight, noticing how desolate the buildings were without animals, and there was not even a bale of straw. The house was empty, and as he walked back to the car a breeze brought with it the smell of the woods and fields. He stood breathing in the fragrance, remembering the good times he had and wishing he could return to the heart of the country again.

His present predicament was too urgent for his dreaming to continue, and he tried to work out where the four men would be by now. He decided they would give up and go home, ready to try again in daylight, which would not be long coming. A glow on the horizon reminded him that it was summer and it would be light in a couple of hours, so he got into the car and started the engine; the smell of his clothes making him feel sick and desperate to get home and change.

* * *

When they had finished eating, Angela felt in the pocket of her trousers for the large button pressing against her leg, took it out and placed it on the table. Remembering where she found it, she spoke slowly. "My God, Jim must have been in that stable."

Peter and Sue had not mentioned her parents' death, and were dreading the moment when Angela remembered what happened. Peter sat down beside her. "Yes, he was there on the night you were injured."

Angela picked the button up and turned it over in her palm. "What happened to me?"

"Well, you were attacked by a man. Jim found you and carried you into the stable, staying until the ambulance took you away."

Angela gripped the button as she saw the leering face of the ginger-haired man clearly in her mind, and stared at the table as the terrible events of that evening came back to her. She choked and whimpered, clasping her head in her hands. Peter and Sue came around the table and he stood beside her, putting his arm around her, although she did not feel him. After about five minutes of silence Angela said shakily. "Mum and Dad. What happened to them?"

Peter's voice was croaky. "Oh Angela, I'm sorry. But they died that night."

Angela, remembered her mother's screams and her father's angry protestations. Sue nodded to Peter and they left the room quietly.

Angela's shoulders began to heave and tears ran down her face. Having cried until her eyes and throat were sore, Angela dried her face and went into the next room to reassure the anxious couple. "Please don't worry. I did wonder why they hadn't come to see me." Now I understand. I must accept what's happened."

Sue got up and led her to the settee.

"Come and sit down and talk if you want to. It may be good for you."

"Yes I'd like to know what happened." She looked straight at Peter.

"What happened to Jim?"

"He found you lying on the ground being beaten by a man. But unfortunately he went mad, killed the man and ended up in jail."

"Oh my God. Poor Jim. I can remember being chased by a ginger-haired man." She went on to tell them what happened that evening, stopping to cry a little when she told how her mother had screamed. They listened in amazed silence, Sue with her arm around the grief-stricken girl trying to comfort her. She sobbed again and said,

"How long did Jim get?"

"One year."

"So he's still in prison. It must be terrible for him."

"As far as I know he is," said Sue.

"We were very close."

"Yes I'm sure you were. And he saved your horses from the fire."

"Did he really. That sounds just like him. He loves animals."

"Obviously."

After telling her all about the fire and the police, it was late when they all finally went to bed. Angela stayed awake first thinking about her parents and then about Jim. She imagined how he would have suffered in prison, and wondered if he was still locked up. She cried bitterly again, but eventually fell asleep.

The next day she walked around the farm buildings, seeing them in a more familiar light. She stared at the new building site, picturing the old house and remembering the last happy meal she had with her parents that dreadful night, but her deep thoughts were interrupted by the building site foreman.

"Morning Miss. Would you like to see the plans of the new house?"

Angela looked at the red-faced middle-aged man with a friendly smile. "Yes, please."

They walked to the wooden site hut and looked at a large plan laid on a sloping desk. It showed a large Georgian house, not as big as the original mansion, but quite impressive. Angela studied the elevations and internal plans for some time and was impressed with the layout and detail.

"How d'you like it, Miss?"

"It's very nice. My parents would have approved."

"Our new boss designed most of it."

"Oh. And who is your new boss?"

"Mr. Garry Osborne."

"My brother's your boss?"

"Yes. Didn't he tell you?"

"No. But then I haven't been taking things in lately."

"Well, he married our boss's daughter just after the governor died, and he's been running things ever since."

"What about Osbornes?"

"He runs that as well."

"What a busy man."

"Yes. And I must say we seem to be doing very well."

Angela left the hut, deep in thought, and found Peter in the farm office. She questioned him about her brother and what had happened since her parents' death. He told her all he knew, but did not say what a pain in the neck Garry had really been.

Angela asked a lot more questions and then said. "Does he try to run the farm as well?"

"He did at first, but soon gave up."

"So he leaves it all to you?"

"He does now."

She remembered the jobs she used to do in the office and spent the afternoon getting the farm records up to date.

That evening there was a warm breeze blowing up the hill, and she sat staring across the wood. The country smells filled her nostrils as she thought about Jim and how he would have enjoyed such an evening. She dearly wanted to see him again

Drink With The Devil

and pictured his wild-looking face in her mind, imagining him sitting near to her and talking about the countryside and his life with the animals. She could almost hear his deep husky voice, which she remembered was like music to her ears.

The following Saturday Garry and Jane arrived and were delighted to hear that Angela's memory had returned. Jane talked non-stop about the things she had purchased for the baby, whilst Garry disappeared with Peter into the office.

Angela was dying to get Garry on his own to answer some questions, and spent a frustrating hour talking to Jane before he returned to the house with Peter. Angela looked straight at him. "Can we have a private chat?"

Garry looked worried. "Yes. Let's go into the office." They walked together in silence and Garry sat down behind the desk.

"What d'you want to know?"

"What happened to Jim Grainger?"

Garry grimaced. "He's in prison where he belongs."

"But he probably saved my life."

"We've no proof of that."

Angela gave him a steely glare. "I want to know exactly what happened."

Garry told her roughly the same story as Peter but added, "Grainger killed Harry Briggs in cold blood and should have been done for murder. I believe he had a hand in the robbery and murder of our parents."

"That's rubbish. He couldn't have had anything to do with it."

Garry took no notice of his sister and raised his voice. "That evil bastard should have been strung up. But instead he only got a year."

Angela stayed calm. "Now you can listen to my version of events."

Garry listened, looking grim, his expression not changing, even when his sister told of their mother's screams. She finished with tears flowing down her face, and they both sat in silence for a minute.

Garry said in an even toned voice. "What d'you think Grainger was doing living in the lodge for so long? Apart from trespassing."

"He loved the countryside."

"Yes. I bet he did."

Angela regained her composure and spoke clearly. "He lost his job when Home Farm was sold, and decided to live on his own in his favourite surroundings."

"He was hiding from the police. And very effectively it seems."

Angela was shocked and her eyes flashed with anger. "Why would he need to do that?"

"I'm not sure. And the police won't admit they couldn't find him."

"That's rubbish. He couldn't have been a criminal."

"Why not? He killed Briggs and probably killed before."

"But he was trying to save me."

"He could have done that without killing him. Besides he was convicted of manslaughter and sent to prison and, no one else has been apprehended for killing our parents, which I can assure you Grainger had a hand in."

"I just don't believe he was capable of a crime."

"Why? What d'you know about him?"

"He's kind, gentle and without malice."

"So you say. But how d'you know he wasn't on the run from some crime?"

"Because he wasn't that sort."

Garry let out a mirthless laugh. "How would you know?"

Angela got angry again. "He's a good man and I love him."

Garry was visibly shocked and stuttered. "D-do you mean you were lovers?"

"Yes, and I'm proud of it."

"How could you associate with that wild looking gypo maniac?" He bellowed.

Angela sat silently staring at the floor and Garry lowered his tone. "Look, Angela, he was hiding from something. And I would guess his temper got the better of him before, and he probably hurt or killed someone. You met him when you were lonely and fell in love. He caught you in the company of another man and killed him in a fit of temper."

Angela looked up. "But I was running away from this man."

"Grainger didn't know that."

Angela shook her head. "I don't believe your theory."

"But it's the only logical explanation."

"I still can't believe it."

"Well, you think about it very carefully."

"Yes I will. Now tell me which prison he's in."

"No idea, old girl. I don't think it matters."

"It matters to me."

Garry decided he had sown enough doubts in her mind for one day and changed the subject. "D'you want to know the details of Mum and Dad's will?"

"Yes. You'd better fill me in."

He explained in detail how the estate was split up and Angela was surprised when he said. "You're the owner of Home Farm House and its buildings, along with the surrounding grass paddocks, and a considerable portfolio of shares — enough to give you a very good income for life with capital to spare." He finished explaining and said, "I take it you'll want Osbornes to continue managing your portfolio?"

"Just for the time being."

"Oh. And what'll you do then?"

"I haven't had time to think yet." She was still stunned by her parents' death and could not think about money.

Garry and Jane went home, and Angela went up to her room to think about what Garry had said about Jim. She churned the matter over for a long time and still did not know what to believe. She realised her feelings had not changed and still longed to see him again.

The next day Peter took her to Home Farm and she looked around the building, deciding that the cowshed would convert to a very good block of stables, and the dairy to a useful tack room. They opened the back door of the house and a damp smell met them in the rear hall. The walk around the house caused mixed feelings for Angela. It was in poor repair, a leak in the roof having brought down one ceiling and rotted the floorboards, but she imagined how nice it could be if enough money was spent.

She walked into a small rear bedroom and knew instantly that it was Jim's old room. A picture of his motorcycle was still stuck to a wall, and she looked around the room with a lump in her throat, walking away from the house determined to see him again.

The following day was Monday and she rang the local police station, who advised her to ring the prison service. After lengthy enquiries she was advised that Jim had been released some time ago. In view of what her brother had said, she was surprised and wondered if he knew he was already out.

Peter came into the farm office and noticed her faraway expression. "Penny for your thoughts."

"Peter, can I borrow the Land Rover this morning?"

"Of course you can. Going anywhere interesting?"

"Back to the hospital for a chat with the staff."

"That's a good idea. They'll be pleased to see you."

"I just want to find out more about the man they say talked to me and brought me back to life."

"Oh, I see."

She set off straightaway and arrived to a warm reception. Nurse Bowen was delighted to see her looking so well. Angela chatted for a few moments and then said. "You met the man who talked me out of the coma?"

"Yes. And I'd like to meet him again."

"So would I. Can you tell me about him?"

She described him in every detail and Angela tried to think about what he would have looked like without his beard and long hair. "That's what he looked like, but what about his voice?"

"Oh, fantastic. Deep, husky and very sexy. To tell you the truth he had me in tears."

Drink With The Devil

Angela knew it was him. "That was my Jim Grainger."

"But why didn't he tell me his name?"

"I don't know and I'd like to find him to ask."

"If you see him, give him my love."

Angela laughed. "I certainly will."

She drove back to the farm desperate to see Jim again, and with no idea how to find him, but then doubts crossed her mind. If he wanted to see her why had he not contacted her? Perhaps he had found someone else. Then Garry's words came to her and she wondered if he was on the run again, but then she remembered the nurse describing his new working clothes.

That same evening Sue noticed Angela's worried look, and Angela told her about the conversation with the nurse. "What d'you think, Sue?"

She thought for a moment. "I don't think he's on the run from some criminal activity. I think you should put yourself in his place. What would you do?"

Angela thought hard. "Yes, I see what you mean. Perhaps he's ashamed of killing someone, and can't face seeing me yet."

"That could be the problem. So I wouldn't try to find him yet."

"I suppose not," she said glumly. The prospect of not seeing him again made her depressed and she went to bed feeling desolate — her beloved parents were dead and the man she loved was somewhere else, and did not want to see her.

Chapter Thirteen

The country lanes were deserted in the early hours of the morning, and Jim took a different route back in case the four men were waiting for him to pass by. He reflected upon the night's events and began to get worried about Rosie, whom he thought must be very frightened, and possibly in danger if the gang visited her on the way back. He pressed on as fast as possible, reaching the narrow streets as dawn was breaking. After parking he put the shotgun in the boot, remembering to wipe the barrel with a duster to remove his fingerprints.

Clutching the bag, he walked through a maze of narrow streets and back alleys until he was able to see the back of Rosie's house. After a few minutes careful looking around, he was satisfied there were no intruders, and he picked his way over the broken back door into the kitchen. The house was quiet and cool, and he walked into the sitting room to find Rosie in an armchair, bent forward with her head in her hands.

"Rosie. Have they hurt you?"

She looked up suddenly. "Jim. Thank God you're safe." She jumped up and hugged him and then recoiled. "Blimey, you don't 'alf stink."

"I know. I could do with a change of clothes."

"And a bath if you ask me!"

Rosie ran a bath whilst he took off his slimy stinking clothes. Twenty minutes later he was dressed again, eating a slice of toast and drinking a cup of tea.

Rosie fussed over him. "You ought to get some rest. Why not go up to bed?"

"I can't do that in case they come back."

"D'you think they will?"

"Yes. I'm absolutely certain." He told her briefly what had happened and then said, "I'm going now. If they return, tell them to meet me in the old grain mill next to the school building site."

"Whatever you say. But I 'ope they don't come back 'ere."

"They won't if I can get to a telephone before they leave." He gathered up Rosie's bag of tools and a coil of rope he had found earlier in the cellar.

Rosie looked at him and frowned. "What d'you want all that for?"

"I want to prepare a surprise or two for them." He walked out of the back door promising to repair it on Sunday. He had the coil of rope over his shoulder, a bag in each hand and he found a telephone box nearby to ring the number he had heard the woman use. After a long wait a gruff voice answered. "Yeah? Speak to me."

Jim spoke clearly and slowly. Jim Grainger here. If Briggs still wants to see me I'll be in the old grain mill building by the new school site."

"Too right, he wants to see you."

"Tell him to be there by 9 o'clock." He rang off, found the black car and sat for a moment, feeling tired and apprehensive. He started up the engine and began the short drive to the derelict old building, parking outside.

He looked up at the tall red brick structure with several doors opening out to the open air. Each door had a small gantry above it, which used to have a chain hoist attached, to lower sacks of flour down to the lorries parked below. Rats and mice scurried about as he strode over empty sacks to a shaky wooden staircase, and went up to the first floor, finding a trap door with a notch in one side. Each floor had a similar wooden hatch, which was used to lift sacks of corn up from the ground floor. A long chain was attached to the full sack, lifting it up, and when it came up against the hatch it was lifted automatically, letting the sack pass on up or be detached on that floor. When the mill was in use the endless chain would run all day. All the metal parts of the mill had been sent to the scrapyard, but the wooden machinery and thick dust remained.

Jim opened his tool bag and started work, stopping to listen from time to time, thinking they would arrive to surprise him. He carried on altering the wooden trap doors until he was on the top floor and, looking down, he could see through the top hatch which was near to the stairs. He could also see out of the top external door, which gave a view across the building site and beyond. When he had finished he sat down on the floor with the money and tool bag beside him. He glanced at his watch to find it was 8:30, and he had just one more job to do.

He got up and looked out the open door to see two cars driving slowly towards the building, stopping fifty yards away. Jim shuddered when he saw eight grim faced men get out, all carrying cudgels. He went across to the stairs, broke the top six treads by stamping heavily with his boot and then scrambled back up to wait. The men had disappeared inside and he heard the sound of hob-nailed boots on wooden boards. He hid the two bags under a pile of sacks and, peering down through the hatch, he heard a voice shouting up at him.

"Grainger, where the 'ell are you?" A lot of swearing followed and Jim's heart thumped painfully as they got nearer. The floor below him creaked as the first man got to the stairs and shouted down. "He must be on the top floor." A voice from below replied. "Right, we're coming up."

Jim lay on the floor, looking down through the slot in the hatch where the chain used to pass through and waited until he heard the voice of Briggs.

"Grainger, get down 'ere right now, or we'll set light to the building."

Jim had not thought about them setting the place on fire, but stayed calm. A man walked across the room and stood directly below him, looking up through the chain slot "He's up there, guv."

Jim heaved on a rope. The man bellowed as the trap door beneath him gave way and he landed on the floor below, with a

Drink With The Devil

bang which echoed through the building.

There was a commotion from below and one of the men shouted, "I'm going up there to kill 'im."

Jim jumped to his feet and threw a coil of rope out of the open door. One end was tied to the gantry above and he looked back to see a red-looking face appear at the top of the stairs. Grabbing the rope and hoping the gantry would stand his weight, he swung out, but as he looked down he saw to his horror the rope was well short of the ground. It was too late to return so he wrapped the rope around his legs and slid down, the bottom of the rope being ten feet from the road. He lowered himself hand over hand as low as possible. He was just about to jump when the rope gave way and he fell heavily, hurting his ankle, with the rope landing on top of him.

He recovered and looked up to see a man peering down with a knife in his hand. Jim hobbled as fast as he could into the building, reaching the stairs just as a man was about to descend. He grabbed the wooden boards which held the stair treads and lifted, as they were not fixed very well to the floor. He then pulled to one side using the wall for leverage, and the two nails he had left in position pulled out easily, the stairs crashing to the floor with a man falling on top. Jim heard a sickly crack as a leg broke on impact. The man screamed and clutched his leg, groaning before passing out. By this time the remaining men were on the first floor, getting very bad tempered. Briggs shouted down through the stair hole. "Grainger, you despicable bastard. I'll kill yer for what you've done."

Jim felt a little more confident. "Come on then. What are you waiting for?"

A man above was trying to open the sack hatch, but found it was nailed shut, so their only means of escape was through the open hole where the stairs were, or a door to the open air on the next floor up. Jim retrieved the rope and threw an end up through the stair hole, one man caught it and shouted down.

"What are we supposed to do with this?"

"Tie it to something and slide down one at a time."

"You must be joking,"

Jim listened as the men discussed their strategy in muffled tones, one of them pulling on the rope and tying it to a timber pillar. Jim stood back waiting patiently, his body tense and his mouth dry. Suddenly a large man appeared above and swung out on the rope, sliding down as if he had done it many times before. When he landed he lunged at Jim, who kept his nerve and crashed his huge fist into the man's ribs. They cracked and the man collapsed in a heap, groaning and clutching his side. The men above watched, horrified by the force of his punch, and started arguing, but Briggs said "Right, who's next?"

"Don't be bloody daft. He'll murder us one by one," said one man.

Briggs got angry. "You're a load of frightened old women. Get down there."

A gruff voice replied. "You're the big boss. You go first."

A heated argument followed and then a fight developed. Jim listened as men cursed each other and fought with cudgels and knives. A man screamed and fell, landing at Jim's feet with a knife buried in his chest and blood spurting out. The man looked at Jim with glazed eyes, his face snow white, and his last words were a feeble "help me."

Jim was sickened at the sight of the man dying and the violence still going on above, but suddenly a group of uniformed police ran into the building, shouting at the men to stop. Jim helped lean the broken staircase back and watched as the policemen advanced slowly upwards.

Inspector Green stood at the bottom of the stairs with Jim and grinned. "Rosie said she thought you might need some help."

"That was nice of her."

"Yes but it seems they're killing each other instead of you."

"Yes. Look at this poor chap."

They bent over the still body and the inspector felt his pulse. "He's had it."

Suddenly a shout from above made them look up. Briggs ran down the stairs with a knife in his hand, lashing out at Jim

Drink With The Devil

and embedding the knife in his left shoulder. Jim gasped and staggered backwards, with Briggs running out towards the school building site, pursued by Brian Green. Jim pulled the knife out and ran after him, his anger overcoming the pain, and he caught up with the inspector who was getting short of breath. It had started to rain half an hour ago, and already the depressions in the ground were filling with water.

Jim splashed forward with powerful strides, gaining on the shorter man who, when glancing back, was stricken with horror when he saw the big man bearing down on him and ran towards a pile of bricks. Jim dived and grabbed a pair of legs with his good arm, and Briggs fell forward with his face buried in yellow sticky mud. Jim sat on him and wrenched his face up so he could breathe. Briggs spluttered and choked but said nothing, and a uniformed policeman handcuffed him before leading the mud-plastered villain away.

Jim was suddenly overcome with pain and tiredness, his shoulder throbbed with pain and his stomach felt weak and queasy. The inspector looked at his pale face and said, "Come on Jim. You must sit down and rest for a while."

Jim just nodded and walked unsteadily back to the old mill building, holding his painful left arm. Blood was trickling down his chest, sticking to his shirt, his knees felt weak and he was relieved to sit in the back of a police car. Brian Green, who was sitting in the front, turned around and looked straight into Jim's eyes. "Now tell me exactly what happened here today."

Jim related the full story from when he was captured the previous evening and then said, "Will I be prosecuted for injuring those men?"

"Good heavens, no. You've done us a tremendous favour."

"Well, what about the money in that bag hidden up on the top floor?"

"You didn't steal it, did you?"

"No, I did not."

"That money was extracted from illegal gambling clubs by Briggs, whose protection racket is well known. And the people he protects will never admit they gave him money."

"Will you try and give it back?"

"Yes, of course. But not until after Briggs comes to trial."

They stopped talking and watched the uninjured gang members being loaded into a police van, handcuffed to police officers and looking very downhearted. The inspector broke the silence. "The ambulance will be here in a minute and, in the meantime, I'll look for that money."

He walked off, leaving Jim feeling relieved that Briggs was captured, but sickened by the unnecessary violence and death. He felt very tired and wanted to sleep, but his left shoulder was painful. Brian Green returned, giving instructions to a police constable before getting into the front seat again.

An ambulance took away the injured men and the inspector drove Jim to hospital where he was stitched up, his left arm put in a sling and a police car took him home. Rosie was delighted to see him and had food ready, but Jim could not face much and went to bed. Waking very late the next morning to the rasping sound of a saw downstairs, he looked out of his window to see one of his building workers cutting a new back door to make it fit. He got dressed carefully and put on his sling. His shoulder still hurt and he felt weak. Rosie fussed over him and explained that Billy Bradford, one of the first workers he had recruited, had called into see him and offered to fit a new door.

Jim was both surprised and delighted. "Thanks very much Billy. Where did the door come from?"

"It's second-hand. Came from a demolition job I did recently."

Jim watched the dark haired man in his twenties work on the door until it fitted perfectly. "Billy, you did that a lot better than I could have done."

"I enjoy working with timber,"

"Why aren't you a chippy, then?"

"I didn't do an apprenticeship. That's why."

"That's a pity."

Rosie cooked a large lunch while Jim explained what had

happened the previous day. The three of them talked a lot, making the meal last until mid afternoon. Jim was delighted to see Rosie back to her old self again. Now that Briggs was behind bars, perhaps they could stop worrying.

Jim spent the next three days at home listening to the torrential rain outside, and resting whilst he worked on his plan for the future. He had saved a great deal of money and was sure that it would be enough to buy a building site.

Billy called in to say he had picked up all the men, but had been sent home because the site was waterlogged and all work had been suspended until the following morning. Jim felt much better about not going to work and arranged for Billy to pick him up in the van the next day. They visited the hospital for a check-up, to find the wound was healing and a new dressing was applied. Afterwards they visited several estate agents and picked up details of building land for sale, and then toured the area looking at different plots of land. Jim bought the local paper and, when he read the property advertisements, he noticed a large run-down house being offered privately for a very reasonable sum. He arranged to see it the next day.

Billy became very enthusiastic. "We could do it up and convert it to flats."

"Yes, that's a possibility," said Jim thoughtfully.

When they called at the old house the next day, they found it was only about fifty years old but badly neglected. The six large bedrooms all smelt damp, wallpaper was peeling off and some of the ceilings were stained brown. Jim suspected the roof leaked and the occupants, an elderly couple, explained they could not afford the badly-needed repairs. Jim was sympathetic. "I don't blame you for wanting to sell. This property needs a fortune spent on it."

"Yes it does. We're looking forward to finding a small flat in the centre of town."

They walked around the house again and Billy was looking fed up. He whispered to Jim whilst the couple were out of sight. "This place'll cost a mint to do up. Let some other mug buy it."

"It is pretty grim I agree, but let's look outside."

"What for? It'll probably be even worse."

They walked around the large overgrown garden, most of which was covered in brambles and stinging nettles. Jim thrust his way through to the boundary fences, stopping to dig his heels into the soil and then pick up a handful for examination. Some of the time he was out of view from the old couple and Billy, who discussed the costs of doing the necessary jobs. They heard Jim crashing though the undergrowth and Billy remarked, "What the 'ell's he doing in those bushes?"

"I haven't been able to go in there for years. The garden's too much for us." The old man replied gloomily.

"You'll be much better off out of 'ere."

Jim emerged, brushing the undergrowth off his clothes, and saw the old couple looking worried. "Your colleague has told us how much it'll cost to repair the property."

Jim glanced up at the cracked walls and rotten window frames. "Yes, it'll be pretty expensive."

Billy had returned to the van and was listening to his portable radio. "Let's go inside and talk about a price," Jim said to the couple.

"Are you still interested, then?"

"Yes. If the price's right."

They talked for a while and Jim offered them what he felt was a fair price. The couple looked at each other and nodded, and Jim thought he could detect a trace of a smile on the lady's face. She said, "Well, it's lower than we'd hoped for. But we realise you'll have to spend a lot on the repairs so we accept."

They shook hands warmly and Jim strode down the weed covered path to the van. Billy grinned when he got in. "So you told them they're out of luck?"

"No. I bought it."

"Christ. What for? The place is falling down."

"Yes I agree. That's why I bought it. We could build four

good-size houses on that site."

"You cunnin' bugger. Why didn't I think of that?"

"You didn't see how much land goes with the house."

"So that's what you were doing?"

"Yes. And the ground is well drained, so we shouldn't come across any problems."

They discussed the price. "You could 'ave got it much cheaper," said Billy.

"Yes, I could have, but I don't like ripping off old folk."

"You're too soft, Jim."

"Maybe. But money isn't everything."

They talked about their next move and went home feeling excited. Grainger Construction was born and Jim felt sure it had a good future.

The next week the stitches were removed from Jim's shoulder. Although it was still painful, it improved every day and he decided to throw away the sling.

After selecting a firm of solicitors, he instructed them to go ahead with the purchase as fast as possible, whilst a local firm agreed to draw up plans and submit them for planning permission. All Jim had to do was wait for all the formalities to be completed.

Two weeks after the stabbing, Jim returned to work to be greeted warmly by all his men, who were working together on the school project. He soon returned to fitness, managing his huge hod as before, but of course the men on the site had heard about his exploits. He was held in high esteem, and noticed how warmly he was received wherever he went. Offers of help with the new building project were numerous and gratefully accepted, but still he could not get on because of the lack of planning permission.

The house and site became his six weeks after seeing the property, so he spent one weekend with Billy boarding up all the windows and doors. Then they started clearing the garden, first cutting down the overgrown bushes and shrubs and leaving them to dry.

The school building project was nearly completed and Jim and his men were asked to demolish the old mill building. Jim accepted and hired a crane with a wrecking ball. All the men were told by Jim they were on a fixed price contract, to be paid when the job was done. Realising what this meant, they pitched into the work with determination. Jim watched as the ball smashed the top floor, sending slabs of wall crashing to the ground, and reflected on the violence the building had witnessed. He thought about the men who had toiled in that building for years, lugging two hundredweight sacks of corn around, crippling themselves in the process and filling their lungs with choking dust, that always hung like a mist in old badly-ventilated buildings.

The site was to become a playground for young children. He smiled to himself as he visualised laughing and squealing youngsters playing happily on ground where so much violence had taken place.

That evening his thoughts turned to Angela, and how he longed to see her again. He rang the hospital.

"Angela has regained consciousness, and is on the road to a full recovery," was the remote reply.

"That's fantastic news. Thank you very much." He spent a large part of that night wondering whether to visit the hospital. But if I do, he said to himself, will she reject me because of my criminal record?

Drink With The Devil

Chapter Fourteen

Jane kept quiet as they drove home from the farm. Garry was obviously in a bad mood, having just talked to Angela. His expression was grim as he gripped the wheel with determination. He was oblivious to his wife's presence and could only think about his sister's relationship with Grainger, the man he hated. He had become bitter and twisted about what he saw as a betrayal of family standards of behaviour and, by the time he arrived home, felt ill and weak.

Jane almost ran from the car and disappeared into the kitchen, a place her husband rarely visited. He trudged through the house staring blankly at the floor, his shoulders hunched forward and hands thrust into his trouser pockets, and slumped into his favourite chair in the study. Cupping his head in his hands, he closed his eyes and imagined his sister making love with that hairy beast of a man who killed his parents, and the vision made him curiously angry. Then he thought what would people say if she met him again and they married — his sister married to a wild gypo convicted of manslaughter, and killer of his parents. He would either be ridiculed or worse, pitied. His family name would be dragged through the mud by cheap newspapers. They would dream up sensational stories about a rich stockbroker's daughter, whose brother was a company chief and stockbroker, having a sordid affair and then getting married after the gypo's release from prison, having served a term for manslaughter. It was almost too much for him to bear. He found his brandy bottle and glass still sticky from his last solitary drinking session. He filled it and gulped half of it at once as he tried to think of a plan to keep the pair apart.

No inspiration was forthcoming, so he dreamed up ways

of killing Grainger — visions of the big hairy beast hanging by the neck on the end of a rope made him smirk before downing the rest of the glass. After filling it again, he considered the best ways of exacting retribution and getting rid of his adversary as soon as possible. More brandy made his bitterness worse and his only relief was thinking of more gruesome methods of torture. Some time after, an empty bottle fell from his desk and as he stumbled forward, failing to reach a chair, his head struck a lamp stand sending it crashing to the floor. He felt nothing but just saw a flash before his eyes as he passed out on the floor, where he remained until morning.

Jane heard the crash but she stayed well clear of the study, going upstairs to the spare room, locking the door securely and then curling up in bed, pulling the clothes over her head to shut the world out. Having slept badly, she rose early and dressed quickly, slipping out of the back door. It was a fine morning. The long walk cleared her head and she returned two hours later hoping Garry had gone to work, but he was still there and greeted her in a croaky and slurred voice as she entered. "Hello Jane. Had a good walk?"

She looked at him clutching a cup of black coffee and leaning against the banister, his bloodshot eyes sunk deep in black sockets. "Very nice, thank you."

"I'm taking the morning off, ole girl. Feeling rather under the weather."

"So I see." She waited until he had gone upstairs and, hearing the shower running, she picked up a shopping basket and slipped out again, this time driving to town for a morning's shopping. She returned after a leisurely lunch to find he had gone, which was a relief.

Garry spent the morning sitting in his study with the curtains drawn, his head ached and throbbed and his eyes hurt when exposed to bright lights. His thoughts were more rational and he considered how he could keep the couple apart. Later he wandered around the house, letting the cleaner clear up the study. He realised Jane was avoiding him and knew she would not

Drink With The Devil

return until he had gone, but this did not upset him as he liked to be alone. His stomach felt bad so he skipped lunch and went to work. Word went around the Blakesbuild offices that Garry looked terrible and should be avoided, and he sat in his large office to briefly read any papers requiring urgent attention and signed them without thinking. He sat back to consider his next move when suddenly an idea surfaced, and he picked up the telephone. The next hour passed slowly as he drank black coffee, brooding slumped in the comfortable chair. When the telephone rang it jarred his nerves. "Yes!" he barked.

"Mr Gordon Simpson to see you."

"Send him in."

A fair haired man in his thirties entered and Garry glanced at him, noticing the paunch hanging over his belt. "Hello Mr. Simpson. I've a job for you."

"Good. What d'you want me to investigate?"

"You may not think this is a job for a private investigator."

"You tell me what it is and I'll try to oblige."

"I want you to impersonate a policeman."

"You've got to be joking! No chance."

"If I pay you enough, you will." They haggled for a while and agreed a price. Simpson was about to leave when Garry announced, "I want you to find a certain Jim Grainger. Find out where he lives and what he's doing.

"That's more my cup of tea."

"Right. Get on with it and report to me as soon as you've found him."

"Yes, Sir."

Garry watched him leave and felt satisfied now that some action had been taken, but he could not get down to work. He left the office early and dropped in at Osbornes.

His secretary put on a brave face when she saw him approach. "Hello, Mr. Osborne. I've put some more papers on your desk which require your urgent attention."

"Right. I'll look at them if I have time." He ignored the pile and headed for the drinks cabinet, telling himself a nip of brandy would settle his stomach. It did not so he had another, then strutted out of the building and went home.

Jane watched him come through the front door and thought she had better make some effort to be nice. "Hello dear. Is all well at work?"

"Yes. Fine." He sat down feeling tired and edgy, but resisted the temptation to be thoroughly nasty when he remembered his promise to be reasonable whilst she was pregnant.

* * *

Angela put on her wellingtons and waterproof coat and, when she pushed open the door, the driving rain and wind took her breath away as it soaked her face even though it was hidden under a hood. She leaned into the wind and walked across the yard towards the stables, not noticing the small black car splashing through the puddles towards her. Having reached the stables, she opened the tack room door and a voice from behind made her jump.

"Miss Osborne?"

She spun around to face a man already soaked and with no coat or boots on. "Hello. You'd better stand in here."

He gratefully followed her inside. "Sorry to trouble you, Miss Osborne. I'm from the police."

"How can I help you?"

"Detective Constable Mike Smith." He flashed a card in front of her with his picture on it, and Angela noticed a picture of a police badge beside the photo. He stuffed the card in his pocket quickly and gave her a searching look. "We're looking for a man called Grainger, and believe you are friendly with him."

Angela felt a shock go through her body at the mention of his name. She gave the constable a straight look. "I haven't seen him for a long time. Why do you want to see him?"

"We wish to interview him in connection with certain offences committed just after he was released from prison."

Drink With The Devil

Her heart sank and tears came to her eyes. "What's he accused of?"

"Nothing yet."

"Well what is he suspected of doing?"

"I'm not at liberty to divulge that information."

She was beginning to get irritated and raised her voice. "What d'you want to see me for? I suppose you are allowed to tell me?"

"No need to get upset. I only asked if you've seen him recently."

"Well I haven't and furthermore I'm unlikely to."

"Why not? You're friendly with him."

"How do you know that?"

"It's in the police file."

"Oh. What else is in the police file?"

"I'm not allowed to say."

Angela turned away and said briskly. "I've got a lot to do, so if you don't mind I must start work."

"Sorry to take up your time, Miss. But you will let me know if you see him, won't you?"

She turned back to look at him, knowing she most certainly would not let him know. "Where do I contact you?"

"Oh, the staff at any police station will be pleased to find out where Grainger is."

"I see. It's that bad?"

"Yes I'm afraid so."

"Oh dear." She stared at the floor in despair.

Simpson thought he saw tears in her eyes and felt guilty about causing such a pretty girl unnecessary suffering. "Sorry to bring bad news. I must go now. Goodbye."

Angela was so shocked she could not speak, and just watched the man turn and walk into the continuing rain. She remained staring as the car turned and drove off. When it had gone she could not hold back her grief any longer and slumped down, crouching on the floor with her back hard against a wall. She cried bitterly with her head in her hands. Her brother's words came back to her clearly and although she had not believed him then, now her worst fears had come true, he was a violent criminal. She kept turning it over in her mind, the man to whom she given her unbridled love was not what he appeared to be. How could she have been so deceived?

She remained crouched for half an hour until cramp set in and made her get up, the shooting pain in her leg bringing her back to reality. She thought about Jim and the way he had treated her. She could not remember him giving any indication of a violent nature in his actions or words, but could only remember his tender care and overwhelming love of animals. She remembered how Gemma had reacted to him — could she have become so attached to a violent man? Surely not, but the policeman would not have come looking for him if he was innocent. Perhaps he had a split personality. Turning away from the doorway, she reached into a large box to pull out a bridle, laid it on the bench and started cleaning. Her thoughts were still intense and half an hour later the bridle was still dirty, so she put it down and walked out into the wind and rain.

She was soon indoors and relaxing in a warm bath. She started to think about the future again, convincing herself she just had to forget about Jim and get on with life with as much activity as possible. With this in mind she later rang a local estate agent and arranged to meet a surveyor at Home Farm the next day.

After the telephone call she borrowed the Land Rover and drove into town, parking in front of a large garage with a forecourt full of second-hand cars for sale. She browsed among the cars in neat rows with prices stuck on their windscreens, but could not decide on a model she liked. Oh well, she thought, here goes, and strode into the showroom. Sitting opposite a smartly dressed salesman she studied and negotiated for an hour, finally buying a new Morris 1000 Traveller, which would be ready in a few days. Driving home she felt much better, having made a positive decision and looked forward to an independent life, which she was determined to enjoy to the full.

Drink With The Devil

Arriving at Home Farm early the next day she studied the farm buildings again and, within an hour, a car pulled up and Angela watched a man with sandy hair and of medium height get out. She thought he must be in his late twenties and keen on sport judging from his slim build, but stopped herself summing him up and said, "Hello. You must be Mr. Reynolds?"

"Mark Reynolds. Miss Osborne, I presume. How d'you do."

His hand was small but firm and she liked his broad smile and blue eyes. They exchanged pleasantries as they walked into the old cowshed building. She looked him straight in the eye. "How much experience d'you have with farm buildings?"

"None at all," he confessed, looking guilty.

"Well, I'll tell you what I want to do."

"Right." He got out a large pad and wrote copious notes whilst Angela explained in detail the alterations required to turn the building into stables. He drew rough sketches and asked a lot of questions about the materials to be used and the dimensions of the individual stables. They went into the house, where Angela explained what alterations and repairs she thought were necessary. He promised to return to do a full survey and prepare a report before drawing up a schedule of works and specification. Angela suddenly felt hungry and, looking at her watch, was amazed to find they had been talking for three hours. She walked back to his car with him, they shook hands and he looked at her shyly. "Do call me Mark."

"Okay. I'm Angela." She was pleased with the outcome of the meeting, and could tell she was going to get on well with Mark Reynolds.

The new car was delivered on time and she enjoyed the new smell and feel of the vehicle. It gave her the independence she needed, and Peter was glad to get the Land Rover back.

Another site meeting was arranged. An old desk and chairs Angela had picked up at a second-hand shop were put in the old dairy so that Mark could lay out his preliminary sketches. The meeting went well. Angela was surprised at how well he had interpreted her ideas, and only a few minor alterations were necessary. They worked all morning until she felt hungry and looked at her watch. "We'll have to finish now."

"That's a shame," came the disappointed reply. "We haven't discussed the house yet."

"It'll have to wait for another day."

He hesitated and then said slowly. "Can I take you out for lunch?"

Angela smiled. "Yes. That'd be nice."

They travelled in his car to a local pub, and sat opposite each other at a small table. The soup was served with bread rolls, and she noticed how slim and delicate his fingers were as they gripped the spoon elegantly. She began to compare them with Jim's huge hands and had to shake her head to stop herself.

"You seem preoccupied, Angela."

"I'm sorry. I do have a lot on my mind. The soup's good, isn't it?"

"Yes. Excellent."

They ate silently and Angela tried not to study him too closely in case he noticed her interest. When they had finished the meal she started asking questions. "D'you enjoy any particular sport?"

"No. I can't stand sport. Do you?"

"I only go hunting and then not very often."

"I haven't much time for hobbies. It's taken all my efforts to qualify."

"So you've only just started to work?"

"Yes. Not long ago."

"That's interesting. How many projects have you been involved with on your own?"

He hesitated. "Yours is the first."

They both laughed and then Angela said. "Why am I laughing? Your first job could be a disaster."

His expression changed to a worried one. "I'll make sure it's a complete success," he said with conviction.

"Don't worry. You have my complete confidence."

"Thank you."

She thought a change of subject would be a good idea.

Drink With The Devil

"D'you live locally?"

"Just down the road from the office. In a rented flat."

"On your own?" She shocked herself at the directness of the question. "Yes. The flat is very small."

When they drove back to the farm, they spent a long time discussing the repairs to the house, and Angela often found herself standing very close to Mark as they walked around looking at the rotting window frames and damp walls.

She thought about him a lot over the next few days, and was delighted when he rang her early one morning.

"Hello, Angela. I've finished the plans."

"Good. When can I see them?"

"Can I come this morning?"

"Yes. What time?"

"About 10.o'clock."

She arrived on time to find him walking around the building. "Hello Mark. You're early."

"Yes. I wanted to look around before our meeting."

They sat on the old wooden chairs in the dairy room looking at the plans, and Angela was surprised at the details he had included, but as she observed his blue eyes, she noticed how tired he looked. "You've put a lot of work into those plans, haven't you?"

"I enjoy this kind of work - converting old buildings."

"So you did the plans in your own time?"

"Yes, but I enjoyed it."

They talked and went through the specification, line by line, and when they had finished he said. "D'you want Blakesbuild to quote?"

"No. It's not their sort of job." She had already decided not to involve her brother, who would try to take the job over and do it his way.

They lunched together again, and this time were more relaxed in each other's company. They sat close together and talked in friendly terms, Angela very interested in his work and what he wanted to do in the future.

"I'd like to start by doing my job as well as possible, and see what comes along."

"But wouldn't you like to specialise?"

"Well, it would be nice to do conversions of old buildings."

They talked about the merits of different local builders and decided which ones to ask for quotes. Just as they were about to leave the pub Mark said, "It's been so nice having lunch with you. Would you be offended if I asked you out one evening?"

Angela tried to hide her delight. "Of course I wouldn't be offended."

"Good. How about tomorrow night?"

"Okay. Where are we going?"

"I'd like you to have dinner with me."

"That would be nice."

That night Angela slept badly, thinking about spending an evening with Mark. Jim kept coming back into her mind, and as she visualised his body so big and well built, she remembered how he had made love to her in the wood and the wonderful feelings she had experienced. She tossed and turned, trying hard to put him out of her mind, telling herself all that had happened was in the past, and eventually went to sleep.

She woke up late. Daylight and activity cleared her mind and she looked forward to the evening. Mark called at Peter's house, dressed smartly in a dark grey suit. Angela wore a simple blue dress and noticed Mark's glances when they met. He drove her to a small country restaurant and guided her to a corner table with a reserved notice on it. She also noticed his nervousness and endeavoured to start a conversation. "It's so nice to come out for a meal in the evening."

"Yes. Much better than eating on your own."

"D'you always eat alone?"

"Nearly always. I don't know many people around here. I lived with my parents in the West Country before getting a job in Sussex. He became more relaxed as the evening progressed, and Angela found herself enjoying the new experience and his company. Having driven her home, he parked in the dark

Drink With The Devil

farmyard, walked around the car to open the door and she got out. Standing close to him she whispered, "Thanks for a lovely evening."

He moved closer. "It was the best evening I've ever had."

"How you exaggerate."

"No. It really was."

Angela felt his arms around her and responded by clinging to his shoulders. They kissed briefly and he held her tight, and after kissing her again he reluctantly broke away. "I must see you to the door." He kissed her forehead before turning to go, and she went in.

The next few days were packed with activity, Mark arriving with different builders. They lunched together regularly and talked about her new stables and plans for a horse breeding business, although he confessed he had very little interest in animals or farming.

The following week he invited her out for dinner again and Angela gladly accepted. That weekend Garry visited with Jane, who looked tired. Angela could tell something was wrong. "Jane, is there anything worrying you?"

"No, of course not. Just a bit tired, that's all."

Angela suspected it was not the truth and noticed the way she looked at Garry. He managed to get Angela on her own and gave her a glowing report on her shares.

"That's good. By the way I'm doing some work at Home Farm."

"What kind of work?"

She told him roughly what she had in mind and he seemed enthusiastic.

"Have you got a good surveyor?"

"Yes. A young chap who's very keen."

"Oh, good. Well, if you like we could quote for the job."

"No, thank you. I'd prefer a local builder."

He did not seem at all upset, but just asked questions about the surveyor.

On their next date, Mark took Angela to the same restaurant

and, as they had both consumed too much wine, they were in high spirits when they climbed into the car to go home. He leaned over and kissed her neck and they cuddled and kissed intensely. It was cramped in the small car and he whispered: "Would you like to see my flat?"

She giggled. "Just for a few moments."

They crept up the stairs to the small one bedroom flat, sparsely furnished, and with the main feature of the living room being a large drawing board. He shut the door and saw her looking around. "Not much, I'm afraid. But it's home."

"I think it's very nice. Angela's thoughts suddenly turned to Jim and their lovemaking. Without hesitating she said, "I must go home now."

Mark looked disappointed. "Yes, of course."

They kissed briefly before she walked quickly indoors without looking back.

Mark drove home depressed, wondering what he had done wrong.

Chapter Fifteen

Gordon Simpson sauntered into Garry's office with a cigarette hanging from his lips. Garry looked up from his desk.

"How did you get on?"

"I've planted the poison."

"How did she take it?"

"Badly. Very upset, she was."

"But d'you think she believed you?"

"No doubt about it."

"Good. I'll see her myself at the weekend."

"What for? To rub salt into the wound? You must hate her guts."

"It's none of your business. But if you must know, I'm doing it for her own good."

"You're right. It's none of my business."

"Now, what about Grainger? Have you found him yet?"

"Give me a chance, guv. I haven't started looking yet."

"Well, don't just stand there. Get on with it."

"I need a few more details."

"Like what?" Garry related all he knew, and Simpson left with a bad feeling about the job he had been asked to do. It took a week of searching and talking to police contacts before he found out where Jim was living, but after that it became easy. He watched the van leave early in the morning and followed inconspicuously. When it turned into a building site, he parked and walked on to the large site with a clipboard tucked under his arm, so as to look official, and no one challenged him. He followed the rough-looking gang to a nearby flattened building, and watched as the remaining structure was reduced to rubble. As he stood beside a pile of old timber awaiting removal, he was spotted, and a man walked towards him, but he looked studiously at his clipboard, glancing up and realising he would have to bluff it out.

"What d'you want, mate?" Billy Bradford asked.

"Just waiting for you to finish, and then I was going to ask who owns the rubble."

"Why. Want to buy it?"

"That's the general idea."

"You're out of luck mate, 'cause it belongs to the main contractor."

"Does he want it?"

"Yeah. For road filling."

"Never mind. I'll find some elsewhere."

"We may have some shortly."

"Oh, yes. Who's we?"

"Grainger Construction. We'll be demolishing a house on Poplar Drive next."

"Where's that?"

"On the other side of town."

"Right. Thanks for your help."

Simpson turned and walked away, chuckling to himself as he drove home to his grubby flat. Just as he started typing his report, his telephone rang and it was Garry, sounding bad-tempered.

"Simpson, when are you going to get off your backside and find Grainger?"

Simpson paused to stop himself laughing, which made Garry's temper worse.

"Well, what have you done about finding him?"

"I found him to-day."

"Where?"

"It'll be in my report."

"Why should I wait for your ridiculous report? Tell me now."

"No. You're just going to have to wait."

"Don't be bloody stupid. I want to know right now."

Drink With The Devil

"I'll bring the report to your office at Blakesbuild in the morning, and you can give me my cheque."

Garry groaned. "If you must play stupid games."

Simpson arrived at nine as arranged and was ushered into the large office. "Well, where did you find him?" barked Garry, looking grim.

"It's all in my report."

"Give it to me, then."

"When you've handed over my cheque."

"Oh, very well." Cheque and report were handed over simultaneously, and Simpson took several steps back and waited. Garry ripped open the envelope and stared at the contents, and in less than a minute his eyes widened, his face went red and he stuttered, "Is this some kind of sick joke?"

Simpson kept a straight face. "Nope. You've been employing him for some time."

"I don't believe it," he bellowed.

"Please yourself, guv. But I'd check with your accounts department before making any rash statements."

"This is bloody intolerable. I can't believe we would employ that evil bastard."

Simpson grinned as Garry blew his top, and walked out making a dash for his bank before the cheque was stopped. Garry stormed into the accounts department and stood before the head of department's desk, the small bald man looking nervously up at him. "What can I do for you, Mr. Osborne?"

Garry struggled to keep his voice steady. "Have we been paying a man called Grainger?"

"Which job would he be working on, Sir?"

"The school contract."

He looked at a file of papers. "Yes, we've paid him a fair amount of money. It seems he produced a gang of men and helped us complete on time."

"I see. And who agreed to this?"

"Our site manager."

"Right. See that no more money is paid to this man."

The man nodded and returned to his work, as Garry walked briskly back to his office, seething with rage. He rang the head of contracts, a middle-aged qualified surveyor. "Gill. Come to my office at once."

Claude Gill almost ran down the corridor. "What's the problem, Mr. Osborne?"

"Did you know we had a criminal working for us?"

"No. Of course not."

"Well, who agreed to take on a man called Grainger and his gang?"

"The site manager recommended him. And I was pleased to agree."

"Why didn't you ask about his previous jobs?"

"The site manager said the man could provide additional men, who were badly needed. And he did us a favour by helping to complete on time."

"The site manager must have known about his record?"

"He may have. I don't know."

Garry cupped his chin in his hands, got up and strode around the office, leaving Claude standing nervously biting his fingernails. Garry broke the silence "I want you to go to that site immediately. Have Grainger and his men thrown off, and then sack the site manager."

"But he's the best manager we've got."

"Managers who take on criminals are no good to this company."

"How could he have known about the man's record?"

"He should have found out." Garry lowered his tone and pointed at the nervous man. "If you don't want to carry out my orders, you can go as well!"

Gill was shocked into silence and swallowed hard. "I'll go to the site straightaway."

Garry sneered. "Huh. I thought you would."

"Who d'you want to take over as site manager?"

Garry stared straight at him again, enjoying his feeling of power. "You phone me when Grainger and the manager have gone, and then do the job yourself."

Claude was about to argue but stopped himself. "Yes, Sir." His face had lost its colour and he edged closer to the door.

Garry glared at him and barked, "Well, what are you waiting for?"

Gill grabbed the door handle and fled. His journey to the site was slow, due to heavy traffic, so it gave him plenty of time to consider his task. He had known Fred Burrows for years and always looked forward to meeting him and listening to his cheerful banter. As he pulled up outside the site and sat in his car debating as to the best approach, he nearly decided to give in his own notice, but thought about his wife worrying about their future. He got out and walked towards the site office, where a big man was just leaving, clutching an envelope.

Fred welcomed him in his usual friendly way, beckoning him to a chair, but his expression changed as he studied Claude's face. "What's the matter, Claude? Lost a pound and found a penny?"

"Is Grainger and his gang still on site?"

"I just paid him off and he's leaving now."

"Good. That means we won't have to order him out."

"Order him out?" Why should we?" That man has saved us penalty payments on this contract."

"Our new boss has discovered Grainger is an ex-criminal."

"So what? He's a damn good worker."

Claude sat down and sighed heavily. "Fred, I've a terrible job to do, and there's no easy way to do it."

"Tell me about it."

"Our nutcase of a boss insists I give you the sack. I'm very sorry."

Fred spluttered, his round face getting redder. "What the hell for?"

"For taking on an ex-con."

"That's a bloody terrible excuse for dismissing someone."

"I know, but he wouldn't listen to me."

"But I didn't know about his record."

"That's what I told him. I'm really so sorry."

"Not your fault, Claude. Thanks for trying. When do I go?"

"Immediately, I'm afraid."

Fred signed in resignation. "Okay, but I expect to be paid what's owed to me."

"I'll see you get paid."

The two men shook hands and Fred walked off the site, looking thoroughly dejected.

Claude picked up the telephone, feeling very angry and upset, and Garry answered in his usual gruff way. Claude just said, "Grainger and the manager have gone."

"Good. I hope we didn't pay Grainger."

"He was paid off before I arrived."

"I see. Well, you just stay there and get on with the job."

Claude slammed the phone down nearly in tears, wishing he had the strength and guts to tell Garry to go to hell.

Garry put the phone down and laughed out loud, knowing how Claude would be feeling. Weak little men, how I hate them, he thought. He settled back in his comfortable chair and thought about his next move, but no inspiration came so he read the investigator's report again, this time taking in all the details. "Grainger Construction — where the hell did he get his money from to start a business, and what is he doing with a site on Poplar Drive?" He grabbed the phone and Gordon Simpson answered. "I want you to find out where Grainger got his money from."

"Hard work, I expect."

"I don't believe it. Find out straightaway."

Simpson had no other work, so he agreed. "I'll try, but I can't guarantee anything."

"You will, or starve."

Garry slammed the receiver down, got up from his desk and paced around the office. Although a large pile of untouched papers were in his in-tray awaiting inspection and decisions, he could not bring himself to concentrate on work. He rang his secretary instead. "Bring me details of the company's purchases

Drink With The Devil

around the Kingston area. In particular, the school job." Next he rang the accounts department. "I want details of all payments made to Grainger."

The information was on his desk within fifteen minutes. First he studied the list of payments and the dates on which they were made, his anger building up again when he realised his company had been paying Jim Grainger since his release from prison. His rage caused the figures to blur before his eyes, so he got up and paced around the room again, swearing and cursing under his breath. He passed the drinks cabinet twice before stopping to fill a glass, gulping it down and returning to the desk with papers strewn all over it. After calming himself down, adding up the figures and calculating how much Grainger would have paid his gang, it came to a considerable figure. As he cursed out loud and thumped his slender fist down on the desk, pain shot up his arm and he cursed again. The unopened file revealed a list of builders' merchants and the amounts spent with each of them during the past year, so he shoved it into his briefcase and walked out of the building to his car, parked in its specially reserved position.

Poplar Drive was a tree-lined road with good-quality detached houses set back from the wide pavement, each with their own tarmac drive. Garry drove down the road slowly, looking at each house. He stopped at the sight of a large house with its windows and doors boarded up, where a gang of men were burning piles of dead trees and bushes. The huge bonfire was sending sparks high into the sky. Garry scanned the site, seeing how large it was, and then studied the men working with a single purpose, each one obviously putting maximum effort into the job.

When he saw a van parked nearby with Grainger Construction on the side, he felt like setting fire to it. His eyes focused on a very big man, stripped to the waist, dragging a tree single-handed to the fire; his tanned body with huge muscles rippling under the strain as he lifted and sent the tree crashing on to the fire, sending a column of smoke skywards. Garry shivered in awe at the physical power displayed before him, and he realised the big man fitted Simpson's description of Grainger. His admiration turned instantly to hatred.

He gripped the steering wheel hard until his hands hurt, shaking his head in disbelief when he remembered that long-haired white-faced man with a beard, who looked so small standing in the dock. He remembered those eyes staring up at him, and a shiver went through his body as the recollection of that day in court returned. He looked again at the bronzed body, once again carrying a huge load. Is this really the same man? Simpson could be mistaken. He studied the other men again before starting the car and driving past the site, glancing across to the fire just as the big man looked up, and their eyes meeting just for a split second. This was enough to convince him that this man was definitely Grainger.

He accelerated away in search of the first builders' merchants on his list. The manager, a young man and very keen, having just been promoted by head office, was anxious to please and rushed into the reception to shake hands. Tea was ordered and Garry was invited through to a spacious office. "What can I do for you, Mr. Osborne?"

"My company has purchased a large amount of materials from you during the past year."

"Yes, indeed you have, Sir. And we're very grateful." He stopped as tea was served by a pretty girl.

Garry did not even glance at the girl, but stared at the manager fussing over the cups. He sipped, put the cup down and spoke evenly. "Blakesbuild will be pleased to continue buying from this and other of your branches if you agree to my terms."

"Well, Sir, I can only speak for this branch."

"That's understandable, but you'll pass this on?"

"Yes. Of course."

"A new building company called Grainger Construction has just started up in this area. It's run by a criminal, and I will not buy from anyone who deals with criminals. Understood?"

Drink With The Devil

"Absolutely, Sir. I appreciate you letting us know about it, and I can assure you we'll cease trading with that company immediately."

"Good. And make sure none of your other branches deals with them."

The manager wrote down the name and said "Is there anything else I can help you with?"

"Yes. You can make sure Blakesbuild buy at the best possible price."

"Yes, of course, Sir."

Garry got up and walked out, leaving the tea on the desk. The remainder of the day was spent visiting the other companies on the list, each one treating him as a VIP, and the results were the same. By the time he arrived home he was feeling much better and greeted Jane with a kiss on the cheek. She was pleased to see him in a better mood and asked "Did you have a good day at work?"

"Not bad at all."

She was really quite worried, having received a phone call from a former colleague, saying Garry had been in a terrible mood and had not concentrated on business for some time. She did not know how to approach the subject without upsetting him but then had an idea. "I was thinking of coming into the office to help out for a few days." Garry guessed what had happened. "No need, ole girl. I'll be going in early to catch up."

"I'll join you later, then."

"Up to you."

Garry left early the next morning to work on the waiting pile of contracts, horrified to find he had neglected his job so badly. It was too late for four of the tenders, which should have been priced and returned a week earlier, so he worked on the others. Jane brought him his coffee and noticed the discarded documents. "What about these?"

"They're not worth bothering with."

She thumbed through the papers. "A lot of time has been wasted here."

"Yes. It's a shame," he said, dismissing the subject.

He worked hard for the next few weeks as he struggled to keep his mind on the job, rather than get twisted up about Jim Grainger. He soon got on top of things again and both companies were running smoothly, with Blakesbuild winning just enough contracts to keep going.

A somewhat nervous Simpson rang to say he could not find the source of Grainger's sudden wealth, but the blasting he was expecting from Garry did not materialise, and he was surprised to hear him say. "Never mind. It doesn't really matter."

"Fine. I can send you a bill, then?"

"Yes, of course."

Garry put the receiver down and resumed the struggle to keep his mind from wandering. He realised how much harm he had done to himself without Grainger raising a finger against him. It's so stupid, he thought. If only I could stop myself getting twisted up.

A further reminder from the past came in the form of a telephone call from Inspector Green, who sounded cheerful. "Thought you'd like to know we've charged a man with robbery and arson."

"Have you really. Who?"

"A man called Briggs. Brother of the man killed on the night of the fire."

Garry was stunned. "Will Angela be called as a witness?"

"No need. He's admitted the crime."

"That's excellent. What about the other man involved?"

"Still at large, I'm afraid."

"I'm still convinced the man you're looking for is Grainger."

"No, Sir. It's definitely not."

"Well, who is it, then?"

"We're still hoping Briggs will tell us."

"And the best of luck to you."

"Thank you, Sir."

Garry sat and thought about his conversation with the inspector, but his thoughts were soon diverted by a thick pile

Drink With The Devil

of papers being dumped on his desk. He looked at the files and started work, determined not to get behind again.

*　*　*

In the meantime Jim had returned to "The Scrubs," but this time as a visitor. Oliver Smythe was surprised at his appearance. "My goodness, Jim. You do look well."

"I feel pretty good. How about you?"

"Looking forward to my release in a couple of months."

"I thought you'd like to know that I've followed your advice and started my own building company."

"Well done. How's it going, then?"

"Reasonably well. I've just bought a building site for four houses."

"How are you managing financially?"

"With money I saved from running my own sub-contract team. The problem now is that, having bought the site, I haven't got enough for the building materials."

"I can help you out," he whispered. "From a safety deposit box with cash in it, but not a word where it came from."

"Of course not. And I'll pay you back with interest as soon as I can."

Oliver pushed a slip of paper across the table. "I'll see you in a couple of months."

"I'll look forward to it."

Planning permission was granted the day Jim finished the demolition contract, and he studied the paperwork until late that night. Four detached houses fitted the site well and he made out a schedule, stating when each stage should be completed, deciding to build two houses and sell them in order to raise enough money to build the other two and secure another site.

The next morning he collected his gang of labourers and delivered them to the new site. A bonfire was made with the contents of the garden, and all worked with enthusiasm, pleased to be part of a new building company. Looking across the site,

Jim saw a red sports car. The man inside seemed to be staring in his direction, but he looked away when their eyes met. Jim continued to watch as the car sped away, and so did Billy who remarked, "It's probably that bloke who wanted to buy some rubble."

"Oh yes. You told him we'd be working here."

"Yes, but I think we'll need the rubble ourselves."

"Yes, we will."

Jim got on with the work and soon forgot about the car. They stripped the house of its lead and copper pipes, together with the lead from the roof, and it was all loaded on the van, which was weighed down to the axles. Jim drove carefully to the nearest scrap merchants, and was delighted with the amount the proprietor was willing to pay.

Within a week the old house was reduced to a pile of rubble, the proceeds from the demolition easily paying the wages and providing some spare cash. The company whose staff drew the plans and obtained planning permission also provided a good on-site service, setting up level markers, taking levels and also producing a detailed specification. Jim purchased a garden shed, which was used as a site hut, and made up a sloping bench on which to lay out the plans. His next move was to get the foundations and drains dug, so he rang the local plant hire companies to hire a digger, and finding they were fully booked, he went back to the site looking very worried. Billy saw his glum expression.

"What's up, Jim?"

"I can't get a digger. They're all fully booked."

"That's funny. I thought they were crying out for business."

"So did I."

"What are we waiting for? Let's dig them by hand."

"Good idea. I'll get some tools." Jim filled the van with spades, shovels and wheelbarrows purchased from the local hardware store. All six men pitched in and worked until dark, hardly any sound audible except metal clanging against stones, and the squeaking of wheelbarrow wheels.

The next day they worked hard again, but by late afternoon all the men were exhausted, except Jim. He looked at the haggard men and said to Billy, "You'd better drive them home."

"Right. what about you?"

"I'll stay until you get back."

He worked on steadily, and by the end of the third day the foundations and drains were finished. He used the van to visit builders' merchants, the first company he visited being the largest in the area and part of a national group. He strode in to the trade counter and said, "My name's Jim Grainger of Grainger Construction. I'd like to open an account."

The man behind the counter looked blank. "Just a minute. I'll be back with my governor." He returned with a young man dressed in a dark suit, who looked Jim up and down and said nervously, "Mr. Grainger, I'm sorry we can't open an account for you."

"Why not?"

"Head office orders, I'm afraid."

"But I'm prepared to pay on delivery."

"I'm very sorry."

"What if I pay cash in advance?"

"Sorry, I still can't."

Jim leaned over the counter and gave the man an icy glare. "Why not?"

"Head office orders," he repeated.

Chapter Sixteen

Mark visited Home Farm with more plans, and greeted Angela nervously, giving the impression he felt guilty about luring her to his flat, but Angela was her usual cheerful self, and they discussed the plans and work schedule. When they had finished the business Mark said, "I did enjoy our evening together. May I take you out again?" Angela smiled. "Yes, I'd like that very much."

They had dinner together, talking almost non stop, and drove straight back to the farm for a brief cuddle and goodnight kiss, which became the set procedure of their social life together. Mark did not suggest another visit to his flat.

* * *

The new Manor Farm House was completed a year after the fire, and was ready for a grand house-warming party. Jane was eager to meet Mark, while Garry did not hide his curiosity either. Every weekend he would aske "When are we going to meet this stout fellow?"

"When I'm ready," was always her reply.

The party was arranged and Jane said to Angela, "You will invite Mark, won't you?"

"Yes, but I can't guarantee he'll come."

"But you must insist."

The occasion was a complete success with local farmers arriving in big cars. Some of Garry's university friends came with their wives and Jane's many friends and relations filled the house with loud talk and merriment. Mark escorted Angela and was greeted warmly by both Garry and Jane. They liked him instantly, and made sure he felt at home. Garry enjoyed the role of host, making sure everyone's glass was full, especially his own.

As the evening progressed he became more and more drunk. Jane saw him staggering towards the bar and tried to stop him filling his glass yet again. She was unsuccessful and was left to say farewell to the guests when Garry disappeared upstairs with a bottle of brandy and a glass. Angela and Mark stayed until midnight.

Garry continued to run Blakesbuild and Osbornes brilliantly when he was sober and in a good mood, but badly when he was drunk and aggressive. The two companies struggled along without managing to expand or improve their profitability.

As Jane became more heavily pregnant, she spent an increasing amount of time with her mother in Wiltshire, and left Garry to his bottle. Sometimes he stayed in his flat, and in his darker moments Jim Grainger still featured as his enemy in many vivid visions of physical violence and torture, each time brandy playing a major part in producing this effect. When he sobered up and returned to reality he was angry with himself for being so stupid. The only times he stopped drinking was when he realised the companies were doing very badly, and then he would hide the brandy, working long hours to retrieve the situation. He always succeeded and felt relieved that his own future was safe again.

Sometimes he dreamed of giving up drinking altogether and building a huge international company in construction and banking. He even drafted a five-year plan to this end, only to digress once again. It was while he was in one of his drunken stupors that the telephone rang.

"Hello, who is it?" he said in a slurred voice.

"Garry, you'd better sober up quickly."

He instantly recognised his mother-in-law's voice. "Hello, Mother. What's the matter?"

"Jane's gone into labour."

His voice steadied. "Right. I'm on my way."

"There's no hurry, so you can sober up first."

"Of course, mother."

He put the phone down, showered and drank a large amount of coffee before driving in the direction of Wiltshire. It was 3 a.m. when he arrived, looking drawn and tired and going straight to the hospital to find the baby had arrived two hours previously. Jane was sitting up in bed nursing it and Garry's face lit up when the nurse announced it was a boy. He sat by the bed looking every inch the proud father, albeit with bloodshot eyes and a grey complexion. He made no attempt to touch or hold the infant, but just stared at his little face in wonder. Clearing his throat, he said clearly, "I promise to stop drinking and look after you properly."

Jane gave him a sceptical glance. "How long will that last?"

"I really mean it, darling."

"Actually I was thinking of moving in with Mother permanently."

He was not surprised at this statement. If it had not been for the baby he would not have minded too much, so long as she would agree to accompany him to social functions from time to time and not demand a divorce. He lowered his tone and looked appealingly into her eyes, "If you would please come home, I'll lay off the booze and try to be reasonable."

"If you really mean it, we could try again."

"I promise to be nice to you."

They named the child William, after Garry's father, and Jane came home to Hampstead accompanied by her mother, who stayed for a month to help out. Garry found it a strain being extra nice to two women, so he spent a lot of time at work, and consequently the two companies benefited. His drinking was confined to long lunch breaks and occasional evenings in his flat.

Jane suspected he was still drinking heavily, but said nothing and their relationship developed into a sort of distant friendship. She no longer craved his love and affection, which made her sad, and she often cried when she was alone.

Garry still admired his wife's beauty and was proud when

she accompanied him to social events, often wishing he could feel in love with her. He still remembered the way she made love when they first met, wanting to take her back to his flat and try again, but knew she would not agree.

* * *

Jim visited all the other builders' merchants in the area with the same outcome as the first, which left him feeling downhearted. Someone has told them all I'm an ex-con, he thought, and sat in the van thinking how different things would have been if that ginger-haired man had not died. Ten minutes later he got out of the van and walked for a while, the physical activity stimulating his mind and stopping him looking back at what might have been. He found himself outside a paper shop and walked in to buy a local newspaper. Having scanned the advertisements, he found a section which nearly leapt out at him – Builders' Merchants Bankrupt Stock Sale. The venue was just out of town and the sale was to be held the next day. He jumped in his van and sped off to find all the materials he needed were there, arranged in lorry sized lots, and he bought a catalogue, pricing each lot carefully.

The Sale day was wet and with only a small group of buyers huddled under a tin lean-to building. The auctioneer got a poor response, selling everything very cheaply. Jim bought much more then he needed and left feeling delighted.

The building materials arrived in a convoy of lorries. Jim and his gang unloaded bricks, blocks, timber and cement in neat piles along the back of the site, where there was only just enough room. The last lorry pulled away and Billy walked up to Jim, his face streaming with sweat, but with a wide grin. "That miserable bastard who tried to bugger up Grainger Construction ought to come and see this lot."

They both laughed, but then Jim looked seriously at his stock. "We'll have to keep a look out for prowlers, snoopers and anyone who looks like a potential thief."

"Yeah. The bloke who got at the builders' merchants might be bent enough to swipe the lot."

"More than likely."

Jim went to see the local police, who agreed to keep an eye open, remembering him from the murder at the old mill and pleased to help. He stayed on site and worked for sixteen hours a day, only going home to sleep. Rosie fussed over and nagged at him to get more rest, but he took no notice and carried on working including weekends. Sundays were his days for sitting in the site hut doing paperwork. The result of all this effort was two houses built in record time and sold by a local estate agent within two weeks of being on the market. The other two houses were built more quickly, Jim continuing to work very long hours with a single-minded determination to succeed. He often remembered being broke, friendless and laying in a police cell not wanting to face life. Some nights he awoke and thought about Angela. He dearly wanted to hold her again, see her lovely face and regularly nearly took a day off to attempt to see her, but always decided not to. After all he was still an ex-con and an ordinary working man, and she deserved someone much better suited to her class.

Before the last two houses were put on the market, a new building site had to be found in order to store the surplus building materials. After days of searching, Jim found a site nearby, with planning permission for twenty houses. He agreed to buy if he could use the site immediately, and spent all night working out if he could afford to buy and build houses before he ran out of money. The only way was to sell the last two houses on the first site quickly, and get on with building the next two before he had to buy a lot of materials. His plan worked and the new site proved a success, so he bought a much bigger site building, which was used as a company office and mess room. The first house on the new site was built with materials from the bankrupt sale, with enough over to excavate the foundations and drains on the next three, but he would soon need new materials. He scanned the papers again, but there was nothing interesting. He thought another visit to the local builders' merchants might be worth while, as maybe they would change their minds due to the amount needed, but the reaction was the same as before. He returned to the site feeling depressed and worried. Billy ran out from the site hut. "Jim, there's a bloke here wants to quote us for materials."

A young nervous-looking man in a smart suit was standing in the mess room and introduced himself as Ron Smart. "We've just started our own builders' merchants and wondered if we could quote for anything."

Jim kept a straight face. "What's your company called, then?"

"B.H.S. Supplies. My partner and I started it a few weeks ago."

"Well, good luck to you. And you can certainly give me a quote."

Ron Smart returned the next day with a list of materials all priced according to the amount to be purchased. A deal was struck and, after an hour of haggling, Jim was pleased with the prices and delivery offered, and Ron was delighted with the business.

Jim spent more time studying the way houses were being built, and soon decided that specialised teams would be an advantage in order to try and create a production line approach. The first team was called the oversite gang — they dug the foundations, laid the drains, built the foundations up to ground floor level and then laid the first rough surface of concrete for the floor. The next team laid the bricks and blocks, followed by the chippies laying the floors and setting the roof. Outside contractors did the electrical and plumbing work, whilst the roof gang laid tiles and the plaster was supplied by a further team.

This strategy worked very well and the houses were built faster than he had first anticipated, and he negotiated a special deal with a local estate agent, who sold the houses as they were completed. He ploughed all the money from the sold houses back into the business, only taking out enough to live on. When ten houses were sold and the others progressing well, he started to look for another site; still using the old van, which was beginning to look battered and rusty, to collect workers and take them home. He found a site for fifty dwellings further south in Sussex, and this time had no doubt about his ability to pay for it. Following this the company progressed at a tremendous rate, due to Jim's enthusiasm and endless energy. Billy was promoted to site manager and worked with equal enthusiasm.

Jim set up his new site office, which he had just finished fitting up with the essential furniture, on a larger site. When he looked out of the window, he saw a familiar figure walking towards the building, and walked out to greet the round-faced man.

"Fred Burrows. How nice to see you."

"It's good to see you. And doing so well, too."

"How are you getting on, Fred?"

"Not so well. Thought I'd see if you could give me a job."

"But what about Blakesbuild?"

"I got the sack for taking you on."

"I'm awfully sorry about that." Jim felt distraught and guilty.

"Not your fault, Jim. The trouble is that bastard Osborne has made sure I can't get another job."

"Why? You're very good at your job."

"I don't know why he got so upset about me employing you. After all you haven't done him any harm, have you?"

"Not that I know of."

Jim took him on as a chippy, which was his trade, promising to let him run a site in the future, and gradually other workers defected from Blakesbuild. He decided to take on two middle-aged women to handle the paperwork, and they worked in the site building attending to accounts and wages, leaving him to spend more time running the business. He bought himself a second-hand Morris 1000 pick-up, and used it for his personal transport, as well as to cart materials about. He was constantly on the lookout for new building sites, trying to find areas that would suit his up-market houses.

* * *

Home Farm House was finished before the official completion date. Angela walked around the house, now fully and tastefully furnished, thinking about her father's long years of working in the City accumulating the money she had just spent, and wondered if he would approve of all she had done. She often thought about her parents, and their loss still made her very sad. She walked around the stables all smelling of fresh paint, and imagined how nice it would be for them to be full of horses with hay and straw in the barn. When she walked outside to view the farmyard, it was neat and tidy, but sort of sterile without animals and people working.

Suddenly she felt very lonely. Everything she had wished for at Home Farm had come true, but the finished house and building were so empty now the builders had left. A gust of wind drove a few dead leaves across the new concrete and they settled at her feet, but when the wind dropped, the silence of the farmyard overwhelmed her. She ran to her car and drove away, back to Manor Farm.

It was mid morning, Peter was working in the fields, Sue had gone shopping and the cows were out to grass. The farmyard was empty and silent, a feeling of melancholy returned and she ran indoors and turned on the radio, but the programme bored her.

She switched off and sat with her head in her hands, realising how desperately lonely she was. In an attempt to shake off this fit of depression, she went into the farm office, hoping that work would fill her emptiness, but her concentration wandered, making work impossible. She rang Mark at his office and his voiced cheered her up. They chatted about how well everything had gone, and then he said, "Can I see you this evening?"

They had a very enjoyable dinner together and then called in at Home Farm for a drink. As they were chatting over a drink in the lounge, Mark put down his glass and took Angela's from her. "Hey, what are you doing?" She protested.

"I'm going to make love to you."

His directness both shocked and excited her, and she trembled as he undid her dress, but then grabbed his hand whispering, "Do you love me, Mark?"

"Yes. Very much."

She released his hand and as he embraced her, their lips met. Mark had dreamed of this moment for a long time, and Angela desperately needed to be loved. Their sudden intense desire for one another was released in a frenzy of passion and they quickly removed each other's clothes, desperate to explore each other's bodies. Mark felt as though he wanted to completely consume her beautiful body, and he kissed her all over before concentrating on her most sensitive parts. Angela lay back on the settee wanting him more and more until she could wait no longer. She reached down and brought his face up to hers and they kissed passionately. As he entered her, they both groaned in ecstasy, and their orgasms came quickly and intensely in an explosion of suppressed emotion.

Long after their mutual climaxes had ebbed away, Angela wanted him to stay close to her forever, feeling that at last she had found the man she loved. They relaxed together, side by side, neither wanting the magic of their experience to fade away, but Angela broke the long silence. "I love you, Mark."

He held her close again. "Do you really?"

"Yes, I do."

Suddenly he got up and knelt down beside her reclining naked body. "Will you marry me?"

She replied immediately. "Yes."

"Oh my God, I can't believe it."

They embraced again, staying together for an hour. Mark suddenly looked at his watch, "Look at the time. I must take you home."

Drink With The Devil

"What for? We can stay here."

"Are you sure?"

"Why not? We're engaged, aren't we?"

"Of course." They made a bed and slept cuddled up together, only needing half the double bed.

The next day Mark did not go to work and they slept late, enjoying each other's company. Later they drove into town to choose a ring and picked up some of Mark's things, as they agreed to cohabit for a while before setting a wedding date.

A month later Angela sat down and thought about the arrangement, which so far had worked quite well; the house seemed to come alive as soon as Mark moved in, and Gemma soon became accustomed to her new surroundings. Mark seemed very happy, setting up his drawing board in a spare room, and most of their evenings were spent pursuing their own interests, but relaxing in the lounge before retiring. Angela was sure Mark was right for her, although their lovemaking sometimes lacked the sort of magic she had hoped for, and had experienced at the beginning.

They agreed to get married as soon as it could be arranged, and the wedding took place in the local church three months later, attended by a few friends and relations. Garry took her arm and gave her away. He was in a very good mood and did not touch a drop of brandy all day; all he drank was a toast in champagne at the small reception held in the Farm House. He even complimented the couple on the work they had done in the house and its buildings. Angela's happy day was tinged with sadness as she reflected upon her parents absence, which was the reason she insisted on a small ordinary ceremony rather than the grand affair her father would have laid on. Mark understood her reasons and was pleased it was not too grand.

Two months later Angela announced she was pregnant and postponed plans to start horse breeding until the baby was born. Mark was delighted with the news, treating her with even more consideration than before, and spending less time at his drawing board in the evenings, preferring to sit and chat.

In her quiet private moments Angela thought about Jim, and still missed him badly. She wondered if she would be able to go through the rest of her life without seeing him again.

Drink With The Devil

Chapter Seventeen

Three years to the day after the fire at Manor Farm and the death of his parents, Garry Osborne stood in his office at Blakesbuild looking out of the window. He was admiring his sleek new Jaguar standing in the parking bay, and feeling very pleased with himself at having produced enough profit to buy the vehicle and expand the company. He sat down and looked at the framed picture of baby William placed in a prominent position on his desk. Although he had never held or cuddled the child, he was very proud of him, and hoped to bring him into the company when he became old enough.

He sat and thought about his present situation. The two companies were doing well, Jane seemed happy, the farm was well managed by Peter French and the new farmhouse was superb. Jane was always pleased to visit the farm at weekends, taking a keen interest in the animals' welfare. His feelings of smug satisfaction were brought to a halt by the telephone.

"Yes," he snapped.

"Mr. Vine for you."

"Hello, Mr. Vine. And what can I do for our solicitors today?"

"I would be grateful if you could come to my office for a meeting."

"What meeting?"

"A delicate matter which can only be discussed face to face."

"I see. But tell me, is it a business or a family matter?"

"Family. Can you come to-day?"

"Yes. Straightaway." Garry ran downstairs and took a taxi to the solicitor's office, wondering what family matter could be so urgent. Perhaps his father had other assets not discovered until now? That would be nice or, maybe he had offshore accounts or even money in Switzerland! If there was, it must be a substantial amount by now, perhaps enough to buy another company. He was bubbling over in anticipation as he entered the office. George Vine shook hands and gestured towards a large leather chair. Garry sat down and made himself comfortable, studying the older man's face, but he could tell nothing from his bland expression.

George Vine stood behind his desk and picked up a brown envelope, fingering it nervously. Garry spoke cheerfully. "Well, what secrets have you to offer about my family?"

"As you know it is exactly three years since your parents' death."

"Is it really?"

"Yes." He looked sternly at Garry. "I was instructed to wait exactly this amount of time before giving you this document."

"When was this instruction given, and who gave it?"

"Your father instructed me many years ago, at the time the document was prepared."

"What is this document?" Garry became impatient.

"It's your adoption details."

Garry was silent for a second and then said in a shrill tone. "What do you mean, adoption?"

The solicitor leaned against his desk, still clutching the envelope and looking Garry straight in the eye. He spoke in a clear, even tone. "Your parents tried for years to have children, but without success. When they thought all hope was lost, they adopted you."

"B-But what about Angela?"

"Your mother became pregnant later, despite the doctors saying it was impossible."

"So she is their natural daughter?"

"Yes."

Garry was stunned into silence. George saw his anguished expression and sat down whilst he digested the news fully. After a minute of staring at his feet Garry said, "Who else knows about this?"

Drink With The Devil

"No one. There are records of course, but they are unlikely to be found unless someone is specifically looking for them."

Garry thought about the situation. "Who are my natural parents?"

"They died years ago, so I wouldn't dwell on that if I were you."

"But I must find out about them."

"I would advise you to forget about them. Just remember Sir William and Lady Osborne brought you up as their son. It would be an insult to their memory to dig up the past."

"I don't agree. Besides they should have told me before."

"They wanted you to settle down in the family business, so that everybody would accept you as their son before you found out."

"Why?"

"So it would be easier for you to accept."

Garry thought about it again and said calmly. "No one must ever find out about this. Not even Angela."

"No one will find out. So forget about digging up the past and get on with the future as Garry Osborne."

"I'll certainly carry on as Garry Osborne, but I do need to know about my real parents."

"Please leave the past alone."

Garry stood up, leaned across the desk and pointed at George Vine. "You will tell me the truth, or I'll find out myself."

"Very well. If you're determined to find out, sit down and I'll tell you all I know. But don't say I didn't warn you.

Garry sat down, but did not relax.

George Vine proceeded. "Your natural parents were farm workers' children. Your mother became pregnant at the age of eighteen and your father was nineteen. They had no money and couldn't afford to marry, so it was decided to have you adopted."

"So I'm a bastard?"

"No, you are not. May I continue?"

"Yes. Go on then."

Your natural parents married two years later and had a son.

When he was one year old, your parents went out to celebrate in a borrowed car, but your father was drunk and a head on collision occurred. Both were killed."

"What happened to the boy?"

"He was at his grandparents at the time. They tried to bring him up, but were unable to take care of him permanently."

Garry showed no emotion. "What happened to him after that?"

"He was less fortunate than you, and taken in by an orphanage." Garry stroked his chin. "What's so terrible about all that?"

"Oh nothing really."

"What was my parents name?"

George Vine fidgeted and then took a deep breath. "Grainger. Tom and Molly Grainger."

Garry spluttered. "Grainger." His face went white and he slumped forward, staring at the floor.

George thought he had better say something. "Your mother was Molly Smith at the time of your birth."

Garry lifted his head slowly and spoke in an unusually deep voice. "What's the boy's Christian name?"

"James."

"You mean he's the same Jim Grainger who killed my parents?"

He didn't kill your parents, but he was there on that terrible night."

Garry stood up, placed his hands on the desk and leaned forward. He spoke in a shrill loud voice. "Christ Almighty. So I'm a bastard and my brother's a murderer."

"That's not true. Now calm down and learn to accept the situation."

Garry straightened up. "So that's why you didn't want me to sue for libel?"

"You had a weak case and wouldn't have achieved much."

"And the very distasteful past would have come out."

"Unlikely, I would say."

Drink With The Devil

"Perhaps you were right to advise against litigation."

"I was right and no doubt about it."

Garry slumped back into the chair, cupped his head in his hands and remained silent. All that could be heard in the room was the loud tick of a wall-mounted clock. After a couple of minutes during which both men sat motionless, Garry slowly got to his feet, reached forward, grabbed the envelope and growled. "The evil bastard should have told me before."

"And what difference would it have made?"

"It would have proved he trusted me."

George Vine just shrugged. "He thought he was doing his best for you."

"He didn't bloody well trust me."

"I'm sorry you see it like that. This news will not alter your life or anyone's view of you. So just get on with running your companies and forget about it."

"It's all right for you to say that." Garry turned on his heels and walked out, slamming the door behind him.

George slumped back into his chair, thinking how badly he had handled the interview. I should have broken the news gradually, he thought. I hope he'll be all right.

Garry did not return to work but took a taxi to his flat where the curtains were still pulled. He sat in the twilight of the stale-smelling room thinking, and all the feeling of hatred for Jim Grainger returned, but was more intense. He suddenly sat upright. What if he finds out he's my brother? he thought. If he finds out others will, including business contacts, associates, friends and relations. Little William is really a Grainger! He almost wept with anger, cursing his mother and father — both natural and adoptive. After a while his stomach twisted up and his thoughts of hatred intensified, his knees felt weak and his hands shook. His stomach and head throbbed as he staggered towards the drinks cabinet, where a new bottle of brandy had rested unopened for a couple of weeks — a record for Garry.

He filled a glass, gulped it down, went back to his seat and closed his eyes, the liquid feeling warm as it slid down inside him, but it did little to untwist his stomach. He tried to imagine both sets of parents being tortured and hung, but the vision would not stay in his mind, always returning to Jim Grainger and ways of killing him. He reasoned that if Grainger had not killed his parents, he would still be living in blissful ignorance of his true parentage. Further large gulps of brandy caused the visions of torture and killing to become real in his mind. He stood up, lifted the bottle to his lips and drank the remaining liquid before crashing to the floor unconscious.

Jane went to bed that night not knowing or really caring where Garry was, but the next morning she found he had not come home. At first she was angry, but then she became concerned, as he always came home eventually. She rang both Blakesbuild and Osbornes to be told that he had not been seen despite an appointment with a client, who was apparently very upset at being let down. She also rang the flat, but there was no reply. Peter French had not seen him and there was no reply at the farmhouse. She thought he would be home for lunch, but by three he had neither returned nor gone to work. She drove to his flat, and recoiled at the stench as she entered.

A mixture of brandy and vomit made the stale air difficult to breathe without making herself feel sick. Garry was laying on the floor, his face surrounded by vomit which had soaked into his hair, and he was groaning. Jane pulled back the curtains and opened a window and then pulled him away from the mess, propping him up against a chair. The empty brandy bottle made her feel angry and, storming off into the kitchen, she filled a saucepan full of cold water, returned and emptied it over Garry's face and head. The shock revived him a little and he shouted out. "That bastard, Grainger. I'll kill him."

"Good God! You're not still on about him, are you?" Jane stood back and looked at her husband to see his white face with his eyes sunk so deep in their sockets that it was difficult to see them. "You pathetic, miserable, inadequate little man," she said in a loud voice. "You think you're so special, but look at yourself now. You're not fit to be called a man."

Drink With The Devil

A squeaky little voice replied, "Oh Jane, my love, I'm so sorry to have let you down so badly."

"Sorry! You're a bloody disgrace to yourself and your family, and not fit for anything but the gutter."

"You're right of course, my love."

"Love! The only person you love is yourself. You disgust me." She walked out, slamming the door, and stood outside to hear him crying and asking for forgiveness. She nearly went back to help him, but resisted the temptation.

Garry eventually rose and staggered to the shower to wash his fully clothed body, before throwing his clothes into a bin. He walked unsteadily to the bedroom, feeling very ill, and collapsed on to the bed. Jane returned home, feeling better having at last told him what she thought of him, but still worried about his health.

When Garry returned home late that night, he drank a glass of milk and went to bed. Jane looked at him lying there, still looking pale and, as she tucked him, in she thought how harmless he looked. She tried to feel compassion, realising how degrading it must be to have to drink until one is ill in order to satisfy some strange need or drown depression.

Although he tried to catch up with work, Garry's mind kept wandering and by mid morning he gave up, and got out the Grainger file from his desk and read it to refresh his memory. He threw it down and cursed. My murdering brother is in the same business as me. I'll have to do something about that, he thought. Grabbing the receiver he rang Gordon Simpson, who answered in a sleepy voice, but Garry soon woke him up.

"Simpson, I want you to find Grainger again and give me an up-to-date report on all aspects of his life."

"Yes Sir, Mr. Osborne." Simpson was at his usual low level of activity, finding customers hard to come by, and he got on with the job straightaway. Going back to find the terraced house in Kingston, he knocked at the door.

Rosie directed him to the new site in Sussex, at the same

time giving him a strange look. "What d'you want to see 'im for?"

"I'd like to sell him some insurance."

"You won't sell 'im anything."

"Why not?"

" 'cause he won't have time to see you."

Simpson walked away smiling cheerfully and drove to Sussex, easily finding the large building site with its wooden site building, and he sat and watched for a while, noticing the activity on different parts of the site with houses at varying stages of completion. Nearer to the site building there was a finished house with a notice over the front door indicating the 'show house.' The garden was laid out neatly and curtains hung at the windows. The row of detached houses nearest to the road was finished, and some were occupied.

Simpson drove in and parked outside the show house, walking in to be accosted by a keen young sales lady, who set about showing him the features of the house, and then led him to a plan of the site showing what houses were still for sale. Simpson listened to her smooth talk and then said. "Tell me about Grainger Construction."

"Oh, it's a go ahead company run by a young man who believes in using the best quality materials and workmanship."

"Have they built many houses?"

"Yes. Two previous sites in Surrey. The houses there sold immediately."

"Will they be building on other sites?"

"Yes, as soon as these are finished."

"D'you know the boss man?"

"Unfortunately not. Jim Grainger works sixteen hours a day and doesn't have time to chat."

"Thank you for showing me around. I'll think about it. Oh, by the way where were the previous houses built?"

She gave him the address and he walked out, glancing around before driving off.

Billy Bradford walked out of the site office with an arm full of plans. He watched the man with a beer gut get into a battered old car and stopped, racking his brains trying to think where he had seen him before. The old car started up and sped off, and suddenly Billy remembered the man wanting to buy rubble, thinking that somehow he did not look like a builder. Billy dropped the plans and scribbled the car's registration number on a scrap of paper, and then picking up the plans walked across to the show house. Once inside he questioned the sales lady. "What did that fat bloke want?"

"He was just being nosy, like a lot of other people."

"What questions did he ask?"

"He wanted to know all about Grainger Construction."

"I see. Thanks dear." He stuffed the scrap of paper into his back pocket and left, wondering if he was being too suspicious or, was this the man who tried to stop the company getting its supplies? He decided to discuss his suspicions with Jim.

Simpson found the new houses near Kingston and counted how many were on the estate. They were all occupied, some with new cars parked outside and all well decorated, and he guessed they would have been bought by middle class families. He drove home, typed his report and that evening Garry rang.

"How are you getting on?"

"Fine. He's still living with the old dear."

"Oh yes. But what about his business?"

"I'm still looking into that."

"Well, hurry up. I want your report by the end of the week."

"Right, Sir." He smiled to himself. It was only Tuesday, and he could stretch the job out for the rest of the week.

Garry had a bad week. Every time he tried to get down to work his mind wandered, and he sat for hours just thinking about Jim and how to get rid of him. All this destructive mental activity took its toll on his health, both physical and mental — his stomach was always twisted up and he could not eat. The only time he forgot about his problems was when he was at a business meeting which demanded his full attention.

Friday morning came and Simpson sauntered into Garry's office, noticing at once Garry's drawn features and tempered glare. "Here's your report, Guv."

Garry reached out and snatched it rudely. "About time too!" Simpson waited whilst he read it, before throwing it down and snorting,

"Huh. So the evil bastard is doing well?"

"So it would appear."

"Yes. We'll have to do something about that."

"What have you got in mind?"

"I don't know yet. I'll call you shortly."

"Okay, but can I have a cheque first?"

Garry agreed and Simpson left to cash it before going home to his flat. That evening he went out for his usual pint, and was stopped on the way home by a pair of big dark-haired men, waiting outside the block of flats. The first one grabbed his lapels and growled, "You're two months behind with yer rent. Now pay up within two days or I'll alter the shape of yer face."

Simpson recognised the man as the leader of a local and particularly violent gang, who normally specialised in burglary and protection rackets. "I promise to pay the landlord this week."

"Well, now you pay me. I've taken over debt collection."

"Okay. I'll pay."

"Yeah. You're bloody right you will."

Simpson staggered up to his flat, his knees feeling weak and he trembled with fear, knowing he could not pay. The weekend passed slowly and miserably, as he tried to think of ways of overcoming his problems. By Sunday morning he had convinced himself the situation was hopeless, and he would have to move out that afternoon, leaving the few items of furniture he possessed in the flat. He had lived alone all his adult life and had drifted from one job to another, never doing very well at anything.

Having been a private investigator some time now, he enjoyed the freedom and this was the job he had decided to stick at, hoping to find a rich client to work for. At first things went well

Drink With The Devil

and he was busy most of the time, but the last year had been dreadful with only a few odd jobs to tackle, mostly for bad-tempered people like Osborne. Lack of activity led him to drink regularly, which made his money problems worse.

He walked home and started packing clothes into two battered old suitcases. Suddenly the door rattled as someone hit it, and his heart sank as he stood still and waited, but the door was bludgeoned again so he ran and opened it before it was broken down. The two big men burst in, knocking Simpson to one side as he asked, "What d'you want?"

The bigger of the two pushed him against the wall. "Yer wouldn't be running out on us, would yer?"

"No, of course not," he lied.

The other man disappeared into the bedroom, returning with the two suitcases. "Look at this. The bastard was goin' to do a bunk."

Simpson started trembling as the nearest man came closer. "You were running out on me, weren't yer?"

Simpson closed his eyes, trying to think of a reply and suddenly he blurted out, "I can pay, and if you leave me alone I'll give you a job that'll pay thousands."

Both men laughed and then sneered. "You miserable little bastard. You're just trying to save yer skin."

"No, it's true. I'll have all the details for you tomorrow."

"What kind of job is it?"

"I've a rich client who wants a man put out of action."

"Okay. We'll give you twenty-four hours to come up with a deal. In the meantime just make sure you don't go anywhere."

Simpson heaved a sigh of relief, and then collapsed on the floor as the big man delivered a hard punch to his stomach. The other man kicked him in the side, and then tore the suitcases to shreds with a long knife, scattering torn clothes around the flat. He did not hear them leave as he felt too ill, the pie and pint he had for lunch reaching his mouth and spurting out over the bare floorboards with some of it disappearing through the cracks. He lay still groaning for a while, and then staggered into the bedroom to spend the rest of the day nursing his stomach and feeling very depressed.

The telephone was ringing as Garry entered his office the next morning complete with hangover and bad temper. "Gordon Simpson here. I've a proposition for you regarding your problem."

"Oh yes. And what is it?"

"Six thousand pounds will make it go away permanently."

Garry was stunned into silence for a couple of seconds and then growled, "If this is some kind of a rip off, I'll have you strung up."

"No rip off, guv. Just meet me with the cash and forget about it."

"Okay. This morning?"

They arranged a meeting place and Garry drew out the cash from the company's account, stuffing it into a large brown envelope. Simpson walked out of the block of flats and looked nervously up and down the street, noticing two men sitting in a car fifty yards away. They followed his car to a large car park behind a cinema where Simpson got out and sat in Garry's car, Garry looking nervously around the car park. "Did anyone follow you?"

"No, of course not," said Simpson.

"What's the deal, then?"

"I know a gang who'll get rid of Grainger for ever."

"Okay. But these are my conditions. Number one, there'll be no contact between the gang and me. Number two, it must look like an accident. Number three, I'll pay three thousand now and three thousand when the job's done. And when I read about his death in the newspapers."

Simpson nodded his pale face. Okay, that's sounds fair. Now give me the money."

Garry handed him the envelope.

Simpson walked quickly back to his car and drove away, looking straight ahead. After a couple of minutes he noticed the car with two men in following, and wondered if Garry had seen it. Anyway back at the flat he sat down worrying about the mess he was getting himself into, and counting the money when suddenly the flat door burst open and two men entered.

"Well, how did yer get on?" said one of them.

"It's all agreed. You get two thousand five hundred to do the job and the same when it's finished."

"Who's the bloke to be topped?"

"A builder called Jim Grainger."

The two men looked at each other for a moment. "Where does he hang out?"

"On a building site in Sussex. For sixteen hours a day."

"What does he look like?"

"A big bloke in his mid twenties, with dark hair."

Further details were discussed and Simpson handed over the money. "This also pays my rent."

"The final payment will."

"Okay. Let me know when it's done."

"You bet, we will."

Chapter Eighteen

The wooden site building was bulging with office equipment and humming with activity. Jim had his desk across one corner of the office, finding it difficult to work with the two ladies chattering as they processed the paperwork. The almost constant stream of men coming in to ask questions and the telephone ringing every ten minutes was beginning to get on his nerves, and he was pleased when everyone went home so he could get some peace.

One evening after the women had gone Billy walked in clutching a scrap of paper. "By the way, Jim, I forgot to tell you about a fat geezer who was nosing around the other day."

"What about him?"

"It was the same bloke who wanted to buy rubble from the school job."

Jim looked up sharply from his paperwork. "I remember you telling me about him."

"Yes. And shortly afterwards we couldn't get any supplies."

"That's right. D'you think he's up to something?"

"I don't know. But he was asking questions about you."

"Was he now?"

"Yes. This is his car registration number."

"Thanks. We'll have to keep our eyes open." Jim changed the subject. "This office is too small. I can't get any work done."

"I'm not surprised with those women chatting all day."

"We'll get some wood sections and build on the end."

"Okay. I'll get on with it."

A week later the extension was finished, and Jim worked on after dark moving his furniture. After Billy had switched on the night security lights which illuminated most of the building site, and gone home, Jim looked out of his new window at the show house opposite. It looked even better floodlit. He could see a lot of the site from his chair and relaxed for a while, reflecting on his achievements. He was very proud of the show house and all the other detached houses he had built. The mature trees on the site had been carefully preserved where possible, making the houses look even more attractive.

His thoughts were suddenly interrupted by a man walking by the window, knocking at the door and walking in. Jim studied the face of a tall dark-haired man dressed in a black suit, and his heart sank when he remembered the man, a fellow prisoner who used to be in the next cell and whom he did not like. Jim got up and shook hands.

"Hello Ken. How are you?"

"I'm fine mate. They said you always work late."

"Yes. That's right."

"Only I was down the local pub and they said you might have a job for me."

"You don't look as though you need one." Jim was trying to think of an excuse to turn him down.

"Well, I do. And I thought you might help a fellow ex-con."

Jim sat and stroked his chin, racking his brains for an answer. "What can you do?"

"Labouring. I've worked on a building site before."

Jim looked at the man's hands, soft and pale, and was about to turn him down when the telephone rang in the next office. He got up. "Sorry about this. I haven't moved the phone yet."

"That's all right mate."

Jim closed the door behind him and picked up the phone to find it was Ron Smart with a list of the latest prices for building materials. He sat down and started making notes.

Ken Bridger, in the next office, paced up and down for a while and then sat himself in Jim's chair, opening each drawer and rummaging about for anything valuable. An expensive pen caught his eye, which he tried on a scrap of paper, not seeing the face peering in the window.

Two burly men walked in and approached the desk. "Hello, Mr. Grainger. We've come to see you about a job."

Ken was taken by surprise. "B-But I'm not Mr ..." His sentence was cut off abruptly as one of the men moved quickly around the desk, and clamped his hand over the frightened man's mouth. They quickly pushed him outside into the shadows and behind a pile of bricks. Whilst one man had his hand over Ken's mouth, the other had a firm grip on his arm, which was twisted up behind his back.

Ken found himself looking at a grinning big dark man, who spoke in a high pitched tone. "Well, Grainger, I've wanted to kill you for a long time. Now I'm being paid for it." He landed a heavy punch to Ken's stomach and Ken pitched forward groaning, whilst the other man stood back laughing. Ken struggled to get up, clasping his painful stomach, but the big man pulled him upright and crashed his huge fist under his chin, his jaw bone breaking with a sickening crack, and he fell unconscious on to the soft earth. The big man gave a short burst of laughter and said, "Right, we'll carry him around the back of that show house."

They picked him up between them and made their way, mostly in the shadows, to the show house back door, which was locked. They dropped the unfortunate man on the concrete path, the big man kicked the door in and they picked him up again, carried him upstairs and left him on a bedroom floor.

After about five minutes Ken regained consciousness and tried to get up, but without success, as his whole body was shaking and he collapsed again. The two men returned after going back to their car for petrol cans, soaked the stairs, floors and all the ground floor carpets. Ken smelt the fumes and tried to crawl towards the stairs, but as he got nearer he smelt smoke and flames billowed up the stairs, meeting him on the landing. Although he tried to cry out, his jaw would not move. The smoke made his eyes stream and breathing difficult. He retreated back into the bedroom but the fire moved faster, catching up with him before he reached the window. He drew breath, screamed and choked. The air was filled with black smoke, flames and fumes from the furniture, and he only breathed in twice more before the poisoned air killed him.

The two men watched from the back of the house as flames leapt out of the bedroom window. This convinced them their job was done, and they ran around the house towards the car parked beyond the site building.

Jim finished his long phone call, and was relieved when he returned to his office and found his visitor had gone. He sat down, thinking Ken must have changed his mind about needing a job, but then he saw his pen on the desk and one of the drawers open. Searching all the drawers he found nothing of value missing, and he sat back wondering why the pen was lying there — perhaps he had not remembered using it. His deliberations were interrupted by a crackling sound, and when he looked out of the window he could not believe his eyes — the show house was on fire.

He ran to the door and for a split second stood staring at the blaze, but a movement around the side of the house averted his gaze. Two men were running towards him, the first was twenty yards away when Jim recognised his face. The last time he had seen that man was on the night of the fire at Manor Farm, and his mind flashed back to remember the man standing over his dead companion.

Jim roared with anger as he ran towards the two men, who saw him and ran back towards the shadows, but Jim ran around the burning house and gained on them. As he looked back at the flames, an explosion rippled through the house and temporarily blinded him, but he turned away and ran on, his eyes gradually adjusting to the darkness again. He saw a figure standing still in front of him and lunged forward, but tripped over a concrete block and fell headlong in the mud. He struggled to get up, but a blow on the back of his head knocked him out.

The smaller of the two men threw down a short length of scaffold pipe and said, "Come on, let's get out of 'ere."

"We ought to finish 'im," said his companion.

"What for? He's only a labourer. Look at his clothes."
"That's true. And he didn't really see us."

They ran for their car just as people from the completed houses were emerging to watch the fire. Jim lay unseen behind a large stack of blocks and bricks. The fire brigade worked all night but were unable to save the house, and all that remained in the morning were the brick walls. They started sifting through the debris at first light and discovered the charred unrecognisable remains of a male body.

Jim regained a sort of hazy consciousness an hour before dawn. Hearing loud noises which hurt his head, he crawled slowly away from the fire not knowing where he was, or in which direction he was going — his only need was for peace, his memory was lost and his past was a blank. When he tried to stand up he collapsed again, giddy and unbalanced, but eventually he reached the edge of the site on all fours. A light breeze blew country smells into his nostrils and spurred him forward to the open pasture fields, and after crawling through a gap in the hedge, he sat still in the half-light watching the red glow of sunrise emerging on the horizon. Birds started singing in the hedge close by and his memory began to return, but only the part appertaining to his life spent in the forest.

Sometime later he felt better and got to his feet slowly, walking unsteadily beside the hedge. As he walked, the memory of his time living among the animals and birds became clearer. He searched the area for trees and saw woodland at the other end of the field through which he was strolling.

It had become light when he reached the wood. He entered it slowly, trying not to disturb the wildlife. The morning chorus reached a crescendo as he walked among tall beech and oak trees, and sunlight filtered through, shining on the droplets of dew clinging to leaves and twigs. He examined a droplet closely, marvelling at the colours contained within its round shape. Then he walked slowly on as though in a trance, sitting for a while on a fallen tree trunk, just taking in the tranquil atmosphere of a forest clearing with flowering heather growing in the sandy soil.

Drink With The Devil

Only thirty yards away, a young deer broke cover on the other side of the clearing. At first she stood motionless staring at Jim, but then twitched her ears forward sniffing the air, and moving forward she nibbled at a tuft of grass, lifting her head with grass hanging out of her mouth. She munched slowly but after a few minutes disappeared between the trees. Jim watched her go as he took a deep breath of air, filling his lungs with sweet tasting country fragrance

Sounds were emerging from the forest all around him, all familiar friendly noises. A rabbit stuck its head out from under the heather, only two yards from him, wriggling its nose about, sniffing and disappearing again. Jim stroked the hair away from his face, and whilst smoothing it backwards his hand touched a big lump on the back of his head, which was sore and throbbed. He got up from his tree trunk and walked to the centre of the clearing, finding a large-leafed plant with water collected on its soft green surface. He bent down low to suck the liquid into his mouth, finding it tasted pure and refreshing.

As he walked into the forest again, over a carpet of leaves and twigs which crackled as he trod, the ground felt springy, making walking a pleasure, and he reached the edge of the forest to look out across a field of grass and clover. Cows were eating nearby and, seeing him standing there, they wandered over. Four of them gradually edged closer, lifting their large noses up to his face to sniff and then breathing out steam through giant nostrils. Jim slowly lifted his hands to rub the nearest cow's ears, and she responded by moving nearer. Then he heard a high-pitched whistle and saw a man in the distance. The cows turned and walked away as Jim disappeared back into the forest. He walked for a while, but started to feel tired and when he came to a clearing again, he curled up in the heather and fell into a deep sleep.

* * *

Billy Bradford turned into the building site with a van full of workers, but stopped suddenly, horrified at the sight of the show house completely gutted. He nearly fell out of the door and ran across to a group of firemen. "When did this happen?"

"Last night," said one of the men. "Are you anything to do with Grainger Construction?"

"Yes. Site foreman."

"Where's the boss?"

Billy spun around and saw the Morris pick-up in the same place as the previous evening. "He must be about somewhere."

A grim-faced fireman moved closer. "We've searched the office and site, but can't find anyone."

"He was here last night."

A policeman intervened. A young plain clothes officer, who stared straight into Billy's eyes with a stern expression. "When did you last see Mr. Grainger?"

"Last night at about 8.30."

"Would he have left the office unlocked and the door open?"

"No. Definitely not."

"We've recovered the body of a tall man from the fire."

"Oh, my God. Is it Jim?"

"We're assuming it's Mr. Grainger."

"Has anyone told Rosie?"

"Who's Rosie?"

"The lady he lodges with."

"No, not yet."

"I'd better tell her before she reads it in the newspaper."

"After you've answered some more questions."

They walked across to the office to avoid the press. Billy answered a lot of questions and finally was asked, "Did anyone have a reason to kill your boss?"

"No one I can think of." He thought for a minute. "Are the Briggs mob still inside?"

"Yes. I know what you're thinking. Perhaps they got someone to settle their old score."

"So you know about his past?"

Drink With The Devil

"Yes of course. I'll check into his known associates."

Billy drove the old van towards Kingston, feeling distraught at having lost such a good friend and worried about how Rosie would take the news. She was standing at the kitchen door as he approached through the back garden. Her white hair was untidy and she looked ill. Before Billy could speak she said, "What's happened to 'im?"

"Let's go inside, Rosie."

They went through to the sitting room and sat down and she said softly. "They've finally got 'im, haven't they?"

"I'm sorry, Rosie. There's been a fire and the body of a man was recovered. They're pretty sure it's Jim."

Rosie slumped forward, head in hands, and cried bitterly. Billy got up quietly and walked into the kitchen, returning a few minutes later with a cup of tea, but Rosie could not be consoled. After about half an hour she stopped crying and just stared at the floor. "I'll be all right now," she whispered.

Billy left the house and returned to the site where men were standing about talking in low tones, and staring at the blackened shell. The firemen had finished damping down and were packing up. He got the men together in the office and spoke clearly. "We're all shattered at the news and none of us feels like work, so we'd better all go home."

One of the younger men stepped forward. "What'd Jim have wanted us to do?"

"Work like 'ell," another man growled.

The others nodded and they filed out to carry on with the construction of houses. Billy was left feeling guilty at his own weakness and worried about running the business. He sat down heavily, thinking about the problems facing him and how he was going to pay the wages. There was all the paperwork Jim used to do late into the night, and he was just beginning to panic when a knock on the door made him jump.

A grey-haired and well-dressed man walked in, who spoke with a public school accent. "I'm looking for my friend, Jim Grainger."

"Oh yeah. And who might you be?"

"Oliver Smythe."

"Oh yes. Jim told me about you. Inside together, weren't you?"

"That's right."

Billy told him the sad story and Oliver digested the news in silence. "That's terrible! Poor Jim."

"Yeah. I hope he didn't suffer."

"Have they positively identified him yet?"

"No. They said dental records would have to be checked."

"That could take days. And in the meantime the company must go on in case there's a mistake, and that body is someone else."

"Not much hope of that."

"Have you contacted the insurance company yet?"

"No. I don't know who they are."

"I can see you need some help."

"That's right. Can you spare the time?"

"I've got all the time in the world for Jim Grainger."

They worked together all day, Billy handling practical affairs whilst Oliver attended to the paperwork.

* * *

After handing over the cash to Simpson, Garry went back to work with mixed feelings — pleased to have taken positive action to get rid of Grainger, but nervous about the possibility of the crime being traced back to him. Work was piling up at Blakesbuild and he still could not force himself to get on with it despite reminders from his staff, which he brushed aside saying he was too busy. His mind was busy, but with a mixture of hatred and a dread of being found out, imagining himself being taken away by the police amid a glare of publicity.

The next day was no better when he went to work at Blakesbuild as usual, after listening to the news. He tried hard to concentrate but without success. He wondered if he would be able to concentrate better at Osbornes, but then remembered he had given Simon Berry a free hand after the recent meeting with his solicitor, knowing he would do a better job than him in his present state of mind. Also, he could not face all the staff now he was not really an Osborne himself, so his mind returned to Jim Grainger again. If he was out of the way there would be no Graingers left, and he could forget the whole nasty business. The day dragged on until the early afternoon when Simpson rang. "Have you seen the late editions yet?"

"What late editions?"

"The newspapers, of course."

"No. What do they say?"

"There was a fire and a body recovered. Too badly burnt to be recognised."

"Did they name the body?"

"The story says it's almost certainly Mr. Jim Grainger."

"Has he been positively identified?"

"Not yet. But it's got to be him."

"I'll see you when he is."

"You'd better see me straightaway or I'll be the next."

"Hard luck, chum."

"It'll be hard luck for you as well."

"What d'you mean?"

"Just meet me in two hours time in the same place. With the money."

Garry rushed out of the office, desperate to get a newspaper. The story was easy to find, showing a picture of a burnt out house beside the caption 'Builder dies in his own house.' Garry read the article several times until he knew every word, feeling elated and free. At last, he thought, I can forget about that evil bastard, and it's even better than I thought possible — he died in a fire the way he killed my parents. All worries about being found out were replaced by a feeling of euphoria and well-being, and he walked briskly to the bank, drew out the money and drove to the cinema car park, arriving early. Simpson arrived soon after, parked next to the Jaguar and slipped into the passenger seat Garry handed over the money. "We won't meet again."

"You're dead right, we won't."

Simpson drove away quickly, and Garry did not notice the car following Simpson's rusty old heap out of the car park. He drove back to the office and immediately got down to work, ordering coffee and sandwiches. Before concentrating on the heaps of paperwork in his 'in' tray he rang Jane. "I'll be working late. Will you meet me at ten for dinner at "The White Swan?"

Jane was taken aback by his cheerful mood and interest in food. "Are you feeling hungry?"

"Ravenous."

"Wonderful. See you later, but please don't drink before you leave."

"I promise to be completely sober."

While drinking coffee after dinner Jane said, "Why are you so happy tonight?"

"I had a good day."

"Really? What went so well?"

"Everything, ole girl."

Jane got up after he had gone to work the next morning and sat in the kitchen, eating a light breakfast while reading the paper. She suddenly stopped eating when she read the name Grainger. That's why he was in a good mood, she thought. He knew about this yesterday. She shivered at the thought of his possible involvement, but convinced herself he would not jeopardise his rich lifestyle on such a risky venture, although in her heart she knew he was capable of killing.

* * *

Miles away in Sussex another person was reading the paper over a leisurely breakfast. Having dutifully given Mark a kiss on the cheek and seen him go to work, Angela ate a bigger breakfast now she was pregnant. She had just finished off a bowl of porridge with the paper spread out to one side of the kitchen table.

She choked on her tea as she read about the fire, sending the cup flying. The story described Grainger as a go-ahead energetic builder, who worked sixteen hours a day to build up a thriving company. No mention of any criminal record was made, and the story went on to say all his workers were devoted to him and devastated by the loss. Angela read it twice before bursting into tears, and was overcome with grief — the person she really loved was dead! She spent the morning almost rigid, not able to move or think of anything else, but during the afternoon she began to get angry with herself. If only she had taken the trouble to find him he might still be alive.

Then she thought of Garry saying he was a criminal and should be strung up, and then there was the detective after him. If he was a criminal, how did he become such a successful builder? Were all the stories invented by Garry to keep her away from him? She was still miserable and depressed when Mark came home from work.

* * *

Simpson drove carefully from the cinema car park back to his flat, with one eye on the following car. He ran upstairs to count out five hundred pounds, stuffing it under a cushion just before the two men came bursting in. They almost pounced on him. "Well, have yer got the money?"

"Yes. It's all here." He handed it over and was silent as the bigger man checked the amount. "Right, you're off the hook for one week, then you start paying rent again."

"Okay, that's fair."

The big man moved closer and pointed a dirty finger at Simpson. "You don't know who I am, do you?"

"No. You didn't say."

"Right. And if you try to find out, you're dead."

"Okay. I know the rules."

"And if you give my description to the police, you'll die 'orribly."

Simpson just nodded nervously. The two men walked out, leaving him trembling with fear, and he did not have to find out who the man was because he already knew.

Charlie Chatfield was well known among the criminal fraternity as a brutal killer. Simpson sat and thought about what he should do next, soon convincing himself that Chatfield would return that night to kill him. He packed his remaining clothes into carrier bags, and began carrying boxes of his favourite possessions down to the car, which was parked outside, as near as possible.

By dusk, the car was full and he locked the flat door. He made sure the money was safely in his inside pocket, but when he got to the outside door of the building he stopped suddenly, holding his breath, and retreated into the building. Chatfield and his companion finished staring at the car and its contents and advanced towards the block of flats.

Drink With The Devil

Chapter Nineteen

As dawn came a light breeze sent waves of fine rain over the treetops and soaked the forest. Jim had slept through the previous day and night, and the cold water on his face woke him. He sat up feeling stiff and cold, studying his surroundings, as slowly the events of the last two days came back to him, together with all his memory. Not realising how long he had slept, he assumed it was still the morning after the fire, and walked around the clearing trying to remember which way he came in. The tree trunk reminded him, and he walked through the trees hoping someone had called the fire brigade. He entered the site through the same gap in the hedge.

He walked towards the show house expecting to see a lot of activity, but everything was strangely silent and the place deserted. He stared at the remains of the house, a black empty set of cracked brick walls without a wisp of smoke or fire to be seen, and walked through the open back doorway feeling the walls. They were cold, and he stood still trying to work out how the fire could have been put out so quickly, but a glance at his watch told him the van with Billy and the men was due. It was on time and, hearing it pull up outside the office, he walked carefully over the debris to where the front door once hung. Billy stepped wearily out of the driver's seat, rubbing the sleep from his eyes, and when he looked towards the burnt out house he froze. All the other men stood like statues, the colour draining from their faces, and no one uttered a word as Jim walked out of the blackened structure.

Billy felt his knees weaken and he started to tremble, but one of the men found his voice: "Is it a ghost or a bloody miracle?"

The sound of a voice made Billy recover and, slapping his

own face, he spoke unevenly. "J-Jim. Is it really you?"

"Of course it's me. This is a fine mess, isn't it?"

All the men surged forward to meet him. Billy spoke first. "We thought you were dead."

"Not yet, Billy. What made you think that?"

"Yesterday morning a man's body was found in the ruins. Everyone assumed it to be you."

"Why me?"

"You were missing, the office door left open and your pick-up was still here."

"You said the body was found yesterday morning. That means I must have slept all day."

"Where were you?"

Jim pointed across the site. "Over there. The other side of the adjoining field. In a wood."

All the men started to talk at once, each trying to tell the story. Jim got the gist of it. "So the police think I'm dead?"

Billy suddenly went pale again. "Oh my God, so does Rosie."

"You told her I died in the fire?"

"Yes. And she took it very badly."

"I'd better go and see her straight away. You ring the police and tell them where I am."

Jim drove off as fast as the Morris would go, arriving an hour later. He ran to the back door, which was open. Newspapers were lying on the front door mat, and he found Rosie in her favourite armchair. She was dead — the shock had obviously been too much for her. An untouched cup of tea was on her small table, and when Jim felt her cold skin he broke down. He loved this old lady as if she were his own mother and he sat on his chair and wept, occasionally looking at her peaceful face. Not having moved from his seat he was still grief stricken two hours later when the police car pulled up outside, and the sound of a loud knock on the front door made him jump.

After wiping his face, he opened the door to be greeted by a young plain clothes officer. "Are you Jim Grainger?"

Drink With The Devil

"Yes. Come in."

"Detective Sergeant Pratt."

Jim just nodded and walked into the front room.

The detective gasped at the sight of Rosie's pale motionless features. "Is she dead?" he whispered.

"Yes. And it's all my fault. Could we talk somewhere else?"

They walked into the kitchen, followed by another plain clothes officer. Sergeant Pratt stood squarely in front of Jim and looked at his red-rimmed eyes. "Why is it your fault?"

"Because if I hadn't gone after the two men I wouldn't have got knocked out. And Billy wouldn't have had to tell Rosie I was dead."

"I see. What exactly happened?"

Jim told his story from the time Ken Bridger arrived.

The sergeant frowned and said sharply. "Why didn't you offer him a job?"

"Because I knew him long enough in prison to know I didn't trust him."

"And you reckon he was the man found dead in the house?"

"He was the only other person on site. And the two intruders probably thought he was me."

"But they must have realised they were wrong when they saw you later?"

"I don't know."

"They would have killed you."

"They nearly did."

"Where did they hit you?"

Jim pointed to the back of his head.

The sergeant looked closely and growled, "There's no sign of an injury."

"The lump's gone down."

"How very convenient, I'm sure," he said sarcastically.

Jim's heart sank even further. "What are you saying, sergeant?"

"I'll tell you what I think. This man Bridger came to see you, and probably threatened to expose you to your business contacts as an ex-con if you didn't pay him off. You had a fight during which you smashed his jaw and killed him. Then you started that fire to make it look like an accident. Just like you did before."

Jim was stunned by the accusations and felt drained. He just shook his head and said nothing.

The sergeant went on. "Very clever of you to get rid of an enemy and claim the insurance at the same time. But you should have dreamed up a better story whilst you were hiding in that wood."

Jim just croaked. "It's all true."

"Rubbish. I'm placing you under arrest on suspicion of murder. And this time you won't get away with it."

Sergeant Pratt went through the formalities and then handcuffed Jim, before leading him through the house to the police car outside. Jim sat in dazed confusion, his mind gyrating from grief at the loss of Rosie, to dread of being incarcerated again. He was taken to the same police station as before and questioned for hours, but he steadfastly denied killing Bridger, although the barrage of accusations and abuse went on and on until he began to wonder if he had killed the man. At last the relays of different police officers ceased and he was taken down to the same cell that he had occupied before. The steel door clanged shut and he was alone to face a night of deep depression and grief.

The next morning he was questioned again until his mind was almost numb, and after four hours was charged with the murder of Ken Bridger, dental records having confirmed that morning the identity of the body found in the house. The newspapers, desperately short of other news, splashed the story across their front pages and pictures of the burnt out house were shown beside different versions of the story. They described Jim as a huge giant of a man, strong as a lion and just as dangerous.

* * *

Jane heard the papers fall on the front door mat and picked them up, reading the headlines on the way to the kitchen where Garry was just starting his breakfast. She stopped at the door and read on and then calmly laid the paper, front page up, in front of him. Giving a short laugh she said, "So your imagined enemy is not as dead as you hoped."

"What d'you mean my ...." He stopped mid-sentence and snatched the paper up, hiding his face from his wife's inquisitive gaze. Then he spun around and stormed out, grabbing his briefcase on the way. Jane heard the front door slam and sat down, amused by his reaction. He must have wanted him dead very badly, she thought. I wonder why? It cannot be for killing that man years ago, but perhaps he still blames him for his parents' death.

Garry stormed into his office and rang Simpson, but no reply. He sat back and fumed over being ripped off, but more importantly Grainger was still alive. He got up and ran down to his car determined to find Simpson, but as he sat in the driver's seat he began to have second thoughts about seeing him again. It could still be risky, he thought, but gradually he began to feel better about the situation. He would never be suspected of involvement in the killing of this man Bridger, and Grainger would be convicted of murder and sent to prison for life – a sentence he richly deserved. All the time he is locked away he will not be in a position to find out about his elder brother, and there would be plenty of time to think of a plan to deal with him when he is eventually released.

By the time he returned home from work he was in a very good mood, having convinced himself the present situation was preferable to the risk of being implicated in a murder. Jane heard the car door slam and ran from the kitchen and up the stairs as fast as she could, thinking he was bound to be in a terrible mood and could even be violent.

He called from the bottom of the stairs. "Jane, Darling, I'm home."

She peered down at him from the top of the stairs, not really believing he was so cheerful.

He grinned and said. "There you are, you lovely lady."

She was taken aback and walked quickly down. They spent a pleasant evening together, but neither mentioned the newspaper story.

* * *

Angela was still engrossed in her private grief for Jim when she read the front-page story, and her immediate reaction was anger. He has deceived me again, she thought. I have spent days mourning his death and now I find he is alive and a killer. "Oh, what a fool I've been again!" she said out loud as she sat in the kitchen, long after finishing breakfast, and occasionally stroking her swollen stomach. She tried hard to hate him, telling herself how much better off she was as Mark's wife, and how proud she was to bear his child, but no matter how hard she tried she could not hate him.

* * *

Simpson hid under the stairs, listening to the two men running upstairs, and waited until a door slammed before running for his life. The car would not start, its tired engine cranking noisily. He sat with his heart in his mouth, sweat dripping from his chin as the engine protested, the battery running out. He was just about to give up and run, when it fired and sprang into action so he crashed it into reverse and turned quickly, driving away from the building with his right foot hard down.

A glance in the mirror revealed the two men running from the building towards their car, but Simpson drove as fast as his old car would allow, without any particular destination in mind just a desperate need to get away. He looked again in his mirror and saw the sleek red car several vehicles back on the narrow and twisting road, which prevented cars from overtaking. His heart thumped painfully in his chest as he racked his brains for inspiration and, when the road widened, he overtook the car in front, his speed increasing as he desperately looked for an escape. He rounded two tight bends, making the car's bald tyres squeal, and a quick glance in his mirror revealed the pursuing car was out of sight. He took a sudden turn left, nearly turning the car over, and sped down a side street to turn into someone's private drive.

Screeching to a halt in front of a garage he slumped forward, resting his head on the steering wheel and clamping his hands over his ears. He closed his eyes and waited, panting as if he had just run ten miles, his temples were throbbing and his knees trembled as he pictured the men closing in. He stayed like this for five minutes to be shaken out of his visions of impending doom by a tap on the window.

Slowly he looked up, expecting to see the face of his killer, but was surprised to see an old lady with a walking stick raised and ready to strike at the window again. He wound down the window and she frowned. "You can't stay there, young man."

"Of course not Madam. I'm just going." He deliberately took his time reversing and drove south, soon finding himself in Kingston, a place he had always liked. He told himself it would be handy to be near London, but far enough away to avoid those villains.

He spent the afternoon looking for a flat, and found one which was just outside the town centre. It was sparsely furnished, smelt damp but was cheap and he told the agent his name was Norman Powell.

* * *

After being formally charged with murder, Jim was returned to the police cell. Now he had time to think. The cell reminded him of the long days and nights he spent in prison, trying to keep his mind active with plans for the future. But no such thoughts came to him now, just the mind-numbing fact that

Rosie was dead and he could not even organise a decent funeral for her.

All the next morning he was left alone to think about what could be done to extract himself from wrongful conviction. An almost cold lunch arrived at noon and when he looked at it he nearly wept, remembering Rosie's superb cooking. He could not eat the food and the afternoon dragged on until he was summoned for more questions by Sergeant Pratt, who was sitting at the table again. Jim looked at the thin-faced, balding young officer and cringed, as he was the most abusive policeman he had ever met.

Pratt spoke with venom. "Sit down , murderer, and I'll tell you what I've been doing." Jim said nothing but just looked on with a blank expression.

"I've been studying the file on the Manor Farm murder."

Jim closed his eyes and groaned, knowing what was coming next.

"You can groan, you bastard. I know you killed Sir William and his wife. And I'll prove it."

Jim shook his head and stayed quiet.

Pratt changed his tone and became more conciliatory. "Just think about it. You're going down for murder anyway. Why not admit you killed them and save yourself further charges in the future?"

Jim cleared his throat. "I haven't murdered anyone."

Pratt stood up quickly, sending his chair crashing against the wall. Pointing at Jim with a quivering finger, he spoke in a high pitched tone, "You're guilty and you know it. You may have fooled the other policemen, but not me."

Jim sat calmly looking down at the table. Pratt sat down and tried the soft approach again, alternating between a soft voice trying to coax a confession and a high pitched burst of accusations. Jim was getting used to this treatment and answered calmly any questions in his deep husky voice, and in an even tone. Pratt went through the events at Home Farm in minute detail, trying to trip Jim up, but he was unsuccessful, and stormed

Drink With The Devil

out of the room in desperation and rage. When he returned, having calmed down over a cup of tea, he started again with the same results, finally running out of questions and stuck for words.

Jim could see he had run out of steam and said, "I want to see Inspector Green."

Pratt went red in the face and nearly screamed. "Chief Inspector Green hasn't got time to see scum like you."

"Oh that's a shame. Because I'll only answer further questions from him."

"You murdering bastard. You'll answer my questions or else."

"Or else what? Mr. Pratt."

"I'll make sure you stay in prison until you rot."

Jim just sat and looked at the red-faced man, wondering why he was getting so worked up and why he was filled with so much hatred. He was taken back to his cell and left alone for two days without further questioning. He paced up and down like a caged animal, trying not to get too depressed, but it did not work and he began to believe the sergeant's words about rotting in jail. On the third day alone, he was in a very low state when he was summoned to answer more questions.

Sergeant Pratt sat grim faced with a file in front of him. He looked up at Jim's pale face and hissed, "Come to your senses yet?"

Jim sat down and gave the sergeant an expressionless glare, but said nothing.

"I hoped your days of solitary confinement would have convinced you that I mean business."

Jim continued with his blank stare.

"Not going to talk, eh? Well, I'll tell you what I've been doing. Yesterday I visited your friend, Briggs 'inside' and he told me you were a member of his gang, who killed the Osbornes. And that bust-up you had on the building site was due to you being too greedy. You wanted more than your share of the Osborne jewellery proceeds and took it — hence the fight."

Jim just shook his head and swallowed hard.

"Yes. You're entitled to look worried. I've hit on the truth, haven't I?"

Jim was fed up with listening to false accusations. "I've never heard so much rubbish in all my life. Your imagination is unbelievable."

"Imagination, is it? Well, tell me where you got the money from to start Grainger Construction?"

"Hard work. Something you wouldn't know about."

"You cheeky bastard. I'll make you eat those words. I'm going to prove that money was not earned, which will prove you were involved with Briggs. If I find the amount of money he says you stole from him was invested in your company, you're as good as booked on two further charges of murder." His mirthless laugh echoed around the brick walls as Jim looked even more downhearted.

Jim was led back to his cell and collapsed on the hard bench, totally dejected and convinced he really would be in jail for the rest of his life. He was kept in solitary confinement for the next three days, his only contact with humanity being a grim-faced policeman shoving unappetising food at him from time to time, which he only picked at. His only contact with the outside world was through the small barred window high up in the wall and out of reach. He stood with his back against the steel door, watching grey clouds roll by, and the only sounds came from heavy lorries thundering by, vibrating the steel fittings on the cell door. This was a regular event and only served to remind him how unbearable the future would be, locked behind steel doors secured by faceless men in uniform.

By the time four days had passed since the last interview with Pratt, Jim was longing just to walk up the stairs to the small room above for a change of scenery, and his wish was granted. Pratt was sitting at the table again with a smug look on his face. Jim sat down heavily and prepared to hear the worst.

"Well, are you ready to be sensible and confess, or do I have to drag the truth from you?"

Jim felt weak and did not have the energy to answer.

"All right. I've really got you this time. I've studied your company records and cannot find the source of your start-up money — in fact when I added up your purchases for the first couple of months, it came to about the same figure as Briggs told me you stole from him."

Jim buried his face in his hands and groaned.

Pratt was ecstatic, laughing in a high pitched ear-splitting shriek. "I've got you, haven't I? Now I want the truth." He disappeared for a few minutes, returning with a large piece of paper and a uniformed officer to act as a witness.

While he was gone Jim thought about the situation. It looked bleak, but Pratt did not really have any solid proof.

Pratt sat down with a sickly grin on his face and whispered, "Right. Take your time and tell me the truth about the events at Manor Farm."

Jim cleared his throat and spoke clearly. "You haven't got a shred of proof I was involved with the murder or burglary at Manor Farm. You're just trying to con me into a confession."

Pratt leapt to his feet and reached across the table, grabbing Jim's shirt with both hands. "You bastard. I'll string you up myself." The uniformed officer pulled Pratt away and marched him out of the room.

Jim was left shocked at the outburst and wondered again why this man hated him so much. He sat alone for half an hour until an officer led him back downstairs to his cell, where he remained until the next morning.

He had only just managed a piece of toast and cup of tea for breakfast before being led back to the interview room again. This time Pratt was joined by another C. I. D. officer. Jim looked into Pratt's eyes, which were red-rimmed and bloodshot, his face a sick-looking pasty colour. The questioning resumed, with Pratt applying the heavy-handed threats and accusations, whilst the other officer spoke in a soft manner.

Jim said nothing, but just cupped his head in his hands and leant his elbows on the table, the sound of the voices droning on and on setting his fragile nerves on edge. He dearly wanted to get up and escape from the brain-washing, as the longer it went on the weaker he felt, becoming more and more convinced that what they were saying was true. When he closed his eyes for a moment, Pratt thought he was going to sleep and knocked his elbows off the table, making him slump forward. He sat up again and Pratt got very worked up, his face going red as he cursed and swore at his victim. By this time Jim had come to the end of his tether and held his hand up to admit his part in the crime at Manor Farm, just to stop the mental torture continuing.

Chapter Twenty

The newspapers reported that formal charges had been made against Jim Grainger, but then dropped the story in favour of a more sensational scandal involving the government.

Garry searched the papers every day for more news but was disappointed. The news of Jim's incarceration had diverted his attention from destructive thoughts to running Blakesbuild properly, and for days he worked long hours catching up with neglected paperwork, realising how close his obsession with Grainger's downfall had brought the company to financial ruin. Some decisions he had made without proper consideration were potentially disastrous, but as usual he managed to scrape through and talk his way out of the problems. The experience had frightened him, and convinced him to be more careful in the future.

After a week he was feeling more confident about the company's prospects, and wondered in which direction to take the company that specialised in large civil engineering and local authority work. His thoughts turned to house building on a large scale; big developments of high quality up-market houses would be very profitable. Then suddenly he sat bolt upright — Grainger Construction — the company would be up for sale soon and was already in the house building market. Oh what a brilliant idea! I can destroy the name of Grainger Construction at the same time and call it Blakesbuild.

He found Simpson's report in his top drawer and studied its contents again, getting very excited as he read how quickly the company had grown. If it carried on at that pace it would soon be the biggest house builder in the country, he thought. After reading it again, he put the file in his briefcase and walked out, announcing he would be gone for a couple of hours.

The building site was easy to find and, driving carefully through the muddy entrance, he parked outside a recently completed house, looking it over from the driver's seat before driving on to the occupied houses. They looked very attractive and were a good advertisement for any company. He drove as far as possible around the site and noticed several gangs of men working hard on half-completed dwellings. The longer he studied the new development, the more he wanted to own it.

Within half an hour he had seen enough, drove to the site office and strode into the office without knocking. Oliver was sitting at Jim's desk, engrossed in a problem concerning a supplier's invoice. He did not look up until he became aware of a man leaning over the desk staring at his paperwork.

He recognised Garry instantly and growled, "What do you want, Osborne?" Garry was taken by surprise and took a second to realise who was addressing him.

"Good God, it's Smythe! When did they let you out?"

"None of your business. I repeat, what do you want?"

"Huh. So a murderer gets put away and another criminal takes over!"

"State your business or get out."

"Are you running this company?"

"Temporarily, yes."

"Right. You'll no doubt have to sell up now that Grainger's inside again?"

Oliver stood up slowly and spoke clearly. "Jim Grainger hasn't been convicted and I don't think he ever will be. He'll be back here running his company as soon as the truth emerges.

"The truth is he's a murderer and should be strung up."

"Go away, Osborne, and play stockbrokers. Perhaps you'll find someone else's life to destroy, like you did mine."

"You deserved all you got." Garry scowled as he walked out, almost running to his car, and drove off, sliding on the slippery surface. He felt angry and even more desperate to get hold of that company, if only to kick Smythe out and tear down

Drink With The Devil

the Grainger Construction sign, removing that horrible name from the face of the earth.

By the time he had arrived at his office he had calmed down but could not get down to work, as his only thoughts were how to obtain that company. He realised that the direct approach would not work, so an intermediary had to be found. The obvious choice was a solicitor, but not one with divided loyalties like George Vine. He pondered the question for some time, before ringing a local one-man firm.

Robert Webster was keen to work for Garry and started making enquiries straightaway. Garry got down to work again, confident that it would only be a matter of time before Grainger Construction would be up for sale, with Webster making an approach before other prospective buyers could find out and cause the price to increase.

Chapter Twenty-One

Jim was about to speak when Chief Inspector Green walked in. He looked straight at Sergeant Pratt. "Come to my office and bring the file on this case." He turned and walked out, followed by Pratt and his colleague. Jim relaxed, clasping his head between his hands, trying to deaden the ringing sound in his ears.

Half an hour later the chief inspector returned and sat opposite Jim, laying the file in front of him and looking stern. "Well, Jim. I didn't think I'd come back from holiday and find you here again."

"I didn't expect to be here."

"Sergeant Pratt brought me up to date with your case, and in particular the murder of Ken Bridger."

"Why is he trying to pin the Osborne murders on me?"

"Because he thinks you did them. Forget about that for a minute and just tell me slowly your account of the Bridger case."

Jim explained in great detail the events on the night and the next few days, while the chief inspector just listened and made notes. He finished his story and then said, "There's one thing I didn't tell the sergeant. It may not be important."

"What's that?"

"Billy Bradford said a fat man turned up and asked questions a few days before the fire. The same man called at the school site just before I started my own company, and I found I couldn't get supplies. Billy took the car number and I put it in the top drawer of my desk."

"As you say, it may not be important, but worth checking." The inspector sat back and stared at the ceiling for a minute, deep in thought, and then cleared his throat. "Well at the moment your position looks grim. The evidence Pratt has produced could convict you of murder."

"What hope have I got?"

"Very little. However, I'm not entirely happy with all the evidence, and I feel a few more questions need to be asked."

"So you're taking over the case?"

"Yes. Now you must go back downstairs."

"Okay. I need a rest."

"Oh, by the way, I'm sorry about Rosie."

"I still can't believe it. She was like a mother to me."

The next day passed slowly and he thought about the grilling Sergeant Pratt had given him, hoping it would not happen again. Each new sound of footsteps on the concrete floor worried him in case the mental torture was about to start again. Later in the afternoon he had a visitor, who noticed his worried look.

The plain clothes woman officer smiled. "Don't worry, I only want a sample of your hair."

"Help yourself."

She snipped a short piece off the back of his head. "That shouldn't spoil your hair style." Jim smiled for the first time since the fire. "Do you want it for your locket?"

"No, but I might come back for another piece just for me." They both laughed as she walked out.

The next day Jim was summoned to the interview room yet again, dreading what would follow and feeling weak before he even got to the room. He sat down heavily, but his anguish was relieved when the chief inspector came in and sat down. He seemed cheerful.

"Hello, Jim. How are you?"

"Could be better."

"I've been on site checking your story, and had a bit of luck. We found the cudgel used to lay you out. Hair still stuck to the rusty scaffold pipe matched yours."

Jim brightened up considerably. "That's good."

"Yes. Not only that, but we interviewed some of the occupants of the new houses last night. One of the men whom we hadn't talked to before said he saw two men running from the scene."

"Why didn't he say so before?"

"He said he'd been away on business. The other news is that the car registration number belongs to a private investigator called Simpson and he's gone missing in a hurry, leaving half his furniture behind."

"So it looks a lot better for me?"

"Yes. But you're not in the clear yet?"

"No. What about the Osborne murders?"

"Sergeant Pratt is too keen on promotion. He cooked up that story about Briggs, implicating you in an effort to make you confess."

"So I won't be charged with their murders?"

"No. You won't."

Jim heaved a sigh of relief and then frowned as he asked. "What's been done about Rosie's funeral?"

"I understand her son and daughter organised it."

"When?"

"She was cremated two days ago."

Jim returned to his cell relieved that things were looking much better, but sad that he missed Rosie's funeral. He thought about her a lot that night, dreaming she was still at home waiting for him.

The next morning dragged by slowly with Jim waiting for more news. At last it came in the afternoon when the chief inspector visited his cell and broke the good news. "The murder charge has been dropped and you're free to go."

"That's fantastic. Thank you very much." Jim shook his hand enthusiastically and gratefully. The inspector grimaced as his hand felt as though it had been gripped in a vice. Jim relaxed his hold. "Sorry about that."

"Never mind."

"Thank God you came back from holiday when you did."

"Yes. I'm sorry about the treatment you received."

"That's all over now."

Drink With The Devil

"I hope so."

"You don't sound too sure."

"There are still two men out there who want me dead."

"Yes. And I'd like to know why."

"Keep me informed if you spot anyone suspicious. And be very careful."

"I will."

Jim ran up the steps and stood outside the police station, breathing in deeply, looking up at the clear sky and feeling the sun warming his face. He was feeling good, with renewed energy surging through his body, but when a hand tapped him on the shoulder he turned to face Sergeant Pratt.

"You bastard. I'll get you, if it takes me the rest of my life."

He walked off, leaving Jim confused and wondering why the man was so bitter. A police car drew up a minute or two later with an officer beckoning him to get in, and he found himself beside the girl who took his hair sample. She brought him up-to-date with the news as they travelled towards Kingston, dropping him off outside the small terraced house which he entered and stood in the hallway. Suddenly the kitchen door burst open and Jim realised immediately that the small lady facing him, a much younger version of Rosie, was her daughter.

Her expression changed to a scowl at the sight of Jim. "What the bloody 'ell d'you want, you murdering bastard? How can you have the cheek to come back here, after killing my mum and that poor man in the fire?"

Jim was shocked and stood still. When she had let off steam he asked quietly, "How d'you know who I am?"

"The police told me you were on your way here."

"Oh, I see." He thought for a minute while she looked him up and down, and spoke softly again. "Thank you for organising Rosie's funeral."

She went red and spluttered. "You, thank me! She was my mother, what else was I to do? Now pack your things and clear off."

Jim turned and saw letters on the front mat, several addressed to him. He picked them up and went up to his bedroom. The room was strewn with his clothes, the chest of drawers left open and the bed was tipped on its side. He tidied up and then sat down to open his mail. The first letter he opened was from a firm of solicitors and enclosed a copy of Rosie's will, which he read through slowly. He was amazed to find she had left the house and all its contents to him. The memory of her and her kindness filled his eyes with tears, and he sat on his bed racked with grief again, but his thoughts were soon shattered by a shout up the stairs.

"Come on, you murdering pig. Get a move on."

Jim rose and walked slowly downstairs clutching the letter and copy of the will, handing it to the red-faced woman who hissed, "What's this?"

"Your mother's will. You'd better read it."

She read it quickly and then, screaming, threw it to the floor. "That evil old bitch didn't leave me anything."

Jim just watched and listened as the woman went berserk, calling her mother all the names she could think of, and many of which he had not heard before. Then she turned to him, "You murdering bastard, you forced her to write that will." Suddenly she ran at him with small fists lashing at his body. Jim just held both her forearms still as she struggled, walked her backwards into the front room and plonked her down into a chair. She was silenced by his strength and listened to his husky voice.

"You can take anything you want, and then leave."

She looked nervously at him. "I've already taken what I want." Jim looked around the room and noticed a lot of ornaments missing.

"So I see."

"I've taken her clothes and things from the bedroom."

"Good. I'm sure she really would have wanted you to have them." Jim watched the sad-looking woman leave through the back door, and thought how different she was compared to her mother.

Drink With The Devil

Jim spent the rest of the day cleaning up the house and then went to his local pub for a meal, which he ate alone while thinking about his future plans. He liked the old terraced house and decided he would stay for the time being, but was worried about his company and about what had happened in his absence. He went to bed early, slept soundly and late, with no Rosie to wake him up. The house seemed empty and silent as he searched for something to eat. The small kitchen smelt musty and stale, and he was pleased to get out into the fresh air. He had breakfast in a transport cafe on the way to the building site, parking his car in the usual place, and then walking into the office.

Oliver leapt to his feet and strode forward, hand outstretched. "Jim, how very nice to see you."

"Oliver. What are you doing here?"

"Minding the shop whilst you were temporarily absent."

"That's very good of you. So you've managed to keep things going?"

"Yes with Billy's help."

"What did you use for money?"

"I gave the company a temporary loan."

"You've paid the wages from your own pocket?"

"Well I knew you'd be back shortly."

Jim shuddered, realising how close he'd come to letting Oliver down.

Billy joined them and shook hands warmly before expressing his sorrow about Rosie.

"I feel very guilty about telling her you were dead."

"You had to tell her something before she read it in the newspapers."

"That's what I thought. But look what happened."

"You couldn't have known she had a weak heart."

"No I didn't know."

Jim did not know either, but it helped to relieve Billy's guilt. They chatted at length about progress on the site and future plans. Oliver joined in and voiced his opinion.

Jim looked at his old friend and said. "Will you stay a bit longer?"

"Yes. If you want me to. I've enjoyed being involved in business again."

"Good. There are several things I need to do, and the most important is to get fit again. At the moment I feel like a limp rag."

Billy grinned. "There's plenty of hod carrying to do."

"That's what I had in mind. The second thing is to find another site. We could be out of here in six months."

Oliver broke in. "That's true. We're ahead of schedule, but more important the houses are all sold."

"Really? How did we manage that?"

"All the publicity you attracted with stories in the newspapers brought the customers flocking in. They all paid deposits on condition we complete on time."

"Good. So we aren't short of money?"

Oliver grinned. "I am."

"Not for long."

Jim wrote out a cheque paying back the loan with interest, and made an arrangement for Oliver to sign the company cheques in case he was away again. In the afternoon he walked around the site. All the men greeted him with enthusiasm, and he thanked them all for standing by him. He left early to do some shopping and arrange for the milkman to call again.

The next morning he was the first to arrive on site, immediately setting to work hod-carrying, using the standard size first and progressing to his own massive hod three days later. He worked all day on site and stayed in the office until late in the evenings, rushing back to his local pub where he had arranged to have a meal ready every night. After a week of strenuous work his body felt like old times, hard and muscular. After having worked all the next week in late summer sunshine, his face and body had become bronzed and he looked the picture of health.

At the end of the second week he was working on the edge of the site, when a voice from behind a hedge attracted his attention. "Hello mate. I had a body like yours once."

Jim walked across to see an old man looking over the top of the hedge. "Hello. How are you?" He said cheerfully.

"Not too bad, considering me age. When I was your age I used to lift two hundredweight sacks of wheat up the granary steps."

Jim listened and noticed the man's bowed legs as he leaned against a stick and that he was obviously not able to stand up straight. He also noticed his swollen knuckles and wrists, and wondered what he looked like when he was younger. Maybe all that lifting he had mentioned caused his present problems, he thought.

The old man eventually stopped talking, looking slowly around the meadow and then back at Jim. His voice was shaky. "D'you think your boss would be interested in buying this field? I can't manage it anymore and I've got no sons."

Jim looked at the flat grassland, which was situated between his building site and a main road.

"How many acres have you got there?"

"Exactly twenty."

"Well, I think Grainger Construction would be interested."

"Good. I'll come round and see your boss."

"You've been talking to him."

The old man laughed. "Well I'll be darned. Nice to see a modern boss not afraid of manual work."

Jim went to see him at the weekend and agreed terms based on the best agricultural price. The old man knew Jim would try to build houses on the ground and wished him good luck. Oliver started negotiations with the Council and they agreed to keep an open mind, pending an application for planning permission.

One morning Jim rang Chief Inspector Green. "Have you found those two villains yet?"

"No, I'm afraid not."

"What about Simpson?"

"No sign of him either."

"Oh dear. Are you still trying?"

"Yes. I've got Sergeant Pratt on it."

"Have you really? Goodbye."

Jim got Oliver and Billy together. "I'll be taking some time off. Can you carry on?"

Oliver answered. "No problem. It's about time you had some holiday."

Billy knew better. "Jim's not having a holiday. I bet he'll be looking for those villains."

Jim nodded. "I'll have a go. The police have got nowhere, and with Pratt looking they never will. I can't just leave it at that. After all, it's their fault that Rosie died, so I owe it to her to try."

Oliver looked seriously at Jim. "Don't forget these men are very dangerous."

"Yes, they are. But I don't want to be looking over my shoulder for ever, waiting for them to attack."

* * *

Garry emerged from a long meeting with his estimators and surveyors, having agreed prices for contract tenders. He was tired and looking forward to going home for a nice meal, but when the telephone rang in his office, he found himself talking to Webster, the solicitor.

"Hello, Mr. Osborne. Sorry to call so late but I thought you ought to know the latest news about Grainger Construction."

"Oh yes. "What's that?"

"They won't be selling in the foreseeable future."

"Why the hell not?"

"Charges against Grainger were dropped this afternoon."

"What? I don't believe it."

"It's true I can assure you."

"They can't do that. The bastard is guilty."

"They have. And it'll be in the papers tomorrow."

Garry slammed down the receiver in a rage, his whole body shaking with anger. He thumped his desk with clenched fists and cursed out loud.

Drink With The Devil

His anger was so intense it affected his whole body, which trembled uncontrollably; tears welled up in his eyes and the muscles in his throat contracted, making speech impossible. Half an hour passed with him leaning on his desk, his thoughts ranging from how badly he had been cheated to his hatred of Grainger — the very thought or sound of that name caused him convulsions.

Some time later, after lowering his brandy bottle, he picked up the receiver to find Jane sounding a bit angry. "Garry, when are you coming home for dinner?"

"Er, right away dear," he slurred.

"Have you been drinking again?"

"No dear," he lied.

"Yes, you have. I'm coming to get you."

"If you must." He put the telephone down and paced up and down the office, feeling ill but still drinking.

Jane walked in half an hour later, unafraid of him but just angry, and this time she was determined to stand up to him. Her face was set firm as she confronted him.

"Why are you drinking yourself silly again?"

"I'm sorry, dear."

"Sorry. You're bloody pathetic. What's happened this time?"

"Nothing, dearest."

"Nothing. So you're drinking for nothing now, are you? Now you listen to me. Our marriage has been over for some time, but you're supposed to be running my father's company. If you start drinking like you did before, I'll come back and stand over you every day."

Garry sat down heavily, shocked by her forceful speech and cleared his throat, speaking as clearly as he could. "You've made your point. I'll stop drinking and concentrate on work."

"We'll see." She drove him home and placed a warmed-up dinner in front of him, which he picked at for a while and then went to his bedroom.

When she read the paper the next morning, Jane threw it down in front of Garry, who was picking at his breakfast. "So that's what it's all about. Because they've let Grainger out."

He picked up the paper slowly, trying to stay calm, and read the story which made him want to shout out loud, but he managed to restrain himself. Even young William stopped eating his cereal as he watched his father's face.

Jane drove Garry to work and warned him as he got out of the car. "You will remember what I said, won't you? And don't forget one more act of violence towards me and I'll leave you. And take William with me."

Garry stormed off without even glancing at her.

Chapter Twenty-Two

Jim sat in his favourite chair, trying to work out how he would set about finding the two villains who had managed to avoid the police for a long time. It would be difficult if not impossible and his only hope was Simpson, the private investigator, who had suddenly vacated his London flat. Where would he go? He thought about the problem for a while, and then decided the best person to find a private investigator would be another in the same business, but where did one find such a person? Just at that moment the local paper was pushed through the letterbox. He searched the advertisements and in the personal column found N. Powell, and immediately rang the local telephone number.

Simpson answered, "Powell here. Private investigator."

"Hello, Mr. Powell. I've a job for you."

"Oh, yes. And what's that?"

"I want you to find a private investigator for me."

"You're pulling my leg?"

"No, I'm serious. The man I need to find is a private investigator."

"Oh, I see. In that case we'd better meet and discuss the case."

"Right. The sooner the better. How about this morning?"

"Shall we meet for coffee? There's a cafe I know just outside Kingston. I didn't catch your name, Sir."

"Jim Grainger."

"Grainger?"

The telephone went dead. Jim tried the number again but it was engaged, and he sat down puzzled by the man's reaction, and wondering why the phone was put down at the mention of his name. Perhaps he had read about the murder and was frightened in case he would be the next victim? No, surely not. He picked up the telephone directory and found several N. Powells, but none with the same number. He thought for a while, wondering why a man would advertise himself and choose to be ex-directory at the same time, but then perhaps it was a new number. He rang the operator, to be informed it was a new number, and he also managed to obtain the address.

Jim jumped in his pick-up and drove to the other side of town, easily finding the small block of flats, where he ran up the steps and thumped heavily on the door. It was opened slowly and then pushed shut, but Jim had his boot in, shoved it open and walked in. The fat man was picking himself up off the floor, Jim towering over him and silently observing the nervous look he was receiving. Both men were silent for a few seconds and Jim spoke first.

"You're Simpson, aren't you?"

"No, my name is Powell."

"Why did you hang up on me, then?"

"I read about you in the papers and was frightened off."

Jim watched his face and eyes while he spoke. "I don't believe a word of it."

"It's true. Please believe me."

"Show me your driving licence, then."

Simpson's expression dropped even further. "I can't. It's away for a change of address.

Jim was getting angry and grabbed the man by his dirty shirt. "You're a liar. Now tell me the truth."

"So, I'm Simpson. Please don't hurt me."

Jim sat him on a chair and growled. "I want the truth about your involvement in the fire on my building site. And what you were doing on the school site, asking questions about me."

"I can't say anything about the fire. If I did my life would be worthless."

"Your life's pretty worthless now. You had to run away once.

Are you going to do it again? How long before someone catches up with you?"

Simpson looked down at the floor and nearly cried. "They'll kill me."

"If you don't tell me the truth, I'll save them the job."

"No. Please don't."

"Speak up, then."

"No, I can't."

"Right. I'm going to throw you out of this window." In spite of his considerable weight, Jim picked up the man with considerable ease.

Simpson struggled but had no chance, as arms like steel girders carried him towards the window. "I'll talk," he spluttered.

Jim lowered him down, and watched as he mopped his brow and regained a certain amount of composure.

"What d'you want to know?" Simpson croaked.

"Firstly, who killed Bridger and set light to my show house?"

"They'll kill me," Simpson persisted.

"No, they won't."

"It was Charlie Chatfield and his mate."

"Where does he live?"

"Brixton somewhere. Near the big pub in the main street."

"Does he drink in this pub?"

"Yes, regularly."

"What's it called?"

"Can't remember. It may be the Dog and something."

"How were you involved with the murder?"

"I didn't kill him."

"I gathered that."

"You were the intended victim."

"I know. But what part did you play?"

"I supplied information to another party about your movements, and that was all."

"What other party?"

"A man 'phoned and sent me money. I supplied him with the information on the 'phone, so I don't know who it was."

"What about the previous time?"

"Same arrangement."

"You'd better be telling me the truth."

"I am. I swear it."

Jim watched the frightened man shake with fear and felt sorry for him. "I believe you, but don't move on, as I may want to talk to you again."

"I'll have to move or Chatfield'll kill me."

"I won't tell him where you are, so stay put." Pleased to have progressed so well, but sorry to have frightened the pathetic man, Jim pressed a fiver into his podgy hand and left.

The next morning was a dark and foggy one, with not a puff of wind to move the moisture laden air, and Jim drove to Brixton. As he walked along the main street, he felt depressed at the sight of dirty cars and lorries travelling slowly through the murky air, and all the shops, buildings and roads looked filthy.

He found what he thought must be the pub, a grey building with dirty windows, and he walked around the area deciding to have lunch in a cafe opposite. The food was greasy and cold and the tea yellow, so he ate a little and pushed it away. A few customers went through the pub's black front door but not one he recognised. After lunch he drove to Central London where he found a shop selling theatrical costumes. He purchased a false beard, wig and plain glasses and put them on, not recognising himself. He kept the disguise on to visit the Brixton pub that evening.

The barman gave him a strange look and served up a pint of shandy. He sat in a dark corner and observed his surroundings, which was difficult due to the poor light. The only illumination was above the bar, but when his eyes had adjusted he discovered the whole place was filthy. The floor had not been swept for days, the brown ceiling had business and visiting cards stuck to it with pins and the old wooden furniture was stained with liquor.

A group of four men sat huddled together talking in low tones and, as the evening progressed, men arrived mainly in couples and sat together engrossed in each other's company. The pub was filling up with only standing room left, and Jim was puzzled by the customers; all very friendly towards one another with not one woman amongst them. When he looked down at the dirty floor he thought I don't blame them for not wanting to come here.

It was nearly closing time, and when Jim got up to stretch his legs and relieve his aching backside, a small man nudged him. "Hey, big boy. Come home with me."

Jim suddenly realised what sort of pub he was in, pushed the little fellow away and walked out into the thick fog. He stood outside and a man heading for the door bumped into him and apologised.

"Sorry, mate. Didn't see you."

Jim instantly recognised the voice. Sergeant Pratt! He stood aside and let the man into the pub. What's he doing here, Jim thought, nearly following him inside but deciding it would be better to wait until drinking up time in ten minutes, when all of the men would come out. He stood in a shop doorway wondering why Pratt was visiting this pub so late —perhaps he was looking for Chatfield as well. After all, that was what he was supposed to be doing, and he convinced himself that was the explanation.

He carried on watching the pub's front door and, after five minutes, men started leaving, some walking hand in hand. Jim smiled to himself, thinking perhaps they thought no one could see them. Another five minutes went by, the last man left and Jim heard the door being bolted. He walked out of the shadows and, looking up at the pub's first floor windows, he wondered where Pratt had gone. The lights were on but curtains obscured his view, and after a few more minutes the bar lights went out, but still Pratt had not emerged.

Jim wondered if he was in trouble and walked around the side of the pub into total darkness, feeling his way along a brick wall until he came to a wooden door which opened with a creak. He walked down two steps to a back yard, a light in the pub's rear kitchen partly illuminating the area, which was strewn with empty bottle crates, barrels and all kinds of rubbish. He picked his way carefully towards the window and peered through to see the barman was making tea. He placed three cups on a tray and then carried the teapot towards the back door, staring at the dregs as he swirled them around in the bottom. He pushed the door open and threw the tea leaves on to the ground. Jim seized his opportunity, grabbing the man's outstretched arm and pulling him outside. He had no chance to yell, as Jim punched him hard under the chin and he collapsed in the rubbish.

Jim walked in and picked up the tray, easily finding the stairs and walked up quietly making his way towards the sound of classical music. The floorboards creaked loudly outside a door from which the music was coming, and a voice called out. "Come on 'arry. Where 'ave yer bin?"

Jim pushed the door open, walked into a large ornate bedroom and was shocked by the sight of two naked men lying on a bed.

Chatfield shouted. "Who the 'ell's that?"

"Your tea, Sir," said Jim mockingly.

Pratt leapt to his feet and spluttered. "It's that bastard, Grainger. I can recognise his horrible voice." He bellowed and launched himself at Jim, who threw the tea and tray in his face. Pratt screamed as the hot sticky liquid got in his eyes and burnt his face, which he buried in the bedclothes.

Chatfield measured his attack and struck Jim on the shoulder with his heavy fist. As Jim leapt to one side he pulled off his beard, threw down his glasses and crouched ready for his opponent's next assault, which came in the form of a blow to the side of his head. Jim fell on the bed dazed and Chatfield jumped on him, but Jim recovered and wrestled the man to the floor. The two big men grunted and struggled for a minute, but Jim's superior strength overpowered his opponent and Chatfield was pinned down, helpless. Pratt lashed out with his foot, striking Jim's ear, which dazed him and he toppled over, allowing

Drink With The Devil

Chatfield to recover. Jim looked up to find the two naked men staring down at him, and Chatfield grinned as he said, "I'm going to kill you very slowly."

Pratt's high-pitched laugh brought Jim back to reality. His ear ached and the sight of the two men leering at him made him feel sick and frightened at the desperate situation he was in. Chatfield reached out and opened a small drawer in a dressing table. He pulled out a long thin-bladed knife, and as Jim's right hand rested on a loose rug on the floor he pulled it sharply, the two men toppling backwards and allowing Jim to get up.

Chatfield recovered first, the grin having disappeared from his face which was set firm with determination, and he crouched with the knife in his hand, ready to strike. Jim grabbed a pillow and moved slowly forward. Chatfield lashed out at the pillow, causing the feathers to scatter, and Jim threw the pillow with the remaining feathers at him, making him choke and splutter. Jim grabbed his wrist and thrashed it down on the dressing table. The knife fell to the floor and Pratt dived for it but misjudged Jim's boot which landed behind his ear. Jim punched Chatfield hard in the stomach and watched him collapse. Pratt was recovering and managed to stand up before receiving a brain-jarring blow to his chin, and he fell on to the bed unconscious.

Jim helped Chatfield to his feet before landing another heavy punch in the guts and he cried out as his legs buckled. Deciding that Pratt would be no further trouble, Jim stood back and looked at Chatfield lying on the floor clutching his stomach and groaning. Jim stood over him. "I want the truth about Bridger's murder."

"Go to 'ell!" was the muted response.

Jim grabbed the man's arm and twisted it behind his back and then gripped his hand. "Now tell me the truth, or I'll break your hand." No reply. Jim squeezed the big hand until it cracked and Chatfield yelled. Jim relaxed a little and said softly, "The truth, or you'll never use your hand again."

"Okay, I'll tell you."

"Go on, then."

"I was paid to kill you, but Bridger got it instead."

"I know all that. But who paid you?"

"A fat bloke called Simpson."

"Oh yes. And who paid him?"

"I don't know, but I saw his car. A new Jag."

"Simpson says he didn't pay you and I'd rather believe him than you."

"Go to 'ell, you bastard!"

Jim squeezed the hand with all his strength and produced two more sickly cracks. Chatfield yelled again and said, "It's true. Simpson set the deal up."

"I see. What about the Osborne murders?"

"Nothing to do with me."

Jim dropped the broken hand and grabbed the other, applying considerable pressure. Chatfield nearly wept. "No, no, not again."

"The truth, Chatfield."

"I was there with the Briggs' boys. We killed them."

"Okay. I believe you."

Jim kept the pressure on Chatfield's good hand, twisted his arm up his back and forced him to crawl towards the bedside telephone. He rang the police and explained the situation, and then allowed Chatfield to lay face down on the bed beside Pratt, who was recovering and groaning. The two men lay close together, Pratt turning his head towards Chatfield and whimpering, "We're finished."

Chatfield's squeaky voice replied. "Yes, I'm sorry." They lay still studying each other's faces and Pratt with tears in his eyes. Jim looked away not wishing to intrude on their silent communication.

They were still in this position when the police entered led by Chief Inspector Green, who looked at the naked pair and then at Jim. He grinned. "Friendly, aren't they?"

"You could say that."

The two men dressed in silence, Chatfield having difficulty, and the Chief allowed Pratt to help. Then he looked closely at

Drink With The Devil

Chatfield's hand and remarked to Jim. "Must've got caught in the door. Shame!"

"Yes. Nasty injury, that."

"And of course the other hand could get caught if we don't get the truth."

"Very true."

The two frightened-looking men sat on the bed and made statements, Chatfield admitting he killed Bridger and naming his accomplice. He also admitted his part in the Osborne murders and robbery, while Pratt admitted shielding his lover from prosecution. Uniformed officers took the two men away and the chief inspector shook Jim's hand.

"Thanks for finding him. I didn't suspect Pratt."

"The pleasure's all mine."

"Now I must pick up Simpson. I take it you found him?"

"Yes I did, but I need to talk to him before you lock him up."

"I'll give you an hour's start. Where does he live?"

Jim gave him the address and directions, which the Chief noted and then said, "I suppose you want to find out who paid to have you killed?"

"Exactly. But I'm not sure Simpson knows who supplied the money."

"He may not. Now Jim, I don't want to find Simpson with a crushed hand when I get there. It wouldn't look good if all the suspects appear in the dock with their hands in plaster."

"Not necessary with Simpson. He's already scared stiff." He walked downstairs to find the barman sitting in the kitchen nursing a sore chin. He left and ran along the murky street to his pick-up.

The journey to Kingston was slow and demanded intense concentration through the dense fog, but at last he arrived outside the block of flats and ran up the stairs. He thumped on the door and listened, but not a sound came from inside. He thumped even harder, rattling the fittings, but still no one came so he shouldered the door open, breaking the lock. He looked around the living room, then marched through into the bedroom and turned on the light to find Simpson curled up in bed with a pillow over his head. Jim looked at the body under the bedclothes, trembling with fear, grabbed the pillow and pulled it away.

Simpson's eyes were tightly closed as he whimpered "Please don't kill me. I didn't tell him."

"I won't kill you unless you tell me lies like the last time."

Simpson's eyes opened slowly and he spoke with a shaky voice. "It's you again. I thought it was Chatfield come to kill me."

"He's safely locked up."

"Oh good." His relief was visible as he sat and looked sternly at Jim. He spoke in a clearer voice. "Did you find him?"

"Yes and I got the truth out of him."

"How did you do that?"

"Painfully."

Simpson winced. "What d'you want to know?"

"The truth about who paid to have me killed."

"I told you. I don't know."

"Chatfield told me you were paid by a man driving a new Jag. Now tell me the truth or you'll have your foot broken." Jim fished under the bedclothes and gripped the man's right foot hard.

Simpson cried out in pain. "His name is Garry Osborne."

"How much did he pay?"

"Five thousand in cash."

Jim released him and sat still thinking, as Simpson rubbed his foot. Then he broke the silence. "The police'll be here in a minute. Chatfield named you in his statement."

Simpson groaned and stopped rubbing his foot. "Oh, my God," he whimpered.

"What did you expect?"

"I don't know."

"Now listen to me. You will not, under any circumstances,

name Osborne as the paymaster. Tell them you didn't meet and have no idea who he is."

"But why not, for Christ's sake?"

"I have my reasons."

"I'd like to keep it secret myself. You never know when that information will come in useful in the future."

"I agree. Now get dressed."

The Chief Inspector arrived soon after with his men and took Simpson's statement. He looked at Jim who was sitting in one of Simpson's armchairs. "So you didn't find out who the person is, then?"

"No. He must have been very careful."

"Yes. And it means you'll still have to be very vigilant."

"I suppose so."

Simpson seemed almost relieved to be escorted away. The Chief watched him leave and remarked. "I see Simpson has a limp."

"Foot and mouth disease, I expect."

"I gather it also affects hands?"

"So I believe."

"Be careful, Jim."

"I will."

He drove home and parked as a glimmer of light began to filter through the fog. It was dawn and he was shattered. He washed, had a cup of tea and fell into bed thinking about the previous night's events. He hoped Simpson would get off lightly and Chatfield a full life sentence, where he could do no more harm.

His feelings about Chatfield were reinforced as he walked downstairs to an empty kitchen, where Rosie would have been cooking a superb meal if she were alive, and they would have chatted happily over a cup of coffee. He left the furniture and fittings exactly as Rosie liked them, with her favourite armchair still remaining in the best place by the fire. He spent the rest of the day doing odd jobs around the house, as he thought about his future and why Osborne would want him dead.

Monday morning was bright and clear, with a few clouds moving slowly across the blue sky. Jim rang Osbornes, but was informed that Garry was at Blakesbuild. He thought about ringing there, but decided to go and visit him straightaway. He parked his filthy pick-up in the visitors car park and marched into the office. The receptionist looked him up and down, gazing at his large boots and working clothes.

"What can I do for you?"

"I've come to see Mr. Garry Osborne."

"Have you got an appointment?"

"No, but he'll see me."

"We'll see. What name is it, please?"

"Grainger. Jim Grainger."

She rang through to Garry, and when Jim moved closer he heard the reply as she quickly moved the receiver away from her ear. It must have been painful as he shouted down the telephone at her. " I don't see murderers. Tell him to get off my premises or I'll call the police."

Chapter Twenty-Three

He had two slices of toast whilst she read on, and then she put the paper in front of him. "I don't know why you're so upset, you ought to be delighted. They have at last caught your parents' real killers."

Garry just grunted and sipped his tea.

She looked at his thin face, wondering how long his body would put up with so much abuse and spoke softly. "You'll have to look after yourself a lot better or you won't make old bones."

He just nodded weakly and stared at the paper.

Jane continued, "Now you can stop blaming Grainger for killing your mother and father."

The mention of that name made beads of sweat appear on his forehead, which he mopped with a handkerchief, and after another cup of tea he left for work without saying a word. His day dragged by slowly as he tried to concentrate and get involved with business, but his mind kept wandering. The next day was not much better until late afternoon, when he was trying to think of a different method of beating Grainger. He decided his own great strength was as a businessman, so why not go into house building on a grand scale and beat Grainger Construction at its own game.

That evening, after eating his first square meal for days, he put the idea to Jane, who eyed him suspiciously. "Why houses now and not before?" she asked.

"Because the market is expanding faster than our usual civil engineering projects."

"I see. Are you sure it's not for some other reason?"

"The only other reason I can think of is profit. The potential is far greater."

"Fair enough, but do a proper study first."

"I intend to."

"Perhaps a new challenge will take your mind off other things."

The next few days went quickly for Garry as he was fired with a new enthusiasm. He studied the house market until late each night, getting excited about the new venture.

* * *

Jane went to the farm at the weekend, leaving Garry working at home. Having taken over Garry's position agreeing capital expenditure, she spent all day looking at the animals and travelling around with Peter French, who appreciated her intereste in the activities and crops. In the evening she stayed with Angela at Home Farm. Young William enjoyed his days on the farm and took particular interest in the calves, especially at feeding time when he helped mix the calf milk, a powder and warm water mixture stirred with a wire whisk. He preferred to use his hands and invariably got plastered.

Angela looked forward to the weekends as it broke the monotony of the usual daily routine which was becoming very tiring, with only a short time before the birth of her child. Jane had never mentioned Jim Grainger, knowing about the past and worried as to how her sister-in-law would react. Angela was relaxing after the evening meal and remarked casually: "Did you see what it said about Manor Farm in the papers the other day?"

"Yes. What a good thing they've caught them at last."

"I agree. And perhaps Jim Grainger won't get blamed any more. He was very badly treated over that murder at his building site."

"Yes. Just because he had a record, Garry was convinced he was guilty of all the murders."

Angela felt angry and tears came to her eyes. When Jane saw her face, she changed the subject quickly.

Drink With The Devil

***

A month after Jim's visit to his office, Garry had purchased his first residential building land. He had appointed a marketing company to project his company's new image as a high quality house builder, and all the staff at Blakesbuild were pleased they were heading in a new direction and expanding. Garry kept his mind fully occupied with this new venture and managed to eat proper meals again, although he still drank several brandies a day. Jane became involved with the company's affairs again, and was particularly interested in the design of the new houses. Their home life was friendly although not intimate, occupying separate rooms and never visiting each other's, but their social life improved with the couple always appearing to be happy.

Garry and Jane were godparents to Angela's baby girl at a grand christening ceremony followed by a large party at Home Farm. They were determined to make up for the rather dull wedding reception and everyone had a good time. Garry tried to stop himself drinking too much and succeeded for a while, but eventually the temptation was too great. He found a bottle of whisky which he had hidden behind a chair, so that he could top up his glass when Jane was not looking. For the first time in his life the drink did not make him aggressive but had the affect of making him merry and randy. He kissed Jane every time she came near and hugged the other ladies — in fact it was the most enjoyable evening he had ever experienced, and he was sad when it was over.

***

Six months after buying his first site Garry held a party to celebrate the opening of his new show house, which was reported in the local newspapers. Customers and sightseers flocked to view the new up-market properties. A temporary sales office was built and buyers were keen to pay deposits to secure the best positions on the site. Garry was overjoyed and looking forward to counting the profits.

After the initial flurry of activity the building programme slowed down due to very wet weather, and as time passed, the buyers started getting angry, with some demanding their money back. Garry became very worried and chased the building workers hard. He visited each of the buyers to assure them progress would improve, which just stopped them from pulling out, but when the weather did get better the project was completed three months late. The costs were much higher than anticipated, and left the company in a break-even situation.

Jane demanded to see the costings and when she discussed their future strategy with her husband, she spoke with a new air of authority. "These figures are not good enough."

"I agree, but it was our first try at houses."

"We'd have been better off with a new school or factory."

"Yes we would. But the experience will be useful for the future."

"So you want to carry on building houses?"

"Yes of course I do. Our next site is ready to start."

Jane gave him a suspicious look. "You only want to build houses to beat Grainger, don't you?"

Garry shuddered at the mention of his name and shouted, "Don't bring that bastard into it. He has nothing to do with our plans."

"No need to go mad. If you think we can improve our profit with the next project, I agree to go ahead."

From that day on Garry spent half his time in the office and the other half looking for the best sites in the south east, negotiating options to purchase while Jane did most of his paperwork. All the time his major ambition was to squeeze Grainger out of the property business. After six months, he had a string of large sites waiting to be developed. His bankers were impressed by his progress and professional approach, and were prepared to advance large amounts of money for expansion.

Drink With The Devil

* * *

After Jim drove away from the Blakesbuild offices, he made up his mind to concentrate all his efforts on his construction company, and went back to his old habit of working sixteen hours a day. Oliver agreed to stay permanently and became the financial director, his expertise at negotiating financial packages with bankers a major asset, which enabled the company to expand at a tremendous rate. Planning permission was soon obtained for the field Jim bought at an agricultural price and, when the development was finished, showed a huge profit.

Although Jim had became very wealthy, he had no time to spend the money and still lived in the little terraced house. The only luxury he allowed himself was a new Jaguar, which he enjoyed driving when looking for new sites. This was becoming a major problem and threatened to halt his expansion. The answer was to go further afield, a policy which worked for a while but added to his costs and lowered profits.

Oliver soon grew tired of working in a wooden site building and put forward the case for a permanent headquarters. Jim agreed reluctantly. Fearing rising costs, he found a run down industrial site in a town central to the area where he wanted to operate. The old disused factory had an office block at the front and a large warehouse at the rear, which fitted in well with his plans, and he set to work renovating the offices. The warehouse was converted to a joinery workshop and stores, enabling timber and other supplies to be purchased at favourable bulk rates.

Jim was pleased to move into his own large office where he could work in peace, but the problem of building sites was worrying. He wondered why most of the best sites were snapped up before he could find them. Research revealed it was Blakesbuild causing the problem, convincing the owners to sign an "option to purchase" agreement. Jim added up all the sites he had lost and found they were in Kent, Sussex and Surrey, but far too many for one company even as large as Blakesbuild to develop.

He wondered what would happen when the time period ran out and they had to buy or pay a penalty, depending on the agreement, and he was still pondering this subject as he looked at a development site only ten miles away in an expanding village. He had just managed to secure the deal, when a man bumped into him as he was leaving the offices of an estate agent. The man staggered backwards and Jim grinned when he saw who it was. "Hello, Osborne. You're too late this time," he said cheerfully.

"Grainger! What the hell are you doing here?"

"I've just bought the site you're after."

"So I'm too late this time."

"Yes. What d'you want another site for? You've too many to develop now."

"I can always sell them."

"That's fine until the price drops."

"It won't."

"Well, if you get stuck with sites you don't want, ring me."

"Ring you! That's the last thing I'll do."

"I see. So it's as I suspected. You're just tying up these deals to shut me out."

"Rubbish. My firm could eat yours for breakfast."

"We'll see."

Jim walked off feeling angry that Osborne still hated him, despite being saved from a murder charge. He thought about his next move and considered telling the police he had just discovered who tried to have him killed, but the reason he did not tell them in the first place was still valid so he dropped the idea, deciding to fight back in a different way. He devoted all his efforts to finding building sites, staying in Hampshire for weeks at a time. This strategy paid off because it resulted in securing enough sites to continue the expansion.

Work occupied Jim's mind day and night. Weekends were the same, as living on his own made matters worse, with no conversation to divert his attention to leisure activities. This situation continued until one day when he was in town visiting

Drink With The Devil

the bank. Having arrived too early for an appointment, he sat in a spacious waiting room area watching the customers coming in, when a girl with a pushchair caught his eye.

She looked familiar. When he realised it was Angela his heart missed a beat and he wanted to get up and hug her, but stopped himself because she was obviously happily married with a child. He watched her every movement as she floated gracefully towards the counter, her hair still as beautiful as he remembered it but longer and reaching her shoulders. She turned, clutching a handbag and putting papers inside. Having closed the bag, she looked around the bank's interior, giving Jim a fleeting glance before returning to the pushchair. He was disappointed that she did not recognise him, but then it occurred to him he had a beard and long hair the last time she saw him. Glancing at the child in the chair he noticed she had dark curly hair just like her mother's, and he wanted to go and talk to them both, but his thoughts were interrupted by a voice beside him.

"Mr. Grainger. The manager is free now."

The following Sunday Jim went out into the country instead of driving to his office, and parked in a field entrance opposite a familiar footpath. He walked for half an hour through fields where he had once walked years ago and which were grass then, but had since been ploughed and sown with wheat.

The path went close to Home Farm house, with only a small grass field and a hedge between, and he studied the house through a gap. It had obviously been restored and he admired it. He noticed hay and straw in the barn but no animals and, when a person came from behind the house and walked into the small field, he was surprised and delighted when he saw it was Angela. She called out a name and stared across the field away from where he stood. A thundering of hooves and a shrill whinny reached his ears before Gemma came into view. As he watched Angela give the horse a titbit from her pocket, fond memories came flooding back, bringing tears to his eyes and a lump to his throat. How he wished he could turn the clock back; now he could only watch and wonder what life would have been like married to her. His thoughts were interrupted by the appearance of a man who walked up to the horse and patted its neck, but Gemma turned away and looked across the field to where Jim was standing concealed behind a hedge.

A breeze rustled the leaves in the hedge, sending Jim's scent across to the horse, and she pricked up her ears, whinnied and trotted away from Angela. Jim saw her coming straight at him and hid behind a thick blackthorn bush, while Gemma stood on the other side whinnying and stamping her feet. He walked quickly along the footpath in case Angela investigated the cause of her horse's interest, but Gemma followed on the other side of the hedge for about one hundred and fifty yards. When a gap in the hedge came into view, Jim stopped as Gemma turned and thrust her head through, and both animal and man stared at each other for a second. Then Gemma whinnied softly as he approached, hugged her big warm head and rubbed behind her ears. She nuzzled up to his face and pressed her soft muzzle into his cheeks, blowing out hot breath. The smell and feel of the affectionate horse made him want to cry out with delight, but instead he talked softly telling her how beautiful she was. He thought she seemed to understand and whinnied in reply, and he stroked her gently, talking for about ten minutes until a voice from behind the hedge called out.

"Gemma, what are you doing?"

It was Angela's voice. Jim wanted to stay and talk but feared she might feel upset at seeing him and be reminded of the painful past. Anyway he was still convinced she would not want to speak to an ex-con, so he moved away quickly and quietly rather than be hurt by a rebuff. He ran down the footpath which skirted around the next field, and heard Gemma whinny loudly as Angela tried to see through the thick bushes. She could only see the outline of a big man moving quickly away, and spent the next ten minutes trying to get Gemma to reverse out of the gap. When she finally walked backwards Angela spoke as she held her head collar. "I haven't seen you like that for years. It was him, wasn't it?" The horse blinked a sad-looking eye which had been scratched by a twig in the hedge, and Angela rubbed her eyelid and led her away.

Angela ached to see Jim again but feared he did not want to see her, and if he did not want to meet her it would be better to try and forget him again. She sighed and felt sick inside, realising how close she had been to talking to him.

Mark saw his wife's sad expression as she passed. "What's the matter, dear?"

"I'm fine, but Gemma's hurt her eye."

Jim carried on walking and thinking about Angela, delighted to have seen her again, but it only made him want her even more. He made his way to his car via a different route.

Every Sunday he found a different footpath through the country, but none near Home Farm, as he wanted to enjoy the countryside without tearing himself apart seeing Angela. Each peaceful walk made him realise how much he missed the open air, the trees, the different landscapes and the animals.

Oliver came into Jim's office with a package in his hand. "Look at this, Jim. We've been invited to tender for a big factory on the south coast of Sussex."

"It's not really our sort of job."

"No, but it's worth looking at."

"Just leave it with me." He studied the plans and specification very carefully for most of the day, and then rang the surveyor in charge to arrange a meeting on site. He said he had another meeting the same afternoon, so Jim rang his secretary to find out who it was he was meeting.

The meeting did not take long, as the site was a flat field which had wheat grown on it the previous year, and he spent all morning looking at the soil. He got down into a ditch and dug up soil from the bottom with a spade. The site was big and he walked all around it, examining the type of grasses growing in patches. He saw a tractor ploughing in the next field, so he jumped over the fence and talked to the driver for some time.

After that he walked up and down the centre of the field staring at the ground, staying until the afternoon when the surveyor returned to meet the next contractor. Jim watched the two men walk around the site chatting and, when the surveyor had driven off, he walked from his hiding place behind a tree and just caught up with the contractor before he drove away. He spoke first. "Hello, Osborne. Nice site, isn't it?"

"Grainger! Don't tell me you're tendering?"

"Of course I am."

"But it isn't your sort of business."

"It is now. And what's more I'm going all out to get it."

"Stick to houses or you'll get your fingers burnt."

"I can't resist this job. After all it's a perfect flat site, good roads and services nearby."

"You don't stand a chance."

"Why not? You muscled in on my business, so I'm going in for big civil engineering jobs. This is just the first."

Garry's normally pale face was beginning to colour as he sneered:

"Your tin pot little outfit will go down the drain on a job like this. And I'll be pleased to fish out what's left, and do the job properly."

Jim grinned and walked away.

Drink With The Devil

Chapter Twenty-Four

A meeting was convened at Blakesbuild in Garry's office. The estimators and surveyors were requested to arrive at ten o'clock to allow Jane time to attend, and they all sat around nervously, wondering what to expect. Garry sat at the head of the table with Jane to his right, and after clearing his throat he began to speak. "I've asked you to attend this special meeting to inform you that we have been asked to tender for a major new factory on the Sussex coast. This is a very important contract because it's the first stage of a large industrial development involving new roads, and could lead to more contracts in the future."

All the people around the table were studying his face, their pens poised to write notes on the pads in front of them. He continued, "The only problem I can see with this contract is the limited amount of time allowed for estimating, and the large penalty clauses written in for late completion. The company we'll be working for is a large multinational chemical manufacturer, who will be very strict when applying the contract terms." He paused and then asked, "Are there any questions?"

Claude Gill said. "I assume the machinery to be installed in the factory will be very heavy?"

"Yes. And the lorries delivering materials."

"So it'll be important to carry out soil tests all over the site?"

"Yes. Provided they can be carried out quickly."

Another person asked. "What's the site like, Mr. Osborne?"

Garry smiled and rubbed his hands together. "Perfect. It's a flat site with good load bearing gravel-type soil."

Jane was the next to speak. "How long have we got before the deadline?"

"Only two weeks."

"Why didn't they send the details before?"

Garry shrugged his shoulders. "No idea, but I expect they want to start production as soon as possible."

Jane frowned and stared at her blank note pad.

They all paused for thought and it was Claude Gill who broke the silence. "Who are we up against this time?"

"I'm not sure yet. But you can be certain all the major civil engineering companies'll be going for it."

Jane looked up from her study of the writing pad. "Did our competitors get the details before us?"

"No. I was assured by the surveyor that we were all informed at the same time."

"So they'll all struggle to tender on time as well?"

"Yes. That's right."

"And if they're already busy like us, they won't tender at all."

Garry hadn't expected her to make this point and desperately tried to think of an argument for going ahead. "B-But that would be very short sighted, bearing in mind the work this could lead to when the site is enlarged in the future. It'll attract other manufacturers who'll want to build, and we'll be well placed to carry out their contracts."

"I suppose so." She replied gloomily.

Garry sprang to his feet hoping to stop any further argument, and looking sternly at his staff he raised his voice. "I want maximum effort on this one. Copies of the plans and contract will be on your desks in an hour's time. When you get them, drop everything else and get on with it. I want results quickly."

They took this statement as a dismissal and filed out of the room in silence. Jane watched the door close and spoke sharply. "I don't agree with blundering ahead without giving ourselves time to do all the checking and other work properly."

Garry knew how to win her over and said softly. "What would your father have done? Turned it down?"

She stopped frowning and thought for a few seconds. "He would have worked non stop until he knew the answers."

Drink With The Devil

"But he wouldn't have turned it down, would he?" Garry persisted.

"No, I suppose not."

"Well I'm prepared to work hard until I have all the answers."

"Very well. As usual, you know best."

Jane left him studying the thick pile of papers that formed the contract and he went on working until late every night, with food brought in so he could keep going.

The other members of the team worked long hours on complicated plans and detailed specifications. Garry stopped himself drinking until half an hour before going home, when he would make up for the rest of the day's abstinence.

His thoughts at this time usually turned to Jim Grainger, when he pictured him sitting in a grubby office trying to understand the details of the contract. He could visualise him getting more confused by the legal jargon, and each time he had his late night drink he became more convinced that a man with no education or experience would either tender too low and bankrupt his firm, or tender too high and lose the contract. Even if by some stroke of luck he got it right he would not have the expertise to complete on time, so would get suffer heavily due to penalty clauses. These comforting thoughts made him cheerful and good-humoured even when he was tired.

With only one day to spare, Garry called a meeting to finalise the price. All the participating parties sat around the table, some looking tired and drawn. The chief surveyor, Claude Gill, looked particularly worried. Garry opened the meeting with Jane at his side, as usual. "I would like to thank you all for the effort you have put in on this contract." The meeting continued for some long time whilst they discussed every detail

Garry questioned Claude about the results of soil tests and he replied nervously, "We've taken samples at four positions and found them satisfactory."

"Good. So we should be okay?" said Garry.

"Yes, in those positions."

He pointed out where the samples had been taken and then

went on. "We ought to take another five samples before we can be certain."

"No time for that, Claude. We'll have to assume the conditions'll be the same throughout the site."

"Yes we could, but it's a risk."

Jane looked up from writing notes and spoke to Claude. "What did you find in those samples?"

"Mainly gravel-type soil. All the samples were the same."

Garry cut in. "So there's no need to worry about more samples, is there?"

There was no reply so he proceeded to the next item. Discussions went on until late in the evening when they agreed a tender price to be delivered by hand the next day.

Jane went home, leaving Garry alone in his office looking through the papers again, and at the item he had deliberately not brought up for discussion — late completion penalty clauses. The cost of not completing on time was frightening, and it made cold sweat appear on his brow when he considered how much it would cost for each week overdue. Jane was too preoccupied at the meeting with the lack of soil tests; it had diverted her attention from this really worrying aspect of the contract. He was pleased she had not mentioned this particular subject.

The tender was delivered an hour before the expiry time, and Garry turned his attention to the house building side of the business. Some of the first deals he had struck agreeing to purchase building land were running out, so he would have to buy the land or let it go to the open market. He thought carefully about it, noting where the land was situated and its proximity to Grainger Construction's head office. There were four large sites all nearby and, as the bank had agreed to finance the purchase some time ago, he decided to go ahead with the purchase of all four sites.

Two weeks after the tender was delivered, a letter advising that Blakesbuild's price was acceptable arrived, and an early meeting was requested to finalise the details. Garry was overjoyed, hugging Jane until she squealed, and went on to spend the day in a state of self-congratulatory euphoria. Jane was much more subdued, remembering her father's words about large contracts with dynamic private companies.

He always used to say your troubles start when you sign the contract and do not finish until the final payment, and then you still have to watch out.

Garry went to the formal acceptance meeting and met the chief architect, Jim Davenport, a small man with piercing eyes and a hooked nose. The American company president looked on as details were discussed, Garry eventually being introduced to the big bull-necked tall man with white hair. Eugene Spence gave Garry an icy stare and growled: "Make sure you complete on time or it will cost both of us."

"We always complete on time, Mr. Spence."

"Yeah, I bet you do." He waddled away, leaving Davenport to complete the proceedings.

Just before the meeting terminated Garry asked Davenport. "Why did you choose Blakesbuild?"

"You submitted the lowest tender and we were impressed by your experience with this type of project."

"I see. Were the others much higher?"

"Some were and some couldn't agree with our conditions."

"What about Grainger Construction?"

Davenport stroked his large nose and thought for a moment before replying. "Oh, I remember. They returned all the documents and plans almost by return of post, explaining they were too heavily committed with existing contracts to be considered."

Garry's face dropped. "So they didn't even bother to tender?"

"No. And even if they had they would have had to be much cheaper to be accepted, due to their lack of experience."

Garry left the meeting with mixed feelings, pleased to have landed such a large contract but annoyed that his efforts at beating Grainger were a waste of time. He remembered Jim saying he was going all out for the job and wondered why. Was it just a ruse to make me tender too low in the hope I would get my fingers burnt? He pondered the subject on his way back to the office, but soon convinced himself Grainger had sent it back because he was too stupid to understand the details of the contract. He should have studied it when it arrived and saved himself a trip to the site.

Garry handed the contract over to Claude Gill with instructions to run it himself and stay on site. Claude protested. "I need to be here in the office with a manager on site."

"I don't want you here getting involved with other contracts. You must work on site with a foreman and concentrate on that job alone."

Claude sighed in resignation, knowing it was no good arguing. He spent the next few days setting up a site office and organising essential services, and within a week the site offices were standing on the edge of the site with a view across the empty flat field. He got more depressed about the job every time he looked out of his window; he was used to being certain about ground conditions before starting, and had a nasty feeling his boss was going to be on his back every day checking progress.

Garry felt happy leaving the job in Claude's hands, knowing how he would worry about details and timing, and it allowed him to concentrate on the house building programme. They had several sites half completed with houses selling quite well, and his only worry was the amount of money tied up in sites and half completed homes.

Another site with an option to purchase needed a decision on whether to buy or not; it was a large expensive site in Surrey and would take all the company's remaining credit with the bank. He gave the matter considerable thought; on the one hand he did not need it and could not build on it for at least two years, but on the other hand Grainger had opted out of the factory job so would need an ever increasing supply of building land, and would probably snap the site up, being so near his headquarters. He decided to buy it without telling Jane, and the feeling of owning so much prime building land made him feel good.

Jane noticed his good mood and wondered if she could love him again. He seemed to have changed so much lately. He had not been violent for a long time, his drinking seemed to be under control and he was reasonably kind to her as well as civil to the staff. Their life at home was improving and he was taking more interest in William, even sitting him on his knee once although the little chap was nervous, obviously wondering if his dad was all right. She wanted another baby but still could not face sleeping with Garry, and comforted herself with the thought that his continuing improvement in behaviour might result in them enjoying a full married life together. He only had to be kind, gentle and stay off the drink and she felt sure they would be able to share the same bedroom again. She realised how badly she wanted to be loved and did her best to be nice to him, awaiting a favourable response. He noticed how hard she was trying, but worries about money made him edgy and he still resorted to the bottle every night.

Two months after starting work on the factory site Garry visited Claude, and they walked around looking at the various stages of construction. The new roads were built with temporary surfaces and work was about to commence on the main structure. The site had been levelled and there were level markers sticking up everywhere, looking as if they were growing.

Garry came away from the site feeling good they were ahead of schedule; the first progress payment was in the bank and the second was due shortly. He went home early and told Jane the good news. She gave him a kiss on the forehead. "I should have trusted your judgement about that contract. You were right, as usual."

"Ah. But you were right to question the haste in arriving at a decision." He sat down in the lounge and read the paper, turning over the pages until a half-page bold advertisement nearly jumped out of the page at him. 'Grainger Construction Quality Homes.' A picture of a beautiful house was featured and followed by a list of sites where it could be purchased. Garry read the very professional advertisement before screwing the paper up and throwing it across the room, his stomach twisted with hatred as he walked towards his study and headed straight for the drinks cabinet. The first full glass joined the wine in his stomach and started familiar visions of doom followed by revenge, becoming more real as more brandy trickled down his throat.

Jane walked into the lounge wearing a pretty dress which flattered her trim figure, and soon discovered the reason for her husband's sudden disappearance. She flattened the paper out and saw the crumpled advert, cursing herself for missing it, and wishing she had removed the offending page as she had previously. She sat down and wept as she realised her hopes for a reconciliation were dashed by his stupid obsession. Her misery turned into anger, and she marched into his study, finding him about to pour another drink. "It'll do you no good to start drinking with the devil again." He just shrugged his shoulders as she walked out.

The next morning he slumped into a chair and ate a light breakfast. Jane looked at his gaunt face and said: "You must stop getting twisted up or it'll kill you."

He looked up at her sadly. "Yes, you're right."

"Well, do something about it."

"What can I do?"

"There are people who could help."

"I'm not going to a shrink."

Jane just shook her head and whispered, "It's up to you of course."

Garry went to work feeling weak and cursing himself for being so stupid, vowing to make a real effort to stop himself thinking about that man. He got down to work and was feeling better by the time coffee arrived. Then the telephone rang.

Claude Gill sounded upset. "Mr. Osborne, we're in trouble."

"What trouble?"

"Running sand."

"I'll come straightaway." He drove fast, consoling himself that Claude was probably panicking over nothing. They walked together to where a huge hole had been dug for a large steel stanchion, which would form an upright for the main frame of the building. The man in charge of the steelwork team stood there, looking grim, as they all peered down the hole. It was only six feet deep, but the bottom looked as though a small stream was running through it.

The steelwork man said loudly. "That's not only running sand, it's a bloody river. We were assured this site was properly surveyed."

"It was," growled Garry.

"Oh yeah. It looks like it, don't it?"

Garry turned to Claude. "Come back to the site office."

They turned and started walking and the steelwork man shouted after them: "What am I supposed to do now?"

They ignored him and walked in silence but once inside Garry said. "What's the answer, Claude?"

"We'll have to dig just far enough away to pump the water. Then we'll have to dig the main hole until we get down to load bearing ground, and fill it up to stanchion base level with concrete."

"Right. Get on with it then."

"Mr. Osborne, I don't think you realise the gravity of the situation."

"What d'you mean?"

"Once we start digging the main hole again, the sides will fall in and we'll end up with a huge hole and no guarantee we'll hit hard ground. The only real answer is a pile driver."

"Don't be silly, Claude. That'll add weeks to the contract and cost a fortune."

"You're right. We'll have to try pumping and digging first."

"Get cracking then!"

Claude walked off to give instructions to the digger driver, and Garry watched as the machine moved to a new position, his brow deeply furrowed and cold sweat trickling down his nose. He mopped his brow and paced up and down the office worrying about the problem, staying on site all day and watching the digger produce another hole deeper than the first and in the direction from which the water was flowing. A large pump was set up and started work, a crowd gathering around the main hole, all smiling as the water stopped flowing, due to the pump keeping up with the underground stream.

Garry heaved a sigh of relief and then shouted to Claude. "Get that digger working in the main hole."

The bucket was lowered and sank easily in the wet sand, but as it was lifted out, a large section of the hole's side caved in, and the digger slid slowly downwards. The driver's face was a picture of horror as he was pitched forward at a gathering pace. The machine eventually came to rest at the bottom and he managed to scramble free before the other side fell in, half burying the digger.

Garry watched in disbelief, his stomach turning over and his knees beginning to tremble. He shouted to Claude who was standing motionless like a stone-faced statue. "Get heavy lifting equipment straightaway."

Claude shook himself out of a trance and ran towards the office to arrange for a mobile crane to arrive that afternoon to lift out the digger. It was quickly cleaned off and the still shocked driver sent to dig another hole for the next stanchion, which again revealed running sand but not so much water.

Garry went home late and drank heavily, not uttering a word to Jane, and slept in his study chair in a drunken stupor. He returned to the site in the morning and was greeted by Jim Davenport, who had been tipped off by one of the steelworkers and arrived early to investigate the problem. He met Garry who was striding towards the sandy holes and said sharply, "What are you going to do about this, Mr. Osborne?"

His sharp tone annoyed Garry who snapped back. "This is why you rushed the tenders through. Just to trick us into missing this problem."

Davenport's small beady eyes blazed as he replied, "You

Drink With The Devil

were recommended to take soil tests, and if you didn't you must take the blame."

"We didn't have time for Christ's sake."

"Then you should have asked for more time, like the others."

"It was sharp practice."

Davenport moved closer and growled. "Don't blame me because you were incompetent. Now I'll tell you what you're going to do about this problem, which'll be tackled entirely at your expense. Remember this is a fixed price contract."

Claude joined them in the site office and took notes as Davenport gave detailed instructions. Garry was almost speechless as he added up the likely cost of the additional work, but all he could do was to stutter his agreement to the proposals. As Davenport rose to leave Garry asked timidly, "Can I request an extension to the contract?"

"No, Mr. Osborne, you can't. This project'll be carried out strictly according to the terms of the contract. If the completion is late, you start to pay."

The extra work took a month to complete which delayed the steel structure being erected, and the cost of borrowing money to pay for the materials was heavy. Claude tried hard to catch up, but bad weather and labour problems added to the delay.

Garry visited the site every other day and always came away feeling sick and depressed, as no matter how hard he tried, progress was still slow. The costs were mounting and progress payments stopped on the grounds that the penalty clause payments would be deducted, leaving nothing to pay Blakesbuild.

Jane knew things were bad but had no idea of the true position, as Garry had managed to conceal all correspondence from the bank, who had extended his loan to cover additional expenses on the factory job. She stayed ignorant of the situation until she heard on the news one morning that interest rates were to rise two per cent, and she rushed into work to talk to the accounts chief, who nervously handed over bank statements. She was horrified to see how much money the company was paying in interest charges, and took all the papers to study them, working out how much extra the new rate would cost and if the huge overdraft could be paid back.

Garry was visiting the factory site, so Jane used his office where she found details of all the land he had purchased and the relevant agreements. By lunchtime she was convinced the company would be bankrupt in a very short time unless all the building sites were sold, which would clear the overdraft, but leave them with no working capital. After eating a light lunch she waited for Garry to return, sitting in his seat trying to work out why he had got them in so much trouble unnecessarily. Suddenly she thought about Grainger Construction and it all fitted in, making her feel very angry.

The bank manager rang requesting an early meeting, and Garry walked wearily into his office as Jane put the receiver down to see she was upset and angry, but managed to keep calm as she rose to speak. "Garry, your obsession with Grainger Construction has just about bankrupted this company. I've been studying the bank statement and we're in deep trouble."

"Yes, I know. The interest rate increase will cripple us."

"You've crippled the company by your obsession. When will we receive our progress payments from the factory job?"

"Never! Time penalty clause payments have swallowed them up and we owe them a lot of money."

"Oh my God, we're finished. My father's company is ruined." She broke down and wept bitterly, but Garry just sighed and collapsed in a chair. Jane suddenly stopped crying and blurted out, "Why did you go for that job without proper tests?" Garry shrugged his shoulders and said nothing. She stood up, walked around the desk and stood in front of him. "Grainger was after that job, wasn't he? That's why you were so keen to get it?"

"Yes. I'm sorry, dear."

"Sorry! Years of work put in by my father ruined by your obsession."

"Not ruined yet, my dear. I'll see the bank manager and then put all our sites up for sale."

Drink With The Devil

"That's not enough. We've still got suppliers to pay."
"We'll manage."
"I can't see how we can avoid bankruptcy."

Chapter Twenty-Five

The prison door clanged shut and Gordon Simpson walked out into the sunshine. He had gained full remission from a shortened sentence. The judge believed his story about being threatened by Chatfield, who had been sentenced to life imprisonment, with a recommendation that he should serve at least twenty-five years.

Simpson had digs waiting for him near his old flat in South London and a couple of interviews for jobs had been organised by a helpful voluntary prison worker, but he had no intention of getting a job, confident that Garry Osborne would provide his monetary needs for some time to come. He moved into a shabby bedroom above a shop, dumped his small suitcase on the single bed and looked at himself in the dressing table mirror. Prison life had not suited him at all and he looked thin and gaunt. His beer gut had disappeared, leaving his clothes hanging loosely around him, and the belt on his trousers did not have enough holes in it, so he tied it in a knot to prevent them falling down. Even his shirt was too big, leaving a large gap between the collar and his neck. The sight of his wasted body made him feel wretched, angry and hungry all at the same time, and after he had packed away a few belongings he went out to find a telephone.

When Garry answered the phone his heart sank when told by the receptionist that it was Simpson. "What d'you want, Simpson?" he snapped.

"As if you didn't know, Osborne."

"I see. Blackmail, is it?"

"No. Just payment for a prison term."

"How much?"

"Whatever you think your freedom is worth."

"Don't play around with me. How much?"

"Half a million as a one off payment. Nothing more in the future."

Garry was staggered. "D-Don't be bloody silly, I can't raise that amount."

"That's a shame. I don't think you'll survive fifteen years inside. Still never mind, I'll visit you!"

"Listen Simpson, let's meet and discuss it."

"No. I'll meet you just once. When you hand over the cash."

Garry paused for a few seconds and then said calmly. "I agree, providing you never come back for more."

"Okay. It's a deal. Meet me on Black Heath, midnight tomorrow. With the money."

They agreed the exact location and Garry sat back feeling desperate, knowing he could never raise that much money. His worst fears had materialised much sooner than he had expected, and when he thought about the problem he could only see two alternatives — one was to sell Osbornes, the stockbrokers, and the other was very risky. His thoughts were interrupted by Jane entering the office with a file in her hand.

Her face looked strained and tears filled her eyes as she said, "Garry, listen to me."

"Yes, dear. I'm listening."

"We've only got two alternatives — the first is to let Blakesbuild go into liquidation. And the second is to sell the farm or Osbornes."

"I won't sell Osbornes. It's my own business."

"And Blakesbuild was my father's own company. So what are you going to do about it?"

Garry looked at the distraught girl and felt guilty. "We'll sell the farm."

Jane collapsed in a chair, feeling exhausted and they both remained silent for a minute. She broke the silence. "I'll miss the farm badly."

"I know you will, dear. And I'm sorry."

"Little William loves the animals."

"You can always stay with Angela."

"I know, but it won't be the same."

"I suppose not. Well, I must get on to the estate agents and go for a quick sale."

Jane sighed, wiped her eyes and walked out.

After telephoning the agents, Garry's thoughts returned to the Simpson situation and, after an hour of scheming, he got up and walked quickly down to his car, driving south to Sussex and finding one of Grainger Construction's sites. He did not stay long, just enough time to study one of their vans which was painted white, with Grainger Construction printed down both sides in blue. Next he visited a hardware store and an army surplus clothing shop. His last visit before going home was to a garage, which hired white vans the same as Graingers. He felt confident his plans were foolproof and would result in his final satisfaction.

Jane saw him looking brighter when he came home and asked, "Are you eating a meal tonight?"

"Yes, I'm hungry."

"Aren't you upset about the farm?"

"Not really, I don't like farming."

"But it was your father's pride and joy."

"Huh. That's a good reason for selling it."

"Good heavens. What did he do to deserve that comment?"

"Never mind. I might tell you one day."

"Tell me what?"

Garry turned and walked out, angry because she had reminded him of his true parentage and the existence of the brother he hated. He went into his study to drink a large brandy before planning the next day, thinking about every move and detail until Jane called him for dinner. He ate well whilst calculating the results of his plans, which made him grin and at one stage even quietly chuckle.

Jane was still very upset at losing the farm and Garry's private mirth made her angry. As she watched him shovelling large

Drink With The Devil

amounts of food into his grinning mouth she asked, "What d'you find so amusing about our situation? We're on the edge of bankruptcy, that beautiful farm is being sold and all you can do is grin."

He stopped eating and looked her squarely in the eyes. "I don't give a damn about my father's precious farm. The sooner it's gone, the better."

Jane was shocked and angry but managed to keep calm. "Garry Osborne, you're a very strange man."

"Yes. Perhaps I am." They finished the meal in silence.

The next day Garry went to work at his usual time, announcing he would not be back until very late that night and so would not need dinner. He visited his bank during the morning and assured them the sale of the farm would be sufficient to provide enough to pay off the overdraft and give the company a much needed injection of capital. The bank manager agreed to continue supporting the company until the sale was completed.

The sale of all but one of the building sites was going ahead, albeit at a substantial loss. Garry was beginning to feel confident about the future, as all the newspapers were predicting interest rates would fall shortly.

Late that afternoon Garry left the office and drove to the van hire garage to find the vehicle he had chosen was ready. He transferred the contents of his car boot and drove away to a quiet lay-by where he changed into a blue boiler suit, boots and a woollen hat. From there he drove to a transport cafe and sauntered up to the man behind the counter, who was clutching a big teapot and said: "Hello, mate. Want a cuppa?"

Garry could not remember anyone calling him mate and grinned. "Yeah, mate, and a bit of cake." He left the cafe as it was getting dark with fog beginning to descend and gather around the trees on the heath, and he watched as office workers hurried home.

The long evening dragged on and he felt the chill of the damp night enter the van and penetrate his clothes, making him shiver and put his suit jacket over his shoulders. Then he put it on, got out to stretch his legs and take a walk, returning later to the van. He drove around warming the vehicle up with the heater, before parking a hundred yards away from the agreed meeting place under a big cedar tree with low branches. The night was dark, damp and foggy with only the muffled sounds of the occasional lorry to be heard labouring across the heath nearly half a mile away. Half an hour before midnight Garry walked from the van, making sure no one was around, and waited with a small suitcase on the ground in front of him.

Simpson appeared out of the gloom on time, having to get quite close in order to recognise Garry in his boiler suit. He grinned. "Hello, Osborne. You'd make a good plumber's mate."

"Simpson, why the hell did you want to meet here at this time of night?"

"I don't want to be seen with you."

"The feeling is entirely mutual."

"Right. Where's the money?"

"In the case on the ground." He pointed downwards.

Simpson bent over and kneeled down to unfasten the case. Garry grabbed an iron bar wedged in the branch of a tree, and brought it down heavily across the back of his head with a loud thud. Simpson gasped and fell forward. Garry repeatedly struck him on his neck and then stood back, panting, and stared at the motionless body. He was unable to move for five minutes, his mind in deep shock at what he had just done. Blood trickled on to the grass from open wounds, making him feel sick, and then a sudden puff of wind brought him back to reality. Simpson was still quite heavy despite losing so much weight, and it was a struggle to lift him into the van, but at last he was laid out on the floor and Garry slammed the rear doors. He jumped into the driver's seat with his heart thumping like a drum and sweat soaking his clothes. The iron bar rolled about on the steel floor as he lurched off towards the road.

He travelled slowly through the patchy fog and began to feel better about Simpson's murder, which had been easier than he thought possible.

Drink With The Devil

With the first stage of the plan a success he congratulated himself on a good job done so far.

When he reached the Grainger Construction site in the early hours of the morning, he drove slowly to where the foundations of a new house had been dug. Having worked out where the next foundations would be dug for the garage, he started digging the sandy ground. It was relatively easy, but as his hands and limbs were unused to manual work he soon began to tire. Sweat poured down his neck and his hands blistered, and after an hour he was worn out. Convincing himself the hole was large enough, he dragged Simpson's body from the van, pushed it down the hole and it landed with a sickening flop. He worked on to cover the body up and make the ground look the same as before and, when he was satisfied he jumped in the van and drove off, arriving outside Grainger Construction headquarters half an hour later.

The side gates were locked so he threw the iron bar over, watching it land in a heap of sand, which partly buried it with just a short length still visible.

He drove away as the first light of dawn appeared on the horizon and headed into the country, where he threw his spade and shovel into a pond and then removed his blood-splashed boiler suit, weighting it with a brick before throwing it in. Next he cleaned the van carefully with a rag, until satisfied that no evidence remained. He returned the van as the garage opened and then drove home to Hampstead, slipping quietly in and up to his bedroom before Jane got up.

He lay on the bed exhausted and unable to sleep, his mind still racing on and re-living the night's events. He imagined the police arresting Grainger, having found another dead body on one of his sites. He was sure the police would not believe Grainger's story about his involvement, but would believe that Simpson was killed by Grainger trying to find out who wanted to kill him. So it would be an ex-convict's story as opposed to his, a person not connected with Simpson in any way. He laughed out loud as he imagined Grainger back in prison again. He changed clothes and walked into the kitchen as Jane was preparing breakfast.

Jane looked suspiciously at him. "Working late again last night?"

"Yes. I think the company will be secure again shortly."

"It will be if I persuade the prospective buyer I'm meeting this morning to buy the farm."

"Oh, so you'e showing someone around?"

"Yes."

"Who?"

"No idea. The estate agent said a person would arrive at eleven."

"Good. Let's hope he buys it."

Jane drove off with William straight after breakfast, leaving Garry to sleep the morning away. She arrived at the farm and broke the news of the sale to Peter, who was upset at the prospect of a new employer or the sack. She felt sorry for him and had to walk away in case she burst out crying. She walked around her lovely country garden, getting very depressed, knowing she was about to lose it all, and William walked beside her silently sensing his mother's grief. They went into the farm house kitchen which still smelt new as it had hardly been used since it was built. She sat at the table sipping coffee, deep in melancholy thought and did not notice William slip out of the back door.

Suddenly she heard the child crying outside and leapt to her feet, running out to be confronted by a tall dark-haired well-built man walking towards her and carrying William. She was shocked by the sight of her precious little boy being carried by a strange man and stammered, "W-What's going on?"

The man smiled as he replied in a deep husky voice, "Don't worry, the little chap fell over, but he's being brave now."

William was gazing into the man's blue eyes and giggling. Jane smiled as she took him into her own arms. "Thank you for bringing him back."

"A pleasure. I've come to look at the farm."

Drink With The Devil

"Oh yes. I'd almost forgotten. I'm Jane Osborne."

"Very pleased to meet you. My name's Jim Grainger."

"Mr. Grainger. Good heavens. Oh dear." She stepped towards the door.

Jim saw her shocked look. "I'm very sorry to have taken you by surprise. I didn't mean to upset you. Perhaps it would be better if I came back another day?"

His voice and manner reassured Jane and she stepped forward again. "No, please don't go. It's my fault for being silly. Come into the kitchen." She put William down and he led the way. The smell of coffee prompted her to say, "Please sit down and have a cup of coffee."

"That would be nice. Thank you." He looked around the large room with its modern appliances all looking as though they had never been used, and then he looked at the tall blond woman, still looking apprehensive but beautiful. She sat down opposite him and they studied each other's faces whilst sipping coffee. Jane broke the silence, "Are you the same Mr. Grainger who owns Grainger Construction?"

"Yes. And my name's Jim. They should have warned you who was coming, so you could be out."

"I'm glad they didn't because I might not have come, and I've wanted to meet you for some time."

"To ask me some questions, no doubt?"

"Yes. Why does my husband hate you so much?"

"That's a question I've asked myself many times. He said it's because he blames me for his parents' death."

"But the real killers are locked up, and you saved Angela's life."

Jim shook his head. "It must be something else, but I can't think what."

"Have you crossed him in business?"

"No. In fact he's been trying to starve me of building land."

Jane cringed. "I know. And to our cost."

"The only thing I did recently was to convince him I was going after that factory job in Sussex."

"Yes, but his obsession goes back long before that."

"I'm sorry. I just don't know."

The sound of his voice and his relaxed easy-going friendly manner made Jane want to talk. She told him all about the farm, going into detail about the cows' production figures and the plans they had for the future. At this point she looked very sad and whispered, "Of course it'll be for others to decide the future strategy, but I'll miss the place very much."

"Oh, Mrs. Osborne, I am sorry. You're making me feel guilty about wanting to buy it, but you can visit any time you want to."

"That's very kind of you. And do call me Jane."

They spent a long time looking around the house and then drove around the farm in Peter's Land Rover, Peter keeping out of sight and not wishing to meet the man who might give him the sack. Jim was delighted with everything he saw and William sat on his lap as Jane drove, obviously enjoying the occasion and smiling at his mother every time she glanced in his direction. She could not believe how good he was, sitting with a strange man, and she understood why Angela had fallen for him.

They drove back to the farmhouse and jumped out of the Land Rover, Jim looking at his watch. "I'm sorry to have taken up so much of your time."

"It's been a pleasure."

"May I come back tomorrow?"

"Yes, of course. What would you like to see?"

"I'd like to go for a long walk in the wood."

Jane smiled as she replied. "You take as long as you like." As she and William watched him drive off, she looked forward to seeing him again, and hoped he would decide to buy the farm.

Jim enjoyed his few hours on the farm and drove home feeling on top of the world. He was still in high spirits when he returned the next morning and knocked on the back door of the big house to be greeted by a smiling Jane.

"Hello Jane, you won't mind if I walk down the track?"

"No, of course not. Drop in on the way back for a cuppa."

Drink With The Devil

She watched him stride away and ran to the telephone.

* * * *

It was a beautiful late summer day with little clouds moving slowly across the sky, the ground hard-baked by days of dry weather, and Jim remembered how different it had been on that terrible night years ago when his shoes filled with water and mud. He found the gap in the hedge he had used before and forced his way through, stepping several yards inside the wood and stopping to find a different world, his own idyllic peaceful paradise. He breathed in and smelt the perfume of the forest, tasting the sweet air, and the ground under his feet felt springy and welcoming.

He walked for an hour along familiar paths, all the time savouring the tranquillity of his surroundings. It was all so beautiful and peaceful as he sat for a while by the pool, listening to the trickle of water over rocks, and the rustle of leaves in the bushes on the side of the hill. He remembered his animal friends with deep affection, wondering if any of them were still in the forest. Shafts of light danced across the water as the branches above moved in the breeze, and he knelt down to taste the crystal clear liquid.

As he approached the rhododendron bushes guarding the lodge, Angela appeared ahead of Gemma, the pair of them having waited behind one of the bushes. Jim stopped for a second, unable to believe his eyes, as it was as if their last encounter had only been yesterday. She looked just the same, smiling as she walked towards him, and he nearly fell over in his haste to embrace her. They clung to each other, Jim burying his face in her hair and breathing in her perfume. Then he realised she was sobbing, and eased away seeing the tears trickling down her cheeks. "Don't cry my love, we're together again."

He kissed her eyelids, tasting her salty tears and then kissed her lips, holding her body gently. The kiss lasted a long time, during which they both imagined it was only yesterday that they had held each other. Eventually they relaxed and walked arm in arm through the trees, the sunlight dancing on the forest floor mesmerising the happy couple. No words were necessary as they sat down on the green and brown carpet of dried leaves, small twigs and vegetation. Slowly and gently they undressed each other and made love passionately, with no other thoughts entering their minds other than their love for each other. Then they relaxed, studying and touching each other's bodies between hugging, holding and kissing. The day was hot and humid and Angela whispered, "Let's go into the pool."

"Yes, that'd be nice."

They walked hand in hand and naked along the path, stopping to cuddle when they felt the need and playing like innocent children in the pool, splashing each other and laughing until the cold water chilled them. They hugged in a shaft of warm sunlight until they were dry and warm, remaining in a kind of trance which blocked out all other thoughts. Both had convinced themselves it was only yesterday when they last met, so everything they did together was natural and beautiful; Angela giggling and squealing with delight and Jim chuckling and grinning as they played in the forest.

It was well past midday when Angela remarked. "I'm hungry. How about some lunch?"

"Why not? In the usual place?"

"Yes. It's all ready."

They lay together in the clearing, eating and talking just as they had before, the sun warming their bodies. They made love again after lunch, even more passionately than before, and then lay together in the sun, just touching and kissing from time to time until late afternoon when a dark cloud covered the sun. Angela shivered and whispered, "Let's get dressed now."

"A good idea, my love."

They dressed and walked towards the lodge where Gemma was waiting, patiently nibbling leaves from the bushes. She whinnied with delight as they made a fuss of her, but suddenly a clap of thunder shook the ground, bringing the couple back to reality. Angela's face was set firm as she said, "We must go now, and never tell anyone what happened today."

Jim nodded gravely. "Of course not, but it'll stay in my memory for ever."

"Yes, and mine." They kissed briefly, turned and went in their different directions.

* * *

The rain started to fall as Jim left the forest and walked along the farm track. The spell had been broken and the bond between them severed, leaving beautiful memories and affectionate feelings. They felt no guilt for what had transpired, just a feeling that it had to be in order that their lives could proceed without deep feelings of regret. Angela felt she could love Mark in the way she wanted and he deserved. Jim was certain he could find a girl to love and marry without comparing her to Angela, and approached the farmhouse with a smile on his face.

Jane saw him coming and called out from the kitchen. "Hello Jim. Had a good day?"

"Yes. Wonderful."

"Come in and have some tea." Tea and cake were laid out on the table, and they sat down and talked about the weather.

Jim looked at Jane and said, "I'm definitely going to buy the farm."

"Oh, good. I'm so pleased."

He could see her feelings were genuine. "You must come and see me often."

"I'd like that. What'll happen to Peter French?"

"I hope he'll agree to stay."

She heaved a sigh of relief. "Can I tell him?"

"Yes. As soon as both parties agree to proceed."

"Marvellous. That's really good news."

"I'm glad you think so."

"Well, it means I can visit and keep in touch with events."

"I'll look forward to your visits," he said with genuine feeling.

Jane frowned for a moment. "The question is, will Garry agree to sell to you?"

Chapter Twenty-Six

After waving goodbye to Jim, Jane rushed back to Hampstead to join Garry for Sunday dinner. Garry wandered into the dining room. "Hello. How did you get on with that prospective buyer?"

"Very well. He's agreed to buy."

"Good heavens. Just like that?"

"Yes. He looked at it on Saturday and returned today."

"How much did he offer?"

"I didn't go into that. He said he would ring the agents tomorrow."

"Good. Who is he?"

"A local businessman."

"That's even better. So he won't have a farm to sell before he buys?"

"I'm sure he hasn't got a farm."

"What's his name?"

"I can't remember. If you want any more information, you'll have to ring the agent."

"I'll do that in the morning."

They did not talk about it or anything else during dinner. Jane watched her husband and wondered why he was holding his knife and fork at unusual angles. He seemed clumsy and was having difficulty cutting his meat. For a split second she saw the palm of his hand and fingers, and noticed how red and raw they were, but stopped herself mentioning it in case he got up and left his food. She tried to imagine what he could have done to get in such a state — it seemed unlikely he had been gardening because he hated it. They finished eating and he disappeared into his study for the rest of the evening.

The next morning Jane watched Garry leave for work and

then walked around the garden. There was no sign of any work done, but she decided not to mention it, bearing in mind what was going to happen later that day; his mood would be bad enough without her stirring him up.

Garry waited until coffee was served and then rang the estate agent, who was very enthusiastic about the sale. "The buyer's agreed to the asking price, and it's a cash offer," he said.

"That's good. What about the live and dead stock?"

"He's agreed to buy the lot after an independent valuation."

"Well, what more can we ask for?"

"Exactly, Mr. Osborne. And he wants to complete as fast as possible."

"The sooner, the better, as far as I'm concerned."

"Right. I'll pass the matter over to your solicitors, and then get that valuation."

"Good. Oh, by the way, what's this businessman's name?"

"Grainger. Mr. Jim Grainger."

There was a second's pause and then Garry exploded. "Grainger! That evil bastard's not going to buy my farm!"

"But Mr. Osborne, he's agreed to your terms. And it's a cash offer."

"I don't care if he offers double the price, I will not under any circumstances sell to Grainger."

"All I can say is you had better have a good reason."

"He'll never get the chance to complete. Put the farm back up for sale." He slammed the telephone down and sat fuming, and was still in a state when Jane brought in another cup of coffee. She put it down on his desk and then stood back waiting for him to speak. She did not have to wait very long.

"What the hell are you playing at? You knew damn well I wouldn't sell to Grainger."

"His money is as good as anyone's. And we need it right now."

"You back-stabbing cow. You let him walk all over my house and farm." The thought of Grainger in his house made him go berserk, throwing the coffee and the cup at Jane and then tipping

Drink With The Devil

the desk over, scattering papers all over the office.

Jane screamed and fled. Cold water stopped the burns turning into scalds and blisters, and she went home wet and angry to change her stained clothes.

Garry paced around his office like an angry lion trying to escape, too angry to work or even tidy his office. The desk remained upturned until he had drained several glasses of brandy, when he felt calm enough to put things straight.

At lunchtime he listened to the news but was disappointed and, during the afternoon, he rang the agents to find out if they had any more buyers, but there were none. That evening he did not go home but preferred a light meal in a local restaurant, and then went to his flat to get down to serious drinking with all the usual accompanying visions. He was too drunk to remember the late night news, but listened in the morning, although his throbbing head and queasy stomach made it difficult to concentrate. No mention was made of a murder. He went to work late and just sat with his head buried in his hands, feeling depressed and bitter. The lunchtime news brought him no comfort, and he began to worry about his well-laid plans.

After a brief lunch he drove south to the Grainger site and stopped outside. Very few people were around, so he drove slowly into the entrance and on to the house where he had buried Simpson. He stopped suddenly when, to his horror, he saw that the area where he had concealed the body was being turfed over. The garage was on the other side of the house, and difficult to see in the dark. He cursed his bad luck and drove away wondering what to do next, bearing in mind no one would miss Simpson and his body could remain undiscovered for ever. In the meantime Grainger would want to know why his offer had been refused, and on the way back to his office he stopped at a call box to ring the police.

The officer on duty said, "What can I do for you, Sir?"

"I want to report a murder."

"Oh, yes? Your name and address, please."

There was a long pause before Garry replied. "Err... Harry

Brown, 6 Lynton Drive, High Barnet."

"I see. Where's the body, then?"

"On Grainger Construction's site. Under a newly turfed lawn."

"And I suppose you know who did it?"

"Jim Grainger." Garry slammed the 'phone down and ran to his car.

The officer sighed and growled, "Bloody nutcase. Ought to be locked up." He made a note of the conversation and then discussed it with his senior colleague.

Garry went back to his flat again that evening, and drank heavily as usual.

The next day there was still no news so he rang the police again, this time giving the victim's identity. The message was passed to Chief Inspector Green on this occasion, whose enquiries revealed Simpson had been missing from his digs since the previous Friday. His few possessions were still where he had left them in the bedroom, and he had not turned up for job interviews.

* * *

Jim Grainger stood at his office window watching a large pile of sand being loaded into a lorry with a new bulk-loading vehicle, which had a large bucket on the front. He marvelled at the rate the lorry was being filled up, continuing to watch as it drove out of the entrance and down the road, when he noticed a car parking outside. The person getting out looked familiar, and his heart sank when he realised it was Inspector Green with two plain-clothes officers.

The policemen reached his office quickly, shook hands and the inspector looked at him with a grim expression. "We've reason to believe your old friend, Simpson, may be in some trouble."

"He was never my friend. And I haven't seen him for a long time."

"I see. Well he's gone missing and a little bird tells me he's been murdered."

"Oh, my God. Poor old Simpson. And I suppose you suspect me?"

"We've been informed that you killed him on one of your sites."

"That's bloody silly. I've no reason to hurt him."

"Not even to find out who was trying to kill you?"

"He didn't know. Have you found a body?"

"Not yet, but with your help we may do so very soon."

"On which site is this supposed to have happened?"

"The one just outside of town."

"Right. Let's go and have a look."

"Good idea. You lead the way." They travelled in the police car in silence, Jim feeling very nervous and distraught at the prospect of being locked up again, and parked outside the site office. Jim got out feeling weak and ill and spoke sharply.

"Where's this body then?"

"Under new turf somewhere."

They found two new houses with recently laid turf, and Jim ordered the site foreman to have the turf rolled up and stacked, and then turned to the inspector, "Right, you can start digging in two hours' time."

"Very well. I'll organise a digging party."

Jim stayed to watch as a team of policemen began to dig, and it was late afternoon when a car drew up and newspaper men jumped out, photographing the officers digging before being ushered away. Jim groaned and buried his head in his hands as he hid in the office, fearing his name would be in the papers again and he would be accused of another murder. A sheet was erected over the site and floodlights were brought in so the dig could continue into the night. It was mid-morning the next day when the body was discovered, buried about three feet down in the sandy soil, and Jim watched as it was carried away. Chief Inspector Green said, "I'll have to ask you to come back to the station for questioning."

"Oh my God, not again?"

He was taken to the same small interview room as previously, and left to sit alone on the same hard chair he occupied before. As he looked around the stark room its walls seemed closer together, giving the impression they would close in on him, and his mind wandered to his previous brainwashing sessions. A shiver went down his spine as he recalled Pratt's angry face, and he remained in melancholy reflection for nearly an hour until the inspector came in and sat down. He asked many questions about the building site, the most important being how long the turf had been laid. Then he asked about Jim's movements over the previous week, and he had just about run out of questions when a plain-clothes officer came in with a sheet of paper. The chief read it and then said, "It seems Simpson was killed last Friday night. Where were you that evening?"

"I was at home after eating at the local pub as usual."

The chief inspector read the report again. "Right. You can go now."

"May I really?"

"Yes, but make sure I can find you at any time."

"Okay." Jim was taken back to his office where he collapsed into a chair, exhausted.

The next day a police search party turned the offices and building site upside down looking for evidence, and Jim was relieved when none was found. The newspapers had pictures on their inside pages of policemen digging with the headline: 'What are they looking for?' But no explanation was offered nor was there any mention of Jim's name.

* * *

Garry read the brief story and cursed loudly. It had been a bad week and Thursday's paper added to his misery with no mention of a man helping with enquiries, or even the acknowledgement of a murder.

It was late afternoon when the phone rang, with the bank

manager sounding very serious. "Mr. Osborne, I'm afraid interest rates are to be increased in the morning and I must insist you reduce your overdraft substantially."

"But they were supposed to be going down, not up."

"They're definitely going up, which is very serious for you."

"Can't you hang on until I sell the farm?"

"Yes. But it had better be a very quick sale."

Garry put the 'phone down and then rang the estate agent, who had no new buyers. "How long would it take to organise an auction?" he asked.

"Weeks, Mr.Osborne. And then you'd have to auction the dead stock separately. And there would be nothing to stop Grainger bidding."

"No, I suppose not. Have you told him I won't sell to him?"

"Not yet. I'm stalling for time."

The next day Jane came into work for the first time since Garry went berserk and, having heard the news about interest rates, she decided to confront him again, walking bravely into his office and standing well back from the desk. "Are you living permanently at your flat now, or is there another woman?"

"I'll live in my flat on my own until I'm ready to come home."

"I see. Now what are you doing about the interest rate increase?"

"Thinking about it."

"There's nothing to think about. The farm must be sold quickly."

"I'm not selling to Grainger, and that's final."

"Why not?" She raised her voice.

"I'm not telling you, you bitch. In fact I might just let the company go bust."

Jane gave him an icy stare and spoke slowly. "You can't avoid selling the farm. I checked with the bank and found you had to put it up as security on our huge loan. A loan that's costing a fortune every day."

He felt trapped and stuttered: "B-But I won't sell to Grainger."

"You'll have to when I tell the bank manager you turned down a very good cash offer."

He slumped in his chair feeling drained and defeated, but after a while he looked up at her with pleading eyes. "Please give me until Monday."

"If you tell me why you hate Grainger."

"I can't and won't. Please don't be a bitch."

"All right, Monday morning it is, but I don't see what difference it makes."

"You'll see."

"How will I see?"

"Something'll happen to alter the situation."

"What will happen?"

He did not answer and just turned his head away.

The next day he arrived at work late and looking ill, sitting in his office all day in a state of deep depression. He rang the agent several times without receiving any good news, and Jane and the staff avoided him all day, heaving a collective sigh of relief when he left early, saying he was feeling ill. He went to his flat and drank heavily, fearing his world was falling apart with enemies closing in rapidly, and it was obvious he could not avoid selling to Grainger if the police did not charge him. Friday's papers reported the murder of Simpson, but just indicated that the police were making enquiries and no suspects were being held yet.

* * *

Jim spent most of Friday trying to get down to work, but as he was still worried about the murder he could not concentrate. In the afternoon the chief inspector called and Jim invited him into his office. "Any news?" he asked.

"Yes. Poor old Simpson was killed some distance from here, transported to your site and buried."

"Good heavens. Why and where was he killed?"

"We're pretty sure it was Black Heath. An old lady walking

her dog reported a pool of blood which matches Simpson's. And his clothes had grass stuck to them."

"But why bury him on my site?"

"I was hoping you could tell me."

"What d'you mean?"

"Well, it's obvious someone is trying to stitch you up with a murder charge. Probably the same person who tried to kill you."

Jim had already worked that out and had spent a long time wondering what to do about it, bearing in mind there were two reasons for not divulging Osborne's name — Angela and Jane — neither of whom he wanted to hurt in any way. He looked at the chief's serious expression and retained his own as he said, "It's the most likely explanation, but as I said before Simpson didn't know who it was. And I've no idea."

"Are you sure?"

"Yes. Why would I keep that from you? After all I'm the one in danger."

"True. If you think of anything let me know."

"I will, of course. Have you got any leads?"

"Yes. A white van was seen leaving the site about the right time that night."

"So he even tried to make it look like one of our vans?"

"Yes. We're checking your vans right now."

The chief left and Jim sat wondering what to do next, relieved because the inspector did not suspect him, and sure it was only a matter of time before Osborne was caught. The next day he went to work to try to catch up with paperwork, but at lunchtime his thoughts turned to Jane, so he finished his sandwiches and rang Manor Farm.

Jane answered and sounded pleased when he asked, "May I come and see you tomorrow?"

"Yes, of course. Come for coffee."

Jim arrived at the farm wondering if Garry would be there and, if so, whether he would be hostile, but was relieved when he found Jane alone. Initially he asked about William.

"He's fine and playing with Angela's daughter."

"Oh, that's nice. Can we have a serious chat?"

"Yes, of course. Come into the kitchen." The coffee tasted good and they ate biscuits together. "I'm sorry about Garry refusing to sell. That's what you want to talk about, isn't it?"

"Well, no. I didn't know about that."

"Oh, so the agent didn't tell you?"

"No, he didn't. But I've been very occupied with other things."

"Oh yes. The murder."

"That's right. Why won't he sell?"

"I don't know. I expect it's his obsession again."

"Oh dear, that's very disappointing."

"Don't worry. He'll have to sell, or else."

"I see. So I'll still be able to buy?"

"Yes."

"Good. Well, I wanted to talk about what happened in the past. I think you should know the truth about your husband so you can be prepared for the future."

Jane sat in silence whilst Jim told her about the attempt on his life years ago. He explained how he had threatened to expose Garry to stop him trying to kill him again. Jane went pale, but stayed silent for a while after he'd finished.

"Why are you telling me now?" she said.

"Please don't think I want to worry you unnecessarily, but I fear for you in the future."

"Why?"

"Well, you read in the paper about that murder? The victim was the same man who was involved in the attempt on my life, and the only person who knew of Garry's involvement."

"Oh, I see. Mr. Simpson?"

"Yes. He probably tried to blackmail your husband."

"Oh, my God. His hands!" She slumped forward, burying her head in her hands.

Jim felt distraught at seeing her like this and said softly, "I'm very sorry to have brought such bad news. I just wish it weren't true."

His gentle words eased her tormented mind and she looked

up and whispered: "So you're sure Garry killed Simpson?"

"As certain as I can be. After all he was the only one to gain. And he tried to implicate me."

"Yes, you're right, I'm afraid. He was out very late last Friday night, and his hands looked as if he spent the night digging."

"That caps it, I'm afraid."

"Oh, this is terrible! But why didn't you tell the police?"

"I felt that if they didn't find out, you and Angela wouldn't have to bear the pain of the terrible scandal."

"But Jim, you could have been convicted of the murder!"

"Oh, well, Chief Inspector Green is too clever for that. He'll track Garry down very soon. That's why I'm telling you about it now, so you can be prepared."

"How long do you think it'll be before the police realise who the killer is?"

"I don't know, but I'm sure it won't be long."

Jane sat in silence for a while before speaking with a shaky voice: "Oh my God. It's too terrible to bear." She slumped forward again, this time crying into her hands.

The sight of her crying filled Jim with compassion and guilt until he could not stand it any longer. He moved from his chair as if by instinct, kneeling down beside her and laying his arm across her shoulders, holding her gently against him. Her crying continued for a minute or so, but then she stood up slowly with Jim still holding her and turned towards him, burying her head in his chest, while he folded his arms around her in a firm but gentle embrace. She returned his embrace, where they remained for some time, with Jane experiencing a warm feeling of comfort, protection and love, which she wanted to go on forever. He buried his face in her hair, kissing her while experiencing overwhelming compassion and affection for the beautiful woman in his arms.

Eventually Jim spoke in a husky emotional whisper. "I'm sorry about all this. Please tell me if there's anything I can do."

She remained pressed hard against his body and whispered, "You've already done too much, and it's my problem now."

"Please call on me for anything."

"I will. But just hold me for a while longer."

She looked at him with tears still in her eyes. He kissed them away and then kissed her lips with a long and lingering passionate kiss, which drove away all thoughts of the problems ahead and delivered them into a brief period of ecstasy. When they finally stopped for breath, reality replaced passion. Sitting down again, they drank more coffee, Jane feeling strengthened and more able to face the future.

* * *

Garry spent a miserable weekend in his flat, working all day Saturday trying to keep his mind off his obsession. He read several newspapers in the evening and listened to the news, hoping to learn that the police had arrested Grainger. Again he was surprised and disappointed to find the media had lost interest, preferring more sensational stories. After going out for a meal which he only picked at, he then went back to his flat for a drinking session and bed alone.

He slept late on Sunday and just ventured out briefly to buy several newspapers and a snack lunch. In the afternoon he read the papers until the words became blurred and he dozed off, waking up in the evening in time to listen to the news again, but he was desperate when there was still no mention of the murder. Only a few more hours and he would have to capitulate and let his enemy have the farm. It was too much to bear and made him so angry he cursed and swore as he reached in his cabinet for a new bottle of brandy. Not bothering with a glass, he just tipped the bottle back to fill his mouth with the comforting liquid, and after two huge gulps was in a different world.

Grainger immediately appeared with a long whip, leering down at him as he lay helpless on the hard ground. He drank again, hoping the scene would change, but it got worse as his arms and legs were tethered to stakes and he could not move. To avoid the stinging blows he took several more large gulps, but it just made matters worse, with his body being slashed to ribbons, blood oozing out of the wounds. He tipped the bottle right back and drank the remaining liquid which sank inside his body, causing a warm glow to reach his limbs and extremities. The scene changed with him wrenching himself off the ground, sending the stakes flying and then beating Grainger unmercifully with his own whip until he was writhing in agony and begging for mercy, and finally dying before his eyes. The vision gradually faded into a warm red glow.

* * *

Jane went to work as usual on Monday and tried to get involved with business, but her thoughts wandered from Jim, and how she wanted to see much more of him, to Garry and worrying about the desperate situation he had got himself into. Her worst thoughts were realised at about three in the afternoon, when Chief Inspector Green arrived. He asked to see Garry and Jane spoke to him truthfully, "He's not here to-day."

"Oh! Where is he, Madam?"

"I'm not sure. but he could be at Osbornes, his other company."

She watched him disappear before phoning for a taxi which took her to Garry's Belgravia flat, as she wanted to warn and protect him. The door was locked so she opened it with a key he had given her years ago, to find the smell of stale drink-laden air was almost suffocating and rushed to a window, throwing back the curtain and opening it wide. She turned to find him in his favourite chair, slumped forward, his ashen face looking in pain. His eyes were closed and one hand gripped the empty bottle lying in his lap. She stood for a second, then felt his forehead, which was sticky with sweat and cold. She bent down to listen to his shallow breathing, then tried to revive him, but without success and he just slumped forward. She was stunned and could not think what to do next.

The sound of a police car with siren approaching shook her

out of the trance and she stumbled towards the door, not wanting to be there when they arrived. Slamming the door, she ran downstairs, just managing to join a crowd walking by as several policemen rushed towards the building. She felt wretched and in absolute turmoil, not knowing what to do but with a desperate need to get away. Without thinking she ran to a phone box and rang Jim, blurting out her story and he said, "Just stay where you are. Don't move, and I'll come straightaway."

She put down the receiver and stayed by the phone box as if commanded by God himself.

Jim arrived an hour later and as she jumped into his car he reached over and kissed her forehead, before driving to a quiet place where he parked and listened to her unload her troubles. She told him all about Garry's drink problem and how he had treated her so badly in the past, the whole story tumbling out as if she could not stop herself. He studied her tormented face, sympathising with everything she uttered, and within an hour, a huge weight had lifted from her slender shoulders and she felt relaxed. Jim with his reassuring manner had made her feel able to face the difficult time that would follow, and he drove her back to her office saying as they parted, "Let me know if I can help in any way."

"Thank you very much, but I must be on my own until this mess is cleared up. It's something I have to do by myself."

"I understand, but I'll be looking forward to seeing you again soon."

Garry was taken to hospital just in time to prevent him dying from alcohol poisoning. He recovered for just long enough to sign the necessary documents agreeing to sell Manor Farm to Jim Grainger, but the strain and anguish of selling to his enemy caused him to collapse with a nervous breakdown, and he was too ill to be questioned by the police.

Three weeks later Jim decided he could wait no longer, as he was longing to see Jane. He rang her office.

"Hello, Jim, it's so good to hear from you."

"Can I see you soon?"

"Yes. Come to the farm on Saturday."

He arrived early on the bright autumn day and walked along the track to a point overlooking the forest below, the trees beautiful with their leaves changing colour. The sunlight heightened the contrasts, making the view quite breathtaking and he stayed for a while before meeting Jane. When she arrived, looking lovely in a blue and white floral dress, they kissed briefly and went into the kitchen, where Jim helped to prepare the coffee as they chatted about things in general, before sitting opposite each other.

"I've good news for you," said Jane. "The sale of the farm is going ahead as fast as possible."

"Good, because I'm dying to move in. How are things at Blakesbuild?"

"Much better now. We've sold all our surplus land and when the farm sale is completed, we'll be back on the road to recovery."

"What's happening at Osbornes?"

"Angela's taking over."

"Is she? I'm sure she'll make a success of it."

They finished their coffee and Jim said, "Come with me to the front of the house."

She smiled and lead the way out on to the patio and Jim moved close to her.

He pointed to the forest in the distance. "Look at that beautiful view."

She whispered. "Yes, it's lovely."

"I want you to share all this with me."

She turned towards him and was in his arms before she could draw breath. They kissed passionately and then drew apart slightly as she whispered, "I would love to spend the rest of my life with you."